I0667642

 Created with Vellum

Paint Me Red

Paint Me Red

TERRAN FERNIZA VALENZUELA

Content Warning

This book contains contents that may trigger some readers, including, but not limited to, child loss, drug use, abuse, assault, death, and murder.

Reader discretion is advised.

Author's Note

First and foremost, thank you for choosing to read my novel. Each word, each sentence, and each chapter is a part of me, a part of my journey. It has taken me years to find the right words to convey my thoughts and emotions, and it is a profound honor to be able to share these words with you.

Secondly, I wanted to address the trigger warnings I have added to this novel. I want to assure my readers that my intention with the content of this book is not for shock value but more of just an honest way for me to express the trauma I have been exposed to.

When I first had the idea for Paint Me Red, I wondered what the story would look like written down on a page and how others would perceive it. I worried about how others would see the actions and ramifications of those actions through my characters. I spent a long time going back and forth, deciding what would be appropriate for the general public.

I was worried about what others would think of me for producing such a work of fiction. Still, the more I wrote, the more I realized that the events in Paint Me Red were less fiction and more a fictitious rendering of what I and those around me have gone through during my lifetime.

With that realization, I felt free for the first time.

This novel has been a salvation to me. It has been a way for me to get the darkness out of my head, and it has been somewhere safe to let it go.

This led me to the decision not to hold back and not to censor myself. Those who have experienced similar events to my characters should not feel the need to censor their trauma or be ashamed of it. I want my readers to know they don't have to hide their pain. You are not a freak, you are not broken, and you are not alone.

That being said, prioritize your mental and physical health above all else. I'll always understand.

There are no chapters in our lives. There was no before you or after you. There was always just you and every step and every second on this earth that slowly led me to the point where I could finally meet you and see the one person who would rewrite my story from a beginning, middle, and end to an ongoing written work. You are endless, my love. And I am yours forever in your endlessness.

"Ever has it been that love knows not its own depth until the hour of separation."

—— Kahlil Gibran

Prologue

LAKE

I step into our apartment's dark doorway and linger with my hand on the doorknob. It's too quiet.

There is always noise in our home as my parents wander from room to room in their drugged way. I don't understand it, but they seem happy. So why should I care?

But today, I care because today is different.

It's too quiet.

I pause in the doorway and take in the silence. The air is too still, and that overwhelming sense of life that I am so familiar with is gone. I know in my heart that they are gone, but I lie and tell myself that maybe they just left for the store or are at the neighbor's apartment, even though they are always home to greet me after school.

I adjust my backpack on my shoulder and close the door with shaking hands. I lock it behind me and pause again, closing my eyes and straining my hearing while hoping and praying they are about to walk into the living room.

1

Silence. Nothing but gut-wrenching silence.

I drop my bag at my feet and take a few hesitant steps forward, deeper into our home.

"Momma?" I call down the hall with a crack in my voice.

Nothing.

"Dad...Daddy?"

Nothing.

I don't want to open the door...

"Just open the door," I tell myself as tears stream down my face.

The door gives way beneath my grip, and I see them lying in bed, still and quiet. They look as if they could still be asleep, except for their half-lidded gaze, staring off into nothing.

I look at them and feel nothing but terror.

Nothing...there is nothing left of them.

I cry silently to myself as I say goodbye.

Chapter One

LAKE

"Here are your things, Miss Lake," the secretary says with a kind smile while handing me a clear drawstring bag.

I try to steady the excited trembling in my hands as I take my belongings from her. Stepping back, I allow myself to take in these surroundings for the last time.

The last eleven years flew by. Eleven years that I initially saw as bullshit, but I guess juries don't take too kindly to fifteen-year-olds setting their foster mom and father on fire in their home.

In hindsight, I got off easy, considering the prosecutor on the case wanted to try me as an adult. Instead, I got to hang out here at Willow Creek Institution for the Criminally Insane on a manslaughter charge instead of first-degree murder.

I turn away from the secretary and face the front doors. My breath catches in my throat as I hear the buzz that signals that the secretary pressed the button for me to walk through the front doors. Steadying my steps to keep from sprinting outside, I see my case worker standing by her gray sedan with the passenger door open for me like a chauffeur.

"Hey there, Shelly!" I call out to her as I pick up my pace to meet her.

Shelly gives me a full-toothed grin as she excitedly waves, knowing I don't do hugs.

"Hey there, kiddo. Ready to see the light of day?" She says as I stop to stand before her and toss my clear bag into the back seat.

"Yes. What do we got planned?" I ask as I slip inside the car.

She leans over me as I buckle up, and I notice for the first time how the sun illuminates her tan skin and blonde hair. Her blue eyes have crinkles around them from smiling so much throughout life. It is nice to see her outside for the first time instead of in a white conference room under fluorescent lighting. She looks more human this way.

I am glad she gets to pick me up today. She is one of the few people who has always treated me with respect and understanding without even knowing me, the real me. I hope one day to repay her kindness.

"Well, we have some time before we have your appointment at the outpatient clinic for group therapy, and from there, it should be time to introduce you to your new roommate. Then you have the night to settle in at your new apartment."

I nod in agreement with the plans as she continues to speak.

"Tomorrow, I will need you up by eight o'clock so I can pick you up for your one-on-one session with your psychiatrist. Before all that, though, what you want to do is up to you."

A smile lights up my face.

It's up to me what I want to do.

Those are some of the most beautiful words I have ever heard.

"Do we have time to stop for a haircut and some shopping?" I ask hopefully.

"I've got just the place in mind."

Four hours later, I'm in the passenger seat of Shelly's car once more, running my left hand through my dark ash-brown hair with my freshly manicured hand.

Shelly decided to take me to a salon that works miracles. I got some long tousled layers added to the length of my hair and some curtain bangs since one of the staff there had said they were one of the newest hair trends. Shelly also kindly suggested that I get my nails done and my eyebrows waxed. I went with a natural look for the brows and a classic French for the mani and pedi.

This was the first time I felt so polished in my life. I can't even remember if I have ever painted my nails before, let alone got a proper haircut.

I gaze out the passenger window and try to still my nervous leg bouncing as I think over the last few hours. Shelly let me get whatever I wanted for clothing as long as I got two outfits for interviews, which was fine with me. I let her pick those out for me, and from there, I made sure to get some more things I've heard are trending right now, such as some cute monochrome styles and a few of my favorite band shirts.

"Are we getting closer?" I ask as a drizzle of rain begins to coat the windshield.

"Yup. I'm pulling up now," Shelly says as she turns left into a parking garage.

Once Shelly parks, I hop out of the car and open the back door to get my bags out. After I gather all my belongings in both arms, I close the door with my knee and run to catch up with Shelly, who is already making her way to an elevator across the garage.

It's a quiet trip up to the fourth floor. The elevator is bumpy and sketchy-sounding, but beggars can't be choosers right now. The state is paying for this place and all the spoils I received earlier as part of some rehabilitation initiative due to overcrowding. It is supposed to help ease the transition and decrease the likelihood of us ending up in the mental ward.

I hear the elevator ding, signaling that we've reached our destination. I follow Shelly down a dark, narrow hallway with a carpet that has a distinct moldy smell. I quicken my pace until we stop in front of a door that looks as worn as the hallway.

Shelly pulls a rusty silver key from her purse and gives me an excited grin. She struggles with the door before pressing on it with her shoulder while turning the key and the knob simultaneously. I commit the action to memory so I don't get stuck in the hallway at some point. Finally, Shelly busts in and looks back, giving me a reassuring smile.

"RILEY!" Shelly shouts.

I jump and wince a bit at the volume. Shelly notices and gives me an apologetic look while mouthing the word *sorry* as a slight woman walks over from the left side of the apartment to greet us at the door.

I try to hide my smile as I gaze upon a JoJo from *Horton Hears A Who* look-alike. She even has gray leggings, black fluffy slippers, and a black and gray sweater to complete the look. It is completely adorable.

I wait for her to say something, but she gazes up at us under short black hair that obstructs her shark-like eyes.

"Riley, meet Lake, your new roommate who came from the same facility as you," Shelly says as she walks further into the apartment through the kitchen area off to the left.

I follow Shelly and put my bags on the counter before turning to Riley and offering her a slightly awkward wave. "Hi. Nice to meet you."

Riley looks me up and down and nods slightly before walking over to my bags. I watch curiously as she unpacks things and lays them on the kitchen counter.

"Oh, um...yeah, those are the things Shelly and I picked up today. If you see anything you like, feel free to borrow it if you need it. When I get a hamper or something, you can toss the things in there when you're done," I say while watching her lay things out by color and style.

Riley nods once more and continues her work. I look up at Shelly for help.

Shelly smiles again. "Riley is a kind soul of few words; some would say that makes her a great roommate."

I nod in understanding. I'm okay with quiet. Only in the past few years did I start talking more to others and having an opinion that didn't just reflect what I thought others around me wanted to hear.

It took me a long time to start to feel okay with even holding eye contact, so I'm not really in any place to question Riley and her demeanor. It might be nice to enjoy the silence for once since my last residence always had a constant stream of noise.

"Come on, let me give you a tour of the place while Riley helps you unpack," Shelly says as she waves me forward.

Leaving Riley behind in the kitchen, Shelly walks past the island into the living room, which has two hallways that break off on either end into a bathroom and separate space. From where we stand, right in front of me is a sliding glass door that opens to a balcony.

"On the left is Riley's bathroom and bedroom, and on the right is your bedroom and bathroom. And where we stand is the living room. Over there is the balcony," Shelly says while pointing out the obvious.

I look around my surroundings and find modest, mismatched black and brown furniture with a bookshelf next

7

to my side of the apartment. I look over the titles from where I stand and notice popular romance novels and horror stories. I nod in approval. I like it. It's refreshing after seeing nothing but white for so long.

I weave my fingers together behind my back and glance over my shoulder to where Riley is still organizing my things. "It looks lovely here."

I see a light blush creep over Riley's pale face as she continues her work.

"Come on, let me show you your room!" Shelly says excitedly.

I take a deep breath, unsure of what to expect, and walk into the hallway on the right leading to my room. The door closed shut behind Shelly, so I lightly press against it to push it open once more. I peek around the edge of the door and see a wooden bed pressed against the far wall under the window with a matching writing desk and nightstand. A Tiffany-style lamp sits on top of the nightstand and casts a nice warm glow to the room. A yellow quilt and soft pillows pile on top of the bed. Across from the bed is a walk-in closet. Walking further into the room, I do a slow three-sixty spin to take in every detail.

"So what do you think?" Shelly asks from my side.

I smile and look up at her. "This is amazing. Thank you."

Shelly clasps her hands together in excitement. "Perfect! I'm sure once you get more settled, this place will feel like home in no time."

I nod, looking around once more. "Is there anything else I need to do tonight before tomorrow?"

"No, just get settled, and I will pick you up tomorrow morning. Last I texted Riley, she told me she had leftovers in the fridge in case you got hungry. Oh! I almost forgot."

I watch Shelly reach into her pants pocket and pull out a simple smartphone. She holds down the power button and waits for the screen to light up before handing it to me with a charger cord.

"Here you go. It is already hooked up to the wifi here, and it has your doctor's number, Riley's, and mine already programmed inside of it. If you have trouble navigating it, I'm sure Riley can show you how to use it. She went through the adjustment you're going through not too long ago, so she should be able to help guide you a bit."

Slipping my phone into my pocket, I sit on the mattress to test its softness. I bounce up and down a bit before looking over at Shelly.

"I don't remember seeing Riley at Willow Creek."

Shelly nods. "She's a bit older than you, so she was kept in a separate part of the facility. She will tell you all about it when she's ready," Shelly states while heading for the door. "It's time for me to head out. I'm glad we set you up for the day before I meet my son. I haven't seen him in a while, so it will be nice to catch up with him."

"That sounds like that will be nice."

Shelly grins. "I think it will be."

I jump to my feet to see her out. Once we start to pass the kitchen, Riley waves bye to Shelly, and I stand awkwardly at the front door as Shelly yanks it open from the inside with some force.

"Damn door. Goddamn fire hazard," Shelly mumbles. "Okay, girls, well, if you guys need anything, you know where to call. I will see you two in the morning."

"Thank you for everything!" I tell Shelly before closing and locking the door behind her as she walks off.

I stare at the back of the door, unsure of what to do next now that I am left to my own devices. Realizing I have been stagnant for too long, I turn to face Riley. She is staring at me with a half-folded My Chemical Romance shirt in her tiny hands. Her head is tilted slightly to the right as if asking me a question.

I force a smile and walk over to her side. "Thanks for helping me unpack. If you load my arms with the folded stuff, I can carry it all into the closet in one go."

Riley nods and starts stacking the clothing in my arms. We make our way into my room and to the closet, where I arrange myself into a sitting position on the closet floor. I put the clothing on the floor beside me since I don't have hangers yet.

"Hey, Riley?" I ask.

Riley leans against my nightstand and looks over at me.

"Could you help me out with my phone? I've never used one like this before, and I need to look someone up," I explain calmly.

Riley arches just one eyebrow at me this time.

"If it's not too much trouble," I add while holding my phone out to her.

Riley pauses for a minute before nodding and retrieving the phone from my grasp. I stand from my spot on the closet floor and shut off the light before closing the door. I go to sit against the bed headboard and curl my legs close to my chest.

Once I am comfortable, Riley settles herself on the desk adjacent to me. After she taps a few things on the screen, she leans over to hold it at eye level, and I am met with a search engine site. Riley leans back in her chair and looks at me.

"I am looking for someone. His name is Malachai Rosemond."

Riley types away on the phone and presses enter. A few seconds pass before the search engine is flooded with results. I jump from the bed to my feet and lean closer to Riley to get a closer look as she clicks on the first article that pops up. My breathing stops as I read the headline at the top of the webpage.

A new gallery will open in the downtown district, owned by the young prodigy Malachai Rosemond.

"Scroll down, please," I ask. "I need to see if it's him."

Riley nods and scrolls as we both continue to read.

Malachai Rosemond is an American artist, entrepreneur, and art collector from Willow Creek, TM. At only twenty-seven years old, he is one of the youngest prominent artists in the United States and has dominated the art scene over the last several years.

Death is a central theme in Rosemond's works. He became famous for a series of artworks in which he only used varying shades of red to depict gruesome images of the dead and the dying. The best-known of these is The Scars Left Behind.

Rosemond first came to fame after becoming the winner of the Bucksbaum Award, Future Generation Art Prize, and the Malcolm Award during the early days of his career. His latest work, Crimson Red, was featured at the Museum of Modern Art in New York, The Centre Pompidou in Paris, and the Guggenheim Museum Bilbao in Spain.

Rosemond will open the doors to a four-story modern gallery to feature space for his productions and rental space for other local artists.

Business hours are yet to be determined.

R iley scrolls to the bottom of the article, where there is a black-and-white photo of a peripheral view of Malachai looking up at one of his works. Riley zooms in on the image and then hands the phone to me so I can get a closer look at him. I smile as I see that his young, boyish features are now replaced with those of a healthy young man. I trace the curve of his nose and lips with reverence.

I glance over at Riley. "It's him."

While trying to commit his photo to memory, I continue

to talk with Riley. "I met Malachai when I was ten after my parents died, and I was placed with my foster parents. He was their biological son. We also had two other foster siblings. I would like to look them up next if you don't mind. But anyway...yeah I...I miss him."

Those are the only three words that have repeatedly played in my head over the last eleven years. They are so simple, but the weight they carry behind them is almost unbearable.

Riley nods in understanding and reaches out to me with her hand. I place the phone in her grasp and watch as she returns to the search bar for more information. We spent the next few hours reading through articles about Malachai and watching a few of his interviews on YouTube.

I nearly melt into the floor at the sound of his voice. He always had a deep voice, even as a teen, but now it has a smoother lilt, as if not weighed down by the pressure of our surroundings anymore.

An aspect of his interview that I find overwhelmingly familiar is his friendly detachment from those around him. He is polite to fans and interviewers but has a way of steering the conversation away from anything too personal in his life. It reminds me of how he used to interact with others during our years in high school. He always held people at a distance.

Forcing myself into the present, I stare at the screen again and lose myself in the interviews.

One question always at the forefront of his discussions is the fire that took his parents' lives, set by his unhinged foster sister–AKA me. Riley gives me a side glance at the mention of that, but I ignore it. I will explain myself if she asks, but until then, that can wait for another time.

Malachai keeps trying to divert from the line of questioning, but this interviewer keeps pushing.

Finally, Malachai sighs before he answers, "I don't know. I can't remember."

His dark eyes show a moment of realness and vulnerability as he says those words.

"What do you mean?" asks the interviewer.

Malachai clears his throat uncomfortably before answering the interviewer. "That night, I was shot in the head and spent a few months in the ICU. Before that night, everything is hazy. I know what the doctors and authorities told me, which is the same thing that was put in the local papers. So truthfully, you all know as much as I do about that."

"He doesn't remember..." I repeat, letting the words and their weight fully sink in.

I look over at Riley, who is giving me a slightly empathetic look as if she just realized the same implication behind those words that I had.

I sit back and inhale. "I wondered why he never called or returned my letters. I was starting to wonder if he was dead after all of this time. But if he just doesn't remember...."

Riley waits for me to nod my okay to her before she presses play to listen to the rest of the interview. We sit in silence after that.

After watching a few more videos and looking through the Instagram of my other foster siblings, I start to feel the emotional fatigue of the day.

"Hey, Riley?" I ask softly.

She turns to look at me over her shoulder.

"I am a bit tired. Can we keep this up tomorrow?"

Riley looks at me while giving me a soft smile and nods before quickly exiting the room, shutting the door behind her with a soft click.

I stare at the door, unable to move. What do I do now? I glance around the room, looking for the answer as I feel my breath catch and warm, wet tears stream down my cheeks. I lift a hand slowly and feel their continuity. I pull my hand from my face and watch as the tears drip from my fingers onto the floor. I can't remember the last time I fully allowed myself to cry.

Why am I even crying now? What warrants tears now rather than all of those dark, cold, lonely nights of my past? I never cried then, even if I should have, even though they wanted me to. If I had, would that have made me seem more human in their eyes? More worthy of kindness and compassion?

I turn and look back at my bed. I have a bed now...not just a hospital bed that mirrored a hundred others under one roof. I walk over and run my hand over the soft material. I inhale before a sob chokes me. Why was life so cruel that only now, after so many years, I finally have my own bed?

I peel my clothing off my body until I am down to nothing but my underwear. I pull back the covers and slip under them with a shiver from the feeling of the cold material pressed against my bare skin. Drying my tears with my hand, I press my face into the plush pillow and let the darkness take me.

Chapter Two

MALACHAI

I lay against the hardwood floor of my studio and stare up at the ceiling, letting the bright overhead lights burn blackness into my vision. Maybe if I stare at them long enough, I will be blind to the failure resting against the studio wall to my left.

I allow my head to lull toward the unfinished canvas. Unfortunately, I have failed to burn out my retinas enough not to see the ugly truth that is waiting for me.

Red...I need more red...

I lift my arms to view them against the light from above, and I see the dark bruising leaking from the needle pricks that trail along the veins in my arms. They look too dark today, meaning I have taken all I can for now.

But it is not enough. I need to get the image out of my head before it turns into the darkness that never seems to be fully lifted from my soul.

I close my eyes and sigh as I see it: the stark white room of the attic, with nothing but a lone mattress lying in the middle of the floor, with hues of red smeared on the surface.

I know the image should elicit dread, but I feel comfort, completeness..., and maybe even love for some unknown reason.

I chuckle to myself at the thought.

Love? How would I know what that is if I cannot feel most of the time?

There is nothing now—just the numbness I can never escape. It is a comfortable numbness, though, and I will take that over the other emotions that, when manifested, leave nothing but destruction and darkness behind.

I relish the image of the mattress, though. I know it has to do with her—the very her that haunts my dreams. They are so vivid that I could almost taste the sweat on her skin and smell the scent of her long, ash hair. I allow myself to picture her on the mattress beneath me, moaning my name, calling me hers.

I will never know whether this is an actual memory or hopeful thinking. My memories and thoughts have been nothing short of fragmented since the night of the fire, but I am obsessed with her nonetheless.

"Lake..."

I whisper the name to myself in the room and allow the noise to echo off the walls until the ghost of the sound comes back to my ears, caressing my skin with the sound of home.

She is the only thing that feels like home to me. She is the only thing that has begun to keep my shattered mind grounded all these years. And she is finally free.

Free to touch, to hold, to mold to my very flesh. Free to be mine.

I resist the urge for the thousandth time to hunt her down myself, just to see if she is genuinely the angel that has haunted my every waking obsession all these years and not just the glimpses of her through iron bars and windows that I have held so close to the black void I have called my heart all these years. But fuck, if those small glimpses of her were not enough to drive me to madness.

My thoughts of worship are interrupted by a soft knock on my studio door, followed by a "Mr. Rosemond?"

My head drifts to the right, and I see Ruby walk into the gallery, hanging back by the door, failing to approach me further, like all other staff here. I am glad for it, though. I'm pleased that Ava has hired a staff with enough self-preservation to listen to their gut when it tells them what they are standing in front of.

A monster.

"Yes, Ruby?" I say as I gaze away from the small, aging woman back to the unfinished canvas.

"I spoke to Riley, like you asked."

"And?"

"She will be here tomorrow with her."

Fuck yes. Finally...

I fain indifference and simply say, "Okay."

Silence hangs in the air before Ruby clears her throat, and I picture her wringing her hands, as she always seems to do in my presence.

"Mr. Rosemond?"

"Yes?"

"Will you...Will you leave my granddaughter out of this? She has been through enough, what with..." Ruby trails off, and I hear her take a few hesitant steps toward the door as if she is scared even to ask this little of me.

I sigh once more, "I will try, Ruby."

I hear her mutter softly, "Thank you," before exiting the studio and closing the door with a soft click behind her.

Lake will be here. She will be within my grasp.

I sit up from my position on the floor and glare at the canvas again as I pull a butterfly knife from my waistband and flip it from one hand to the next.

I need more red...

Chapter Three

LAKE

"Lake?"

I look up from the spot on the floor that I have been pretending is fascinating as I count the tiny carpet fibers. I know the social worker has called my name a few times now, but I don't understand why she's waiting for me to hold eye contact to tell me what she's here for.

I already know, so this is a waste of time. They should just get on with it.

"Are you ready to meet your new family? The Rosemonds are just outside and excited to finally meet you after hearing all the great things about you from the staff."

I look back down at the carpet and don't answer her. I doubt the staff has told the Rosemonds anything remotely close to the truth about me. There is nothing remarkable about me. I'm an average kid with average grades, forgotten by my friends, and I no longer talk to anyone.

The social worker clears her throat uncomfortably before

standing up from the office table across from me and leaving the room. A few minutes later, I hear the door click open again, and two adults in their late thirties walk into the room.

My gaze first falls on the man who is too perfect-looking. He is wearing a tailored blue suit that fits him like it was made for him and no one else. Looking at the shininess of his shoes and the glistening watch on his left wrist, the suit probably was. His dark eyes crinkle at the edges as he gives me a white, full-toothed smile.

I look at the woman and see she is just as clean-cut as the man. She wears a bright green dress that costs more than anything my parents ever owned. Diamonds shine from her ears and left ring finger. Her makeup is clean and neat, just like her dark brown hair that doesn't have a strand out of place. She also gives me a broad smile, but it doesn't reach her eyes.

"This is Penny and Michael Rosemond. You are familiar with Mr. Rosemond and his wife; it's election time, and his ads are all over TV lately," the social worker says while gawking at the couple.

I stare blankly at them because I have no idea who the fuck these people are. I have never seen them before in my life, let alone on TV.

Penny is the first to greet me. "Hi, sweetie. I'm sorry to hear about your parents; that is a tragedy. But Michael and I are so happy to welcome you into our family."

She holds out her hand, and I grasp it to be polite, but she pulls me into a hug instead. I stiffen slightly at the contact as her perfume chokes me.

When I don't hug her back, she squeezes me before letting go and stepping back in line next to Michael, who greets me next.

"Hey, kiddo. Welcome," is all he says.

I nod at them both and grab my backpack with the few things I brought from home to the foster center.

As I stand up, a movement behind Michael catches my eye. I

lean slightly to my left to get a better view and see a boy about my height and age leaning against the wall with his hands in his black hoodie pockets. His head tilts slightly to the side as he looks me up and down before locking his eyes with mine.

His curly hair hangs in his dark eyes, which look exactly like Michael's. The main difference is that they don't look as lifeless and fake.

Michael follows my gaze behind him and gives me a more forced smile this time. "This is my son Malachai. He came with us today to meet you. Ava and Gage are your other siblings, but they are at school today for a test, so you will have to wait to meet them until dinner time."

I nod again and follow them out as the staff says goodbye, which I ignore since none of them had ever interacted with me before today. Malachai falls in step next to me, and I can feel his gaze burning a hole into the side of my head as we walk out to the car.

I'm not surprised when we walk up to a brand new Range Rover that Penny is gushing about to me, but her words get lost in the sounds of the busy street across from the parking lot. Michael opens my door, and I slide into the back seat and place my bag on my lap.

Malachai slides into the seat next to me and closes the door gently to prevent the shiny new paint from being disturbed. Penny and Michael wave to the staff with bright smiles, but their smiles slip as we leave the parking lot.

My stomach drops as I notice the sudden change, and I look over to Malachai, who is holding eye contact with his father in the rearview mirror. Unspoken words pass between the two until, finally, Michael looks away and focuses his full attention on the road. Malachai seems to relax in his seat, reaching over to my lap and pulling my hand into his.

I glance down at our hands, subtly tucked away into each other's, out of Penny and Michael's view. For the first time, I *notice the varying shades of bruises on the back of Malachai's hand, trailing up his wrist and disappearing under his hoodie.*

Wake up... You need to wake up...

My heavy eyes open, and I inhale deeply as I start to rub my face hard enough to try to block out the memory. I let my arms drift back to their resting position before I spent the next few minutes staring at the wall on my left until I could feel my limbs again and move breaths in and out of my lungs.

Slowly, light begins to peek through the blinds, and I feel the dread of waking up day after day sink into my chest again. I want to stay in bed until I can shake the dream that is closer to memory than not.

Sighing, I drag myself out of bed and into the bathroom to scrub clean, and brush my teeth. After achieving that incredible feat, I dab the bare minimum of mascara and blush onto my face.

While staring at my work in the mirror, I tousle my hair so it falls in waves down my sides to dry naturally. It looks good enough to leave as is, and for that, I am relieved. I don't have the mental energy to achieve much more appearance-wise than I have already this morning.

Next, I venture back to my room and pull on a black long-sleeve turtleneck with matching tights and a skirt paired with the same old pair of Chucks I've had since the beginning of my stay at Willow Creek. They fit only how an old pair of shoes you should have thrown out years ago could fit: snug but molded perfectly just for me.

I unplug my phone from the nightstand charger and scroll through Shelly's messages. Her saying, *I'll be there asap, leaving now, 10 minutes out, up the street,* etcetera...I get to the last message when another message pops up where Shelly tells me she's here.

I reached Shelly after battling the front door as Riley watched me struggle. She tried to hide her smirk from her spot on the couch where she was nestled in with an Alternative Press magazine clutched in her hands.

I fought the urge to roll my eyes at her as she waved good-bye. I hustled down to Shelly, who had her nose buried in her phone, as I approached her and opened the passenger's door.

"I'm sorry. I was just replying to my son," Shelly says, grinning broadly. "Are you ready?"

I plaster a smile on my face and lie through my teeth. "Always."

After what feels like the longest day of my life, sitting and talking with my psychiatrist and then going to group therapy, I find myself waving bye to Shelly once more.

Shelly spent the day excitedly babbling about her son and how well he was doing when she saw him, and I couldn't help but be envious of their dynamic. I can hardly remember my mother's face at this point, much less her ever showing pride in my accomplishments.

What would that have been like? I want a mother like Shelly who takes the time out of her busy workday carting around a criminal like myself to speak to her child and show them love and affection.

I wish I had someone like that to share my days with.

I'm abruptly pulled from my thoughts as I feel a light nudge on my elbow and damn near levitate to follow my soul that just left my body. With wide eyes, I whip around and look into Riley's startled and apologetic eyes.

"Holy fuck," I gasp and then chuckle at my own overreaction. "Are you okay?"

Riley nods as she dangles a pair of car keys in front of my face and signals me to follow her. I walk after her without question and hop into the passenger seat of a dated black Bug from the early nineties. It takes a few turns of the ignition before the engine kicks on, and then we peel off down the road at slightly illegal speeds.

I look over at Riley, who has a smirk that shows she is pretty pleased with herself. I don't trust that look in the slightest, but I try to go with the flow until, after a few turns, my anxiety gets the best of me.

"Okay, what gives? Where are we headed?"

Riley reaches into her pocket, pulls out two small slips of paper, and hands them to me excitedly like she was waiting for me to ask. I read them over closely and nearly choke on my saliva as I realize they are VIP tickets to Malachai's art Gallery to see his new exhibit, which is currently closed to the general public.

"Holy shit! Where did you get these?" I ask incredulously.

She just shrugs and keeps on driving.

"Riley, I can't go there. What if we run into him? He probably doesn't even remember who I am."

She ignores me and taps her fingers on the steering wheel.

"Riley!"

"Stop being a pussy and just go."

I stare at Riley in stunned silence before bursting into laughter. Tears spring to my eyes, and I clutch at my stomach. Whenever I look back at Riley and see her giving me the side eye, I laugh again—a full minute passes before I inhale deep enough to speak.

"That... That is the first thing you say to me. Out of anything...." I sit up in my seat and dry my eyes with the back of my hands. "Fuck I haven't laughed that hard in, like...well, ever."

Riley gives me the side eye again and picks up speed until we pull into a parking garage across from the gallery. I watch Riley park and shove the car keys in her pocket as she unbuckles her seatbelt. I watch her in nervous silence as she slides out of her seat and slams the door.

She waits for me to follow her at the back of the car, but when it becomes apparent that I will not make any motion to move, she walks over to my side and yanks the door open.

"In all seriousness, though, I can't just walk in there, Riley," I say, trying to put as much finality into my voice as possible without being rude.

Riley rolls her eyes as she reaches over me, unbuckles my seatbelt, and grabs my arm to remove me from the vehicle physically. I try to pull my arm out of her grasp, but she's alarmingly strong for being so teeny. We grapple momentarily while I pull myself back into the car before a security cruiser pulls up next to us.

"Everything okay here?"

With a final light slap at Riley's prying hands, I turn and close the door. As I answer the security guard, I fix my clothing and hair in the window's reflection.

"Yup. Everything is fine. We're just on our way across the street."

Riley smirks triumphantly as we walk past the security guard. He glares at us as he slowly rolls up his window before driving off.

We walk in silence as we avoid any oncoming traffic, which, unfortunately, doesn't manage to take us out. At least that would have ended the never-ending anxiety that's growing more and more unbearable as the distance between us and Malachai decreases.

Once my feet hit the sidewalk on the opposite end of the street, I see in great detail an abstract, tall glass building glistening in the afternoon sun. I look through the glass and see multiple people on different floors, looking from one piece of work to the next.

I swallow as my eyes trail from the tallest floor full of people down until I am finally met with my reflection.

I have the same features I've always had, but there is a difference there that wasn't before. Just like my appearance, I know I have changed over the years as a person. What if he doesn't like who I've turned into?

What if he doesn't love me anymore?

I glance at Riley for words of encouragement, but she holds my gaze for a moment before walking into the gallery. She keeps the glass door open for me and makes a sweeping gesture with her free hand, ushering me forward.

Shaking my head in disbelief at where today has brought me, I step forward, expecting something dramatic to happen as I walk through the doors. Instead, I'm met with the smell of sawdust and a hint of a metallic tang in the air. I glance around as Riley walks over to an employee dressed all in black and hands her our tickets.

The gallery is everything you would expect of a modern art gallery. Wood floors, sharp edges, bright lights, and more employees walking around offering people champagne glasses as they murmur to themselves in hushed voices.

I take a few steps forward and see that the gallery has opted to hang Malachai's art by fiberglass wires from the industrial-looking ceiling, causing the life-size canvases to look like they're floating. The setup complements the canvas images that portray nearly all shades of red on the color spectrum as possible. Webs of red thread connect one work to the next, making each painting look like a continuation of the next. I am urged to reach up and run my fingers along the threads, but I refrain as I walk forward to take a closer look at Malachai's art.

Riley steps beside me as I continue from image to image. I see the works from yesterday's article in person and a few others that weren't mentioned. I stay on those the longest because they're the most abstract images.

I feel like I'm in on a sick secret that those around me are unaware of as I listen to the people around us whispering to themselves, trying to guess what the impressionistic images must signify since Malachai didn't leave any descriptions next to the titles of his paintings.

While looking at the first image, I see a horrifyingly familiar image of floorboards and smeared blood stains from where someone was dragged on the floor. The perspective is slightly higher than my memory, as if the person doing the dragging had this moment burned into their memory.

I clear my throat a bit due to the tightness I feel as I look over to the second image. This one is simpler. There are broken, thin lines with shades of red seeping out from them in a circular pattern that entwines in on itself. I stay on this image the longest as I subconsciously trace the mirror image that stains my left wrist like a fucked up bracelet made from pain.

Malachai used to run his fingers along them at night as we lay beside each other. I never knew what he thought of the marks, but I used to feel a sense of soothing when he would trace them as if he was showing that part of my body that had been abused the calm and gentle touch it had deserved from the beginning.

I feel Riley gently pull my hand away from my wrist and enclose it in her hand in a light, pleasant manner to stop the anxious rubbing of my scars. I spare her a glance and see she is staring at the image before she glances down at my scarred wrist and back at the image.

We stand there in silence for a few more minutes as the crowd starts to move on to the next image without us. I let Riley lead the way from one embodiment to the next. A few are more lighthearted, but most are more intense than the first few images we viewed. As we continue, the weight in my stomach grows heavier and heavier with the importance of the memory behind each image.

It seems on some level that our past has burned its way from Malachai's subconscious onto the canvases before us as if they refuse to be let go of or forgotten.

While I stare at the details of a familiar willow tree on one of the canvases, Riley pulls out her phone from her pocket and glances at the time. She nods to herself lightly and unexpectedly changes direction away from the exhibits before us.

Confused, I follow her as she walks up a flight of stairs to an empty floor with only a few office spaces at the far end of the corridor. One office has a few lights on inside it on the other side of a closed door.

Riley walks up to the door and taps on the glass before stepping away a few feet so I'm standing in her direct path instead of hers.

Before I can ask her what's happening, the door opens, and I'm greeted by an older woman dressed in black like the other employees. She is quite a bit shorter than me and looks like a cute old grandma.

"Hello there. Lake De Leon?" She asks with a friendly smile.

"Yes?"

"You are right on time. Come on in," she says while turning to walk back into her office.

I glance at Riley, who slides down the glass window into a crouching position to make herself more comfortable as she plays with the string on her hoodie. Seeing that she would not give me any other answers, I walked into the office behind the woman and closed the door with a soft click.

"My name is Ruby. I am head of facility management here alongside Ava Roybal, Malachai's sister and cofounder." Ruby says as she sits behind a clean, orderly desk in this new barren office center. "I am also close with Riley. I'm her grandmother."

Sitting across from her, I stare at her in stunned silence when she mentions her relationship with Riley and Ava.

"I usually don't set up interviews based on word of mouth alone, but Riley filled me in on your situation and sent me a copy of your resume. I understand you are part of a rehabilitation program."

I nod as I nervously clasp my hands together in my lap.

"Seeing as Malachai and Ava like to employ those in similar positions, such as yourself, I thought you would be a good fit for a starting position on our nighttime cleaning crew. Do you have any problems sweeping, lifting boxes, taking out the trash, or anything else?"

I clear my throat and answer her as calmly as possible. "Um, not at all. I don't mind that kind of work."

"Perfect. As you can see, we are a newer gallery in the area, and we are just getting started on getting established, so there is a lot of room for growth, especially with the new foundation that Ava will be proposing soon to our investors. If you are a hard worker and prove yourself, we can see what other positions open up."

"Oh, I mean...I'm more than grateful for what you're offering me already," I tell her honestly. I'm more grateful than she can imagine.

"Perfect. Our starting rate is fourteen dollars an hour. Are you able to start this Friday evening? The hours are from seven pm to seven am. We are working on a bit of a skeleton crew at the moment, so for the first few weeks, you are going to be some of our only staff on shift at that time, but I will be here for the first few hours of your first day to go over what needs to be done and how to do it."

"That works perfectly for me," I tell her with a genuine smile.

Ruby pulled a stack of papers from her desk and slipped them into a manila envelope before handing them to me. "Fill these out and bring them back to me at the beginning of your first day."

Ruby starts to stand, so I follow suit and reach my hand out to her to shake hers. "Thank you for this opportunity. You won't be disappointed."

Ruby gives me a polite smile as she grasps my hand. "We will see you on Friday."

Ruby ushers me out of her office and shuts the door behind me with a final wave. I look over to Riley, who is grinning from ear to ear from her spot on the floor.

I feel a grin creep onto my face as well. "Goddamnit, Riley."

Chapter Four

MALACHAI

"Did you hear how beautiful her voice was?" I ask Ruby from where I sit alongside the wall under her desk.

I situated myself here long before Ruby even arrived in her office, and I can tell by her posture that she is less than pleased that I took the liberty to do so.

But it was necessary. I needed to meet Lake on her terms as much as possible. I wanted to hear her voice and how she communicates with the world around her without the shock of seeing me eclipsing her natural reactions.

Ruby would not have understood this if I had explained this to her beforehand.

Ruby swallows and nods without further words. She just stares at me as I move from my position on the ground and stretch.

"She speaks so softly. It sounds like the echo of music lost on a rainy day..." I lean against Ruby's desk and roll up my sleeves on my dress shirt. "And she smelled like cherry blossoms. Fuck, I wish I could have seen her head-on. What did her eyes look like?

Ruby clears her throat nervously and takes a step away from me. "They were brown."

"And full of warmth, I assume?"

"Sure," she answers deadpan.

I roll my eyes and run a hand through my hair, tearing through the curls. Of course, she couldn't see anything beyond what was right before her. No one else seems to notice those small, minute details that make an individual them, but I always seem to feel like I am drowning in them.

I need to see her. Now.

As I approach Ruby, I transfer my weight from the desk to my feet. "Where are they going now?"

Ruby steps away from me until her back is pressed against the wall. "Home, I'm sure."

"Where do they live?" I ask.

"You said you would leave Riley out of this," Ruby states, looking up at me as terror fills her gaze.

"I said I would try. And for now, I am. But you don't understand, do you? I need to see her like I need to breathe. Are you really going to get in between us?"

Ruby swallows. "No, Mr. Rosemond."

"Good. Text me the address then. Goodnight, Ruby." I say as I step away from her and leave the office.

A few minutes later, I found myself in my car, on my way to see the address that Ruby had sent me. I speed through the streets with what I think must be excitement. I rub a hand against my chest as if the physical contact would still my racing heart.

This is... exhilarating. I do not think I have felt this much in ages. I feel...Scared, excited, and an unquenchable need. I need to see her, touch her, hear her voice again.

I need to feel her.

She lives only a short distance away from the gallery, which feels like a sign from the universe confirming to me that she belongs near me, with me, underneath me.

What if I am overthinking this? What if she doesn't match the girl I see when I close my eyes? What if she doesn't love me?

I shake my head. No, that all is impossible. Just the sound of her voice confirmed to me what I have known since I first started dreaming of her in the hospital.

She is mine.

And tonight, I will have her. I need to have her.

I follow my car's GPS directions to the less well-off part of town, where I find a run-down apartment building that seems to be where she lives.

I pull into the deserted garage and park before looking around. She should not be living here. It feels...dangerous. Anyone could have access to this building.

Anyone like me.

My phone starts buzzing in my pocket, and I look down to see two missed calls from Ava and four from my mother. I roll my eyes at them as I open the text notification from Ava that is illuminating my phone screen.

> Answer your fucking phone, or I am hunting
> you down within the hour.

I send a simple text letting her know I am fine and not up to my usual haunts.

Hardly two seconds later, another call from Ava rings, which I silence before putting my phone on Do Not Disturb.

I sit for the next two hours, watching the clock tick down and entertaining myself on my phone to make the time go by faster. This should be enough time for Riley and Lake to settle in for the night.

Finally, I slip from my vehicle and take the stairs up to the fourth floor, where I run my fingers along the dirty paint and doors, relishing the knowledge that she walks these halls daily.

Once I reach her door, I let my hand linger on the cool, peeling paint. I sigh as I press my ear against the door and listen for any movement on the other side, but I am met with none. I glance at the gap at the bottom of the door and see no light peeking out from underneath. They must be asleep. If not, that doesn't matter either way, does it?

I pull some tools from my wallet and quickly work the lock before entering the apartment. I walk around, running my fingers over as many surfaces as possible to ensure that I touch everything she has possibly touched.

She has likely only been here for over a day, but that is long enough for her scent to linger in the air. Cherry blossoms. My new favorite scent.

Off to the left of the living room, I hear metal music on a low volume coming out from a light-filled door. That must be Riley's room. I remember overhearing Ruby complain about her taste in music while making small talk with one of the other gallery workers so that she could ignore my presence. I was annoyed then, but now I am grateful for that information.

I turn to the right and see no other lights from the twin door. I smile as I walk over to it and test the doorknob. Locked. Smart woman.

But then again, that wouldn't stop someone who wanted to get inside. Someone like me, whose heart is pounding out of their chest with the mere thought of seeing her in the flesh.

I also work on this lock, keeping Riley's door in my peripheral vision in case she decides to leave her room. Soon enough, I hear a soft click that signals it is time to enter.

I stretch and stand to full height as I open the door and walk a few paces before I stop dead.

"Oh fuck..." I whisper to myself.

Lake stirs in her bed and rolls from her left side, giving me a full view of her beautiful bare chest. The comforter of her bed rides up between her legs, showing off her right hip and stomach. I clench my fist at my side to dull the ache of needing to run my fingers along her bare thigh.

Moonlight peaks through her window, making her pale skin and ash hair glow in an ethereal way. She unconsciously licks at her thick, full lips and groans in her sleep, causing me to grow immediately hard.

Why the fuck is she sleeping naked?

The irrational part of my brain tells me she did this for me. She must have known I would find her here, and she is presenting her beautiful self to me as a gift, an offering, one that I need to take.

I close the door behind me before walking closer to the side of Lake's bed. She breathes heavily and groans once more. I wonder what she is dreaming about.

"Malachai..." My name escapes her lips in a soft whimper.

Oh fuck she has me. More than I thought she ever could have, which feels impossible.

I let my hands drift from my sides to the zipper of my dress pants, where I slowly free the length of myself, sighing in relief to be absent of the pressure of my clothing.

I stroke myself slowly, not daring to take my eyes off of her as I brace myself with my free arm against the wall. I bite my lip to contain my groan as my fist tightens and I quicken my pace.

I haven't felt this way ever. No one has even given me a hard-on, not for the lack of trying on their part. I was starting to think I might just be asexual, but within minutes of seeing her, I want her. I want every inch of her. I want to make her mine.

My gaze drifts from her to her nightstand, and I see she has laid out her clothing for tomorrow, with a pair of cotton underwear lying on top. Perfect.

I grab them and wrap them around the length of myself as I reach my release. My body shutters, and my eyes flutter as I try to quiet my heavy breathing.

As the pleasure slowly starts to dissipate from my body, I rub my fluids deeper into the fabric before returning the underwear to its original spot on her nightstand.

"Fuck, Lake," I whisper breathlessly.

Her only answer is to groan once more and roll onto her left side, facing away from me. I cover myself before kneeling beside her bed, where I start to count the individual strands of her hair, which fans out against the mattress.

She is so beautiful...

Chapter Five

LAKE

"Stop, stop, stop, please—I'm sorry!" I scream as Penny yanks me down into the wine cellar.

I stumble in her gasp and try to regain my balance against the wall, but fall onto all fours as I scramble away from her.

Tears spring to my eyes as she grabs me by the back of my neck and yanks me back into a standing position. I try to grasp the wall for balance as she pries open the cellar door and tosses me in before slamming it shut and dead-bolting it from the outside.

I run a shaking hand through my hair and try to calm my breathing as I stare at the door. I slowly turn to where I know Malachai is chained to the brick wall behind an empty wine case that obstructs him from view. I take slow and delicate steps to ensure I do not startle him.

I find him sitting up, his arms propped up on his bent knees, and his head leaned back against the wall. He smirked at me playfully as he saw me approach.

"*That has to be a new record for you. You lasted three days against Penny,*" *he says without any humor.*

I sigh and walk over to him. He opens his arms for me to bury myself in them. Three years have passed since I came to live with the Rosemonds, and Malachai has become my only place of comfort. He is the only person who can soothe my pain with the touch of his hand or voice. He has become my family, and I love him more than words express.

His skin feels cold against mine, so I pull our shirts up enough to free some of my skin to press against him to warm him up. He sighs at the feeling and relaxes into me as he pushes his face into the crook of my neck.

"*I'm sorry. I wasn't able to bring you food today,*" *I apologize while trying to hide the shakiness in my voice.*

"*I am just happy to have you here, Lake. It is lonely without you.*"

A blush heats my cheeks as I change the subject. "*Ava or Gage will bring us something if they can.*"

He smiles against my neck. "*I know.*"

I pull away from him slightly enough to inspect him to make sure he isn't any worse than when I saw him last night. He looks exhausted and malnourished, but the wounds on his neck from where the chain rubs against his flesh finally look like they are on the mend.

"*Are you holding up okay?*" *I ask him.*

He chuckles to himself and gives me a lopsided grin. "*I am in perfect health, Lake. I have never been better.*"

I frown as I rest my head against his. "*Fucking liar.*"

He sighs and murmurs, "*I love you too.*"

I steady my breathing before sitting in bed and looking for my phone. I find it lying beside me, buried in the sheets, and I groan as I notice missed calls from Shelly.

Fuck, I'm going to be late.

I decide to skip a shower as I rush to pull on the clothing I had laid on my nightstand the night before. I pull on a black bra before pulling on the underwear, pausing at their slight stiffness. What the hell?

I decided against changing them since I got them straight out of the package. They may soften once I run them through the wash at the laundromat. Ignoring the odd texture, I pull on the rest of my clothing and call Shelly to let her know I'm on my way downstairs.

An hour later, I wondered why I was rushing to make it on time for this appointment.

"I know this is rather unexpected, but I appreciate your flexibility," Dr. Fiyero mutters as I plop down into my usual spot on a dusty futon in Willow Creeks' outpatient psychiatric facility.

Dust puffs up in the air as I try to rub the sleep from my eyes. Sleep has been almost non-existent due to vivid dreams since I left Willow Creek.

I feel like crawling out of my skin.

I try to suppress my annoyance as I ask, "Where's Dr. Luis?"

"They are taking a brief sabbatical due to a family emergency, so I will be taking over their caseload for the next few months," Dr. Fiyero murmurs with a sigh at the end as he sits down across from me.

"Oh."

Dr. Fiyero crosses his legs and then laces his fingers over his knees while peering at me over his glasses. He looks like any stereotypical psychiatrist you would see in a drama on TV.

"So tell me what happened to get me up to speed."

What happened...

That's an agitating way to put it.

"Did you not read over my file?" I ask, leaning against the futon to see the ceiling.

"I did, but reading it from someone not involved in the situation can be rather convoluted."

"Which part?" I ask in a monotone voice.

"All of it. So start from the beginning," he says, matching my tone.

I resist the urge to roll my eyes. "Define beginning."

"Well, what was the beginning for you?" he asks.

I pause momentarily before letting my head roll to the side to hold his eye contact. "That is hard to pinpoint, and I feel like there were multiple beginnings to everything."

"Tell me about them then. All of them."

I look back up to the ceiling. "There is always the beginning, being how my parents met and got to the unfortunate decision of having me. Then there's when they died, and then when I went to stay with the senator and his wife."

"How did you feel about your parents' deaths?" he asks.

"Which set?" I retort.

"Your biological parents. After reading your file and the court reports, I don't think it would be deemed appropriate to call the senator and his wife your parents, let alone the parents of any other children involved at the time."

I nod a bit and answer him. "It was sad but not unexpected. They both had a bad heroin problem and got a bad batch. Happens all the time."

"Who was the one that found them? Was it you?" he asks.

I swallow and try to answer him without emotion. "Yeah."

"How did you take it at the time?"

I sigh and look back over at him. "I was sad. What ten-year-old wouldn't be sad to lose their parents? Why are we bringing this up again? I've already worked through all that grief three therapists ago."

"Do you not want to explain it to me?"

40

"No."

"Why?"

I sit up and meet his studious gaze. "Because I am exhausted. You're not the second, third, or even fourth psychologist I have told this to. There were the paramedics, then the cops, and then more cops, and the doctors, and then multiple lawyers and jurors, and I could continue with the lists of strangers I have had to bare my soul to and tell my most humiliating and dehumanizing moments to over and over again just to explain why I am the way I am and how I ended up here. It's exhausting to be pitied and gawked at like some cautionary tale of how fucked up things can get for one person."

"You think people are gawking at you?"

I scoff. "They always have been. People love tragedy, and it's entertaining for them until they have to hear it repeatedly and deal with the consequences of someone else's actions. I never asked for any of this, and it's exhausting to be the one who has to apologize for it constantly."

"You don't have to keep apologizing."

I roll my eyes. "Of course I do. Why do you think you and I are even talking in the first place? I have to be babysat and act as if I deserved to be locked up in the first place."

"Do you think what you did to your foster parents was justified?" he asks.

"After reading the court reports, do you? What would you have done if you were in our shoes?"

Dr. Fiyero smiles a bit. "This isn't my therapy session."

With my hand on the futon's arm, I prop my head up and hold his gaze until he continues talking.

"Have you talked with your foster siblings about what happened?" he asks.

"You know I haven't. I tried sending letters, but I don't know if they ever even got them."

"I mean since you got out? From seeing how adamant you were about talking to them when you first arrived at Willow Creek, I figured you would have tried to find them as soon as possible and reach out."

I hold his gaze evenly and answer as carefully as I can. "I wanted to, and I still do. But I haven't spoken to them."

He smirks to himself again and continues talking. "I did some research about them, and I figured telling you a bit about them in a controlled setting would be best rather than wandering the streets yourself to find them."

I didn't have to wander far, thanks to Riley.

I keep my face as neutral as possible. "Oh yeah?"

"Gage, Ava, and Malachai were adopted into the same family after they were released from the hospital. Gage stayed with his adopted family until he turned twenty-two, where he seemed to fall off the books. Ava and Malachai seem to be doing well, especially Malachai, from what the newspapers and magazines have to say about it. Ava works for him at his company and seems to have a big share in it."

I nod and wait for him to continue.

"You must be proud of her. How old would she be now?" he asks.

I clear my throat. "I am proud. She and Gage would be twenty-five."

"And Malachai?"

I clear my throat again to try to remove the frog in it. "Twenty-seven. He is a year older than me."

"How do you feel about missing out on the years between now and when you last saw them? It must be difficult," he says in a sympathetic voice.

I blink back a few tears and lean back once more on the futon. "Difficult is an understatement, Dr. Fiyero."

"Do you think they feel the same way you do about them?"

I don't hesitate to answer. "Yes, of course."

"Then why haven't you reached out yet?" he asks pointedly.

I look down at my shoes and don't answer him.

Dr. Fiyero sighed as he reached over to scribble a note in my file. " I don't think you will have to worry about the timing not being right for long. Your siblings are probably closer than you think."

Chapter Six

LAKE

The day after my appointment with Dr. Fiyero, Riley drops me off in front of the *Galleria De Rosemond*. Before walking inside, I stare at the newly hung gold calligraphy lettering above the entrance. I stand awkwardly by the door for a minute before I decide to ask the ticketing woman to let Ruby know I am here for training.

I clutch my manilla folder tightly to my chest and try to make myself as small as possible if Ava or Malachai are near working on some sort of business.

I glance around and watch the ticketing woman return with another manilla folder in the crook of her arm and a frown on her face.

"Everything okay?" I ask her as her scowl deepens.

She hands me the folder. "Here. Ruby left this for you. She left early today. These are the instructions for you and keys to lock up the place at closing at nine."

As I grab the folder from her, the keys fall onto the floor

with a loud plop. I give her an apologetic smile and grab them from the floor. Before I even straighten up fully, she is already walking back to her post, which means I am on my own now.

I open the folder and pull out the instructions as I go to the back of the gallery, out of sight of the roaming guests. The directions are everything you would expect from a night crew cleaning job. Simple and straightforward.

I make my way up to the top floor, which is full of empty studios for artists to paint. I find the supplies closet and work from the studio closest to the stairs to the one farthest away at the end of the hallway. The rest of the studio spaces were left open except this one. I flip through the keys that Ruby left for me until I find the right one and open the room there.

I gasp lightly at the beautiful space. It's cast in a warm glow from the sunset, illuminating the few canvases that are a work in progress. This one is pristinely clean, unlike the other studios that seemed to be occupied by different artists. Not a speck of paint is on the hardwood floor, and there is no sign of a drop canvas or other art supplies. The room has a few plants along the peripherals and the large paintings' easels.

A catwalk hangs from the ceiling so the lights can be adjusted to complement the paintings. Gazing up at it, I walk over to the glass wall and peer down at the people walking along the sidewalk on their way to wherever they're going. They all look so serene from up here.

I pull myself away from the window and look over to my left, where I see an office with a black door. The other studios did not have this in them. Curiosity wins out as I walk over to it and try the door to see if it unlocks—no such luck. I try the keys on the key ring, but none work. I pull my debit card out, courtesy of Shelly, shimmy it above the lock, slide it in and down, and simultaneously pull the door towards me. I feel the door give and swing open with a satisfying click. I quickly inspect the card to make sure I didn't ruin the magnetic strip, but it looks fine even though it has a few scratches on it now.

As I walk in, I am met with another spotless room. It has a black desk with a hutch pressed against the far wall. Under the desk is a mini fridge. I walk over to it and open it, wondering what snacks this person may choose to have in here.

Instead, I find containers of red liquid. Four, to be exact. I tilt my head to the side in confusion, and then I remember the slightly metallic smell I first encountered while coming to the gallery for the first time.

Blood. I was smelling blood.

I scrunch my nose and realize this is Malachai's office and studio. No one else would be painting with blood.

I remember watching Malachai leaning over me on a bloody white mattress, painting flowers along my skin while he whispered sweet and soothing words.

It is a disturbing memory but beautiful in its own right.

I shake the image away and look around the office to see if there are more signs of Malachai besides the blood. The only indication I see of him is a photo of my foster family sitting on his desk, and I pick it up to inspect it closer. The faces and hands of the senator and his wife are burned out, and I wouldn't expect anything else. I'm sure if he wasn't the one to do that, it must have been Ava.

I run my fingers lightly over the faces of Ava and Gage in the photo. They look so young and small here—more petite than they should have been. It was taken in July after my fifteenth birthday, so they should've been fourteen in this photo, but they looked much younger, so much so that they could have quickly passed for being under ten years old. They have fake smiles plastered on their faces, which we were trained to put on for public events.

I grimace at the image and look over to where Malachai and I are standing in the photo. I am a mirror of Ava and

Gage, with slightly deeper circles under my eyes. Malachai, on the other hand, is looking off past the camera with a straight face. No fake smile that doesn't touch his eyes. I remember the senator's wife being pissed about him ruining the photo.

Looking at it now, I wonder what he must have been thinking. Did he see freedom off in the distance beyond the camera's lens?

My stomach starts to turn the longer I gaze upon the photo, so I put the image down quickly as if it were beginning to burn my hand. Trying to find a distraction from the picture, I open the drawers in the desk and find vials of heparin with a thermometer inside. I assume that is to keep the blood from clotting.

In the other drawers are IV kits and eighteen-gauge needles. It also doesn't take a genius to guess what those are for.

I close the drawers and leave the office, ensuring the door locks behind me. Although it looks like there is nothing to clean in the rest of the studio, I still wipe down all surfaces before I sweep and mop the floor. I even take a few extra minutes to water the plants and ensure they are in perfect condition before locking up behind me.

I move on to the other floors and clean the place almost neurotically just to distract myself from my thoughts, which are taking darker turns as the hours pass. I'm out of breath and shaky as I finish the last items on the list.

As I put away supplies a few hours before the end of my shift, I hear the beep of the front entrance alarm and the lock turning in the door. I quickly shut the supplies closet before stepping behind one of Malachai's canvases, which obscures most of me besides my feet. I had dimmed the lights hours ago after closing and locking up the place, so I hope whoever's coming in now quickly walks past and leaves me to finish my shift alone.

I hear the front entrance lock once more and the alarm being reset. I hold my breath as I hear familiar footfalls. I would know the sound in my sleep. The sound is almost blocked out by my heart pounding in my ears, and I don't dare move a muscle as the footfalls get closer and closer.

Finally, he walks past the canvas I am hiding behind and continues towards the stairs leading to the upper floors. If he were to alter his gaze slightly to his left, there is no way he'd miss me where I'm standing. I almost want him to do so so I can lock eyes with him again. I want that as much as I wish for him to continue walking because I have no clue what I would even begin to say to him after all this time.

Why didn't you write?

Why didn't you visit me?

Why...Why did you leave me all alone?

As he reaches the stairs, his steps slow to a stop with his left hand on the rail. He pauses for what feels like a lifetime before continuing up the stairs without a glance behind him.

I wait a minute while staring at the outline of Malachai that my brain has imprinted itself with from where he hesitated on the steps. After I hear the sound of doors opening and closing above me, I follow him up the stairs to the top floor.

The hallway that leads to his workspace is pitch black, which allows the door at the end of the hallway to be brightly outlined by the lights within. I walk down the hallway to the door and leave my hand lingering over the door knob. Should I knock? Should I just walk in?

I remember the catwalk above his studio that I saw while I was cleaning. Most exhibit areas had the catwalk available, but this was the only studio with one. I step away from the door and take a few minutes to explore this floor before I find the entrance to the catwalk in the utility closet. I slowly make my way up the steep ladder and ignore the fluttery feeling in my stomach because I see how high up I will have to climb.

Once I am up the ladder onto the catwalk, I slowly move from my hands and knees up to unsteady feet. I take one slow step after the next, rolling my feet as I walk so they make virtually no noise. After a minute, I stand above Malachai as he stares at one of his canvases with only a few shades of red splattered onto it.

I slowly crouch back down to a sitting position. As I get as comfortable as possible, I rest my chin on my knees and wrap my arms tightly around myself as I watch him. He stands so still that I could almost imagine him as a Greek statue of one of the gods.

His wild black hair gleams under the lighting of his studio as it curls gently around his earlobes, the length of it just barely kissing his shoulders. I flex my fingers slightly as I remember the feel of how those curls would wrap around my fingers when I held him close to me. They were soft, like silk, and as black as a raven's wings.

I smile, glad for the familiar feature, but his changes also take my breath away.

As a teenager, he was tall and slim, but now, as a man, his shoulders are wide and broad. I can see the outline of muscles under his black button-down shirt. I want to run my hands over them to learn the changes in his frame and then commit them to my memory.

He wears glasses now. I always told him he needed to check his vision, but I never thought he would have the chance to. Now I see they complement his face nicely. The black frames sit on his straight nose perfectly, bringing out the deep black of his eyes, which were always like sharks', deadly and mesmerizing all in one. I miss looking into his eyes.

When he looked at you, he made you feel like the only person in the universe.

And when he would look at me...He looked at me like I was his savior, his lifeline; all the while, he was mine.

Suddenly, Malachai steps away from the painting and pulls a cell phone from his black dress pants. I watch him scroll briefly before he presses on a few things on the screen. I soon hear music flow from the speakers hanging from the catwalk. A lonely, melancholy tune surrounds us, perfectly complementing this moment.

I watch Malachai enter his office and step out with one of the containers I saw earlier. I stop breathing as he grows closer to the canvas below me. I watch as he sets the container on the ground and slowly unbuttons his shirt.

Once he reaches the last button, he lets the shirt slip from his shoulders down to the floor, where it pools at his feet. I hold my breath in anticipation as he reaches towards his waistband and pulls out two paint brushes stained red on the ends. After he moves the brushes from his right to his left hand, he picks up the red container and approaches the canvas.

I exhale at the sight.

Beautiful. He is so very beautiful...

For the next few hours, I sit and watch Malachai paint like I used to when we were younger. I feel at home listening to the music he chooses to inspire him, and I get to selfishly stare at his body as it stretches up or down to reach different parts of the canvas.

For the first time in years, I long for the feeling of charcoal in my hands to capture how Malachai's muscles move under his skin. I long to blacken my hands in an effort to recreate the beauty of every extension and flexion of his body. Maybe if I could acutely recreate his visage, he could finally stop haunting me.

All too soon, I see the sunrise in the distance. I know it's time to pull myself from my perch, but I am stuck with a nearly unbearable ache in my chest at the thought of leaving him.

Standing slowly, I spare one last glance at Malachai while blinking back tears before making my way out.

After my feet are firmly back on the ground, I hurry to the main floor and say my goodbyes to the day cleaning crew before passing the keys to them.

I leave the front doors of the gallery, making sure to stand off to the far side of the left of the building as I wait for Riley to pick me up so that if Malachai looks out the window down at the people like I had been, he won't see me.

I don't wait long as Riley pulls up in front of me and reaches over to the passenger door to open it for me from the inside. She raises her eyebrows at me in a questioning way.

"I saw him," I say with a grin.

Chapter Seven

MALACHAI

"I saw her," I tell Ava from where I am lounging on the black sofa in her office.

Ava chokes on the coffee she has been nursing behind her desk since seven this morning. Once she has composed herself, she looks over to me, completely forgetting the budget for the gallery's upcoming year. "When? Where?"

"Last night...Well, technically, the night before that, too."

"What did she say?"

"Nothing. I just followed her and her roommate home. Do you know she likes to sleep naked? Did she used to do that when we were younger?" I ask her.

Ava runs a frustrated hand through her perfect hair as a shadow passes over her expression. "Not by choice, no."

I sit up and lean forward towards Ava. "Please tell me that I gave my father the gruesome death he deserved."

"Not gruesome enough, in my opinion," Ava mutters.

"Fuck."

Ava clears her throat and looks me over. "What else happened?"

I think back to the image of her in bed and how the fabric of her underwear felt around my cock. "Nothing."

Ava stares at me unblinking, seeing right through my bullshit, per usual. "And last night? Where did you see her?"

"Here. You know the new night cleaner I asked you to hire?" I say, a grin spreading on my face.

"You fucking didn't."

"I did. Well, technically, Ruby did."

"She would do anything you ask her to. She's scared as shit of you."

I wave off her comment. "They all are."

"With good reason to be."

I stand and walk over to where Ava is sitting in her chair. She swivels to meet me and looks at me with deep, crystal-blue eyes. I gently caress her face while tucking the hair behind her ear. "But you are not. You never have been."

Ava closes her eyes and leans into my gentle touch. "I've tried to be. But I can't. Even after everything you've done, I would still do anything for you. This is why I am ignoring the large donation made to Lake's facility last month."

"They weren't going to let her out, and you know she didn't deserve to be there in the first place."

Ava nods. "I know."

I smile down at her. "That is why I am asking you to let her stay. The staff fear me but respect you. If you asked Ruby to make her leave, she would, out of loyalty to you. So please, for me, let her stay?"

Ava's eyes open, and I see that fire again, which only appears when I mention Lake. "Why, though? She forgot about us. She moved on. I haven't heard a word from her in eleven years, and now she thinks she can just come into our lives again. It's fucked, and fuck her too."

I force my expression to stay neutral as I try to quell the rage I feel at Ava speaking about Lake with such venom. "Ava..."

Ava notices the change in my gaze and lightly pushes my hands from her face. "Nevermind, Malachai. She can stay. I just don't want to see her myself, okay? Keep her away from me."

I nod as I watch her pretend to go back to working on the budget. I take that as her dismissing me, and I approach the door before pausing.

"She is your sister, Ava. You will have to talk to her eventually. If not for me, do it for yourself."

Ava keeps her gaze glued to her paperwork, but I can't help but notice how her breath catches a bit as she bows her head lower so I cannot see her face.

I decide not to push her further and exit, returning to my office. I will have to fix the rift between us sooner rather than later.

Especially with Gage.

Which reminds me...

I pull my phone from my back pocket and scroll through my contacts until I find the name of the facility I am looking for.

The line rings a few times before a perky voice answers.

"Hello, this is Malachai Rosemond. Is my brother available?"

The perky woman quickly agrees, and she puts me on hold.

After a few minutes, a gruff voice answers. "What the fuck do you want?"

I smile, glad to hear his voice again. "It's time to come home, brother."

Chapter Eight

LAKE

I let out a sigh of relief for what feels like the first time in years. Penny is going to meet Michael in DC, and she left the cellar door unlocked, allowing us out for free reign of the house.

Once the coast is clear, Ava and I run to the kitchen to start working on our feast for the evening.

While we try not to burn the house to the ground, I hear the sound of laughter from outside. I stop what I am doing and walk over to the large kitchen window, where I see Malachai and Gage playing some botched version of football. Gage laughs hysterically as Malachai trips over a sprinkler and loses his grip on the ball, enough for Gage to steal it right out from under him. Gage's blond hair and blue eyes glisten in the sunlight as he does a victory dance, making him look angelic and blissful.

Malachai jumps to his feet and takes off after Gage with the biggest grin I have seen on his face yet. His joy almost blocks the sight of the dark circles under his eyes and pale skin from being *malnourished for so long. My heart flutters at the image of him running free. This is how he should always be.*

After preparing our meal, we call Malachai and Gage to eat at the big Victorian table that Ava took extra care of setting so that it would look like a dinner party. She and Gage sit at one end together and gush over the food and fresh ingredients while Malachai pulls up a chair next to me and scoots in close enough so that our knees are just barely brushing. I inhale deeply and allow myself to smile at the contact.

The rest of the dinner continues in silence as we devour our meal. Ava and I are probably not the best cooks in the world, but after having scraps for so long, this tastes like heaven. Especially the cake that we managed to bake. It came out better than expected on our first try.

Once we are finished, I grab some non-perishables from the kitchen and take the time to hide them in various nooks and crannies of the cellar. I also make a trip to the back of the linen closet to find things I know Penny will not miss and stash those for us. I have been doing this on a smaller scale every time I am out, but this seems the perfect time to do some significant stashing. I also make sure to toss in a few books and playing cards since playing rock-paper-scissors to pass the time so much has almost brought all of us to blows.

I am about to head down to the cellar with my newly found items but hesitate as I walk past Michael's office. I pause at the door before making my decision and open the door lightly and as quietly as possible. I enter the office, grab a stack of paper and a few pens, and add them to my pile of goods. Malachai might like these for something to pass the time with.

Satisfied with my work, I go across the house back to the kitchen to find the others. I pass a few maids and gardeners along the way. They take extra care not to look at me since they're under the thumb of Michael and his checkbook. I honestly stopped acknowledging them since they've been so complacent about the treatment of us, disregarding the abuse they see.

When I return to the kitchen, Ava and Gage turn on the radio to some old-school jams and dance as if this were a real party. We all take turns as partners, but I would be lying if I said I wasn't more excited to dance with Malachai whenever the chance arose. My hands fit perfectly with his as if they were made for him and him alone.

Finally, I tuck Gage and Ava into one of the guest rooms after they shower and get comfy for the night. They are fast asleep when their heads hit the soft pillows.

Closing the door with a soft click, I go to the guest bathroom down the hallway and start to run a bath with the hottest water and most bubbles I can manage. I have dreamed of this moment for months and will enjoy it thoroughly.

I strip out of my clothes and leave them in a neat pile on the floor as I dip into the water and slowly submerge myself fully. I hold my breath under the water until my lungs scream for air before sitting up with a gasp. I rub the water from my eyes and see Malachai leaning against the wall with his arms folded, watching me with a slight tilt of his head.

I stare at him with wide eyes as he straightens up and pulls his black hoodie over his head.

"Turn around," he says firmly.

Unable to do anything besides what he says, I scoot myself in the large tub until my back faces him. After a moment, I hear the water shift as he joins me. I sit as still as possible, knees tightly against my chest, as I feel the skin of his back gently press against mine. Another hesitant moment passes before he settles more fully against me and rests his head on my shoulder.

"Today is the best day," he murmurs.

It really is...

. . .

After another night of broken sleep, I sit on the catwalk above Malachai's studio again. He isn't painting today. He is just sitting on the ground, staring at the traffic with his back to me. His shoulders seem tight as if he's troubled by something. I watch as he moves from one position of comfort to the next as he watches those below him.

While I lightly adjust my cramping legs, he stands up abruptly and walks out of his studio with a slam of the door. I jump a bit at the noise.

Wondering what could be troubling him, I wait for him to return.

I start to fidget a bit, deciding whether to leave my current position, when I feel the hairs on the back of my neck stand up.

I feel the phantom light graze of fingers in my hair. The pressure of the feeling increases, and I jump up from my sitting position and turn to face Malachai as he straightens up from where he is crouching behind me. He stares at me blankly with his head tilted slightly to the left.

My throat tightens up as I hold his gaze. I open my mouth several times, hoping to form the right words. But standing here, there is still nothing.

He tilts his head to the other side and continues looking at my face. "What are you doing here?"

"I've missed you," I state honestly.

"Why?" he asks as he steps slowly toward me.

"Do you remember why?" I ask, taking a step away from him and onto the catwalk.

He thinks about that before answering. "Not completely."

"Do you know who I am?" I ask, trying to steady my quivering voice.

He takes another step towards me. "You are the girl that I dream about."

58

"What else?" I ask hopefully. "Please tell me you remember more...Please..."

Malachai stares at me with that hauntingly blank expression that looks so unfamiliar as he lets my pleading hang between us. It looks like a mask placed over his usual kind, smiling features.

Wrong...this is wrong...

Unable to bear this drastic change in his demeanor, I try to walk past Malachai as he steps further into my path. I try to avoid touching him, but he reaches out and lightly holds my forearms to keep me from moving further. The familiar pressure of his grasp nearly breaks the floodgate of tears I am trying to withhold.

Malachai tightens his grip as he pulls me closer to him. "What did you miss about me?" he asks in a tone that is too smooth.

I pull away from his grip and steady myself against the catwalk's railing, trying to avoid looking down while also trying to avoid looking at him.

He steps closer again and presses his body against mine while placing his arms on either side of me to hold me in place. "What did you miss about me, Lake?"

Hearing my name from his mouth causes me to snap my gaze up to his and hold it. It almost sounded how he used to say it, with such love and reverence.

"Everything," I whisper honestly.

I stare at him momentarily before lightly pressing my hands against his chest to distance us. I hold his gaze while stepping away before turning and going down the catwalk with hurried steps.

There is something wrong with him....

Once my feet hit the solid ground, I make my way out of the utility closet. I look back to see if Malachai is following me down the ladder as I run full force into someone in the hallway. Their small frame hits me squarely in the ribs, knocking the breath out of my lungs. I double over with my hand clutching my chest and gasp a nearly inaudible apology.

I glance behind me again to see Malachai jumping from the ladder and landing lightly on his feet. He locks gazes with the person I ran into over my shoulder, giving them the same odd, blank expression that he had been giving me. I turn back to them and finally look into the face of the person I ran into. When I realize who is standing before me, the breath is knocked out of me all over again.

"Ava," Malachai says in greeting to her.

Her deep auburn hair is cut above her chin and sways slightly as she regains balance. She looks prim and perfect in a business suit and black stilettos, paired with a pearl jewelry set adorning her delicate neck and ears. Her pale skin contrasts with her red lips and blue eyes, glistening with frustration. I feel the smile that had been forming on my lips at the sight of her healthy glow falling from my face as suddenly as it had appeared.

"I got your text, Malachai." Ava straightens up fully and lifts her chin at me. "What are you doing here?"

I step back from her as the venom in her voice bites into me. This was the same question Malachai had asked, but it holds so much more emotion behind it.

"I missed you," I answer her, as I had answered Malachai.

Ava turns her gaze away from me with disgust and looks at Malachai. "Make her leave, or I will."

Stunned at her reaction, I turn from her without looking back at Malachai and make my way from the floor down multiple flights of stairs until I find the emergency exit that leads outside at the base of the stairwell. Luckily, the alarm did not sound during my escape.

Feeling lost and shocked by what had just transpired, I walk down the street toward Riley's and my home. I have a few more hours before Riley picks me up, and I am sure she would come for me if I called now, but my head is swimming with chaos, and I need to clear it.

I slow my walking and finally stop when I cannot look back and see the clear crystal of the gallery behind me. Tears fail to fall from my eyes, but I feel a distinct quiver in my lower lip. I try to steady my breathing as I get odd looks from the people on their early morning walks down the sidewalk.

Trying to avoid eye contact with them, I hug my arms to myself and continue walking to quiet my thoughts. The morning chill bites deep into my bones to the point it is almost as painful as the void in my chest, but it is welcome. I would rather have the physical pain than the mental pain that leaves phantom traces all over my body.

Since leaving Willow Creek, I have slowly felt myself slip back into that void where nothing but seeing Malachai and being near him would fill. I haven't slept or eaten much, and I know that that is taking its toll now just as much as the pain of Ava's rejection or Malachai's unfamiliar gaze.

After walking almost endlessly, I see the outline of my apartment against the pale gray sky. I speed up until I am locked securely inside the elevator leading up to the fourth floor. I lean against the wall and let the warmth of the metal panels seep into my skin. As the doors opened to deposit me onto my floor, I realized I had left my purse with the apartment keys and phone back at the gallery.

With a frustrated groan, I knock on our apartment and wait for Riley to battle the door to open it for me. I hear a few crashes and rattling on the other side of the wall until Riley opens the door and peaks around it.

Riley lets out an audible sigh of relief as she opens the door and steps into the kitchen. I step inside after her and watch her toss a steak knife that she had answered the door with onto the counter.

Riley stops and turns back to face me to look me over. Worry washes over her face at the sight of me.

"I'm okay, just ah, spoke with Ava and Malachai," I state for lack of a better explanation.

Riley nods and gestures me over to the couch, where she has set herself up with a warm cup of coffee and a fluffy blanket. As I sit beside her, she passes me the blanket, which I gratefully accept.

"Do you want to talk about it?" she asks softly.

I nod and reiterate the interaction with Malachai and then the confusing confrontation with Ava.

After I told Riley everything, we turned on the TV across from us and put on a random baking show while I tried to warm up.

As time passes, we make a plan for me to go pick my stuff up from the gallery, but for now, it is nice to hang out and try to settle my thoughts.

When I can feel my toes again enough to walk, I get up and go into the shower to clean up a bit.

While passing the mirror, I strip off my clothing in defeated motions before slipping into the shower. The scalding water calms me almost as much as the cold bite of the air outside. I reach down to the faucet to make the water hotter, just to drown out all other feelings.

I do the bare minimum to make myself look human before shutting off the water and entering my room. I lock the door, drop the towel around me to the floor, and slide naked into bed, too tired to do anything else.

I count in my head until, finally, the darkness takes me.

Chapter Nine

MALACHAI

"Where are you going?" Ava asks me with a mixture of hurt and rage in her voice.

I continue down to the garage where my car is, slightly agitated at the fact that it takes Ava two steps for every one step I take to keep up with me. It's odd to be agitated about this, but I can surmise that it's not just her shortness making my stomach churn with my rage but everything about her.

"After her. Did you see her face?" I ask in a hollow tone as I arrange Lake's belongings into one arm so I can pry open the car door with my other.

Where the fuck did she go? Did her roommate pick her up? No... She doesn't have her phone. She must have walked.

Maybe I can find her.

Ava wedges herself between me and the door. "Wait, Malachai."

I look up at the ceiling, praying for patients to a deaf god. "Move. Now."

63

"No, I told you to keep her away from me, and you fucking tricked me into running into her by telling me to come meet you in your studio. You don't get to be pissed off at me for what you did!" Ava glares up at me with that stubborn expression of hers.

"I can, though. And I am. Now move before I move you." I tell her, holding her unblinking gaze.

She shakes her head at me and lifts her chin defiantly, holding her ground. If at all possible, my anger deepens to unspeakable depths. I lean close to her face and allow my face to twist into the sneer I have been holding back.

"Tell me this, Ava, why, if she didn't give a fuck about us, would she take a job at a company that we run? Why would she be stalking me at work from the rafters?" I lift Lake's phone to Ava's eye line and scroll to the internet history. "Why would her search history be full of nothing but our names? And why the fuck would she look so happy to see you when she ran into you earlier? You are smarter than that, so use your fucking head."

Ava deflates in front of me. "I don't understand..."

"No, you don't. You are too blinded by the bullshit everyone else has been spewing about her based on the lies WE told everyone."

Ava shakes her head. "She never reached out..."

"Can we know that for sure?" I demand. "Who was the one person who told us over and over not to speak with her? Who would have the power to block us from communicating?"

Ava's eyes widen. "Mom wouldn't have..."

I scoff at Ava. "She would. You know she would if she thought it was for our benefit. Ask her and see what she says. Now move."

Finally, Ava moves aside and slowly returns to the gallery. I watch as she pulls out her cell phone and makes a call.

64

I watch her make sure she makes it back into the gallery safely before I get into my car and speed down the streets toward Lake's apartment, hoping to find Lake walking down the way. Slowly, the anger starts to dissipate from my limbs, and that comfortable numbness is back, allowing for clear, coherent thoughts once more.

This will all pass. Ava and Lake will understand, and Gage will be home. Soon, we will all be a family again, and this nightmare will finally end.

Chapter Ten

LAKE

I push my food around on my plate and bounce my leg repeatedly, willing myself to take another bite even though my stomach churns at the thought.

I keep my head down at the cafeteria table while sparring glances up at Malachai. He sits beside some boys from his class, indulging them in mindless conversation. He makes sure to smile and laugh at all the right places.

I feel a light pang of jealousy, wishing I could do the same and blend in. Maybe then I could make more friends and not be such a freak to everyone I encounter.

I want to not flinch at every sudden movement. I want to be able to let people shake my hand in a friendly manner and not feel repulsed by the feeling of their skin touching mine. I want to make friends and be able to hug them close when they need comfort.

I want to be normal...

I scoop some food onto my spoon and place it in my mouth. I

force myself to chew and swallow it, resisting the urge to choke on it. There is nothing wrong with the food, but I couldn't eat over the weekend. Neither could the others. Penny found our stashes and put locks on all the cabinets again.

After not eating for so long, the food hits my stomach like a rock, and I cannot inhale the food like I wish I could.

I look at the others and see they barely touched their food. Just a few bites here and there. I notice Gage pushing his food around his plate while he talks with a girl from his class. Ava briefly looks down at her food, and I see a quick wince covering her features so fast that if you weren't staring directly at her, you would have missed it.

This is so unfair...

My thoughts are interrupted by a stray elbow catching me in the back of my head. I close my eyes at the distinct ache that takes place where the contact was before looking up to see the culprit.

"Whoops," a girl from my class says with a smirk.

I look at Laurie and her posse of carbon copies. They snicker and whisper to themselves as they continue to walk. I roll my eyes at Laurie and return to not eating my food.

"Fucking anorexic freak," she says over her shoulder before continuing behind her friends.

Red clouds the edges of my vision as I stare down at my food. Our table had gone quiet at the commotion, and I look up, locking eyes with Malachai. He gives me such a look of utter sympathy and defeat that my rage grows.

Images of Penny putting locks on the cabinets and laughing, fucking laughing about it, dance across my vision.

Anorexic?

Before I know it, I am on my feet and grabbing Laurie by the hair. She is on the ground quicker than anyone has time to react, and I pin her as I repeatedly bring my fist down.

I didn't ask for this. I didn't ask for any of this.

I hate being so fucking helpless all the time and can do nothing but watch my family starve in front of me.

I hate Penny.

I hate Michael.

I hate Laurie.

I want Laurie to hurt, and I want her to hurt like I have been hurting, and I NEED her to break.

Screams fill the cafeteria, and I feel Ava clawing at my clothing, trying to pull me off Laurie.

Malachai steps into my line of vision and grabs my raised fist before it can make contact with Laurie's bloody face again.

"That's enough," he tells me gently.

I inhale and exhale rapidly, freezing while straddling Laurie's limp body.

It's not enough...Nothing will ever be enough to make this stop hurting.

I need to wake up...

I feel the fog of nightmares begin to lift as I toss and turn in bed. With my eyes closed, I feel the heat of the early afternoon sun beating against my face through my window. I groan, knowing full well that I did not get nearly enough sleep as I roll away from the light. As I switch positions, I feel a hot, soft pillow the length of my body against me. I bury my face deeper into it and take a deep breath as the familiar scent lulls me back into sleep for a few more minutes.

I wake up enough to realize that I do not have a heated body-length pillow in bed with me. My eyes fly open while I shoot into a sitting position in bed, inhaling enough air to let out a scream. The shriek gets lost in my throat as I meet the smirking gaze of Malachai, who has made himself at home in my room and in my bed while I was asleep.

"What the fuck is wrong with you?!" I hiss at him. "You scared the shit out of me."

Malachai ignores me and continues scrolling through my phone, which I had left at the gallery this morning. I pull my comforter closer to my chest and press myself into the wall further away from him. He looks utterly relaxed, like nothing he is doing is currently wrong.

I kick at him lightly with my foot. "Hey, answer me."

He pauses his scrolling and sets the phone in his lap as he looks me up and down. His gaze lingers on where I have the comforter pulled tightly to my chest. "You look uncomfortable," he states.

"Well, no shit," I laugh incredulously at him. "How did you get in here?"

He rolls his eyes at me and lifts my house keys out of his coat pocket, dangling them in front of my face from his index finger. I snatch them from him, making sure not to disturb the comforter from its position.

"How do you know where I live?" I ask while tossing the keys onto the floor by my closet away from his grasp as if it will change the fact that he is already in my room and apartment.

"You work for me. I have your address," he says while putting my phone back in his pocket like it's his.

He scoots down the headboard until he rests lightly on my pillow. I settle more against the wall away from him and pull my legs away so that no part of our bodies are touching, which is problematic since he is so tall that he takes up most of the bed.

A blush burns my cheeks, and I look away from him toward my bedroom door. "Where is Riley? Is she okay?"

Malachai rolls over on his side and props himself up on his elbow. "Asleep soundly on the couch. I didn't wake her."

"My bedroom door was locked..."

He chuckles again. "It's just a lock."

I glare at him, but he ignores my displeasure as his gaze trails back to the comforter.

"Stop that," I state while pulling further away from him.

"Stop what?" He asks, smirking at me fully now.

"You can't just break into my home while I'm sleeping and then look at me like that and act as if you did nothing wrong."

"Why not? It's fun," he states as he trails his free hand lightly against the comforter and takes a fist full of the fabric into his hand. "Do you always sleep naked?"

I clear my throat and try to make it less evident that I am looking around the room at anything but him. "I usually don't. Lesson learned, though."

He chuckles again. "Why do you say that? I like it."

"Go get me clothes since you are here and have the audacity to make yourself so comfortable," I demand while gesturing to the closet.

He makes a dramatic sigh while pushing himself up from the bed. "You are no fun."

This time, I chuckle and bury myself deeper into the covers as I watch him rummage through my closet. "I was never fun, and I distinctly remember being morbidly serious all of the time, which has continued to be the trend."

"Ava says differently," Malachai throws back from the closet.

"Oh, and what does Ava say?"

"You were obsessed with me," he states calmly.

Face fully aflame now, I sit up and glare in his direction as Malachai walks out of the closet with some warm clothing for me. Considerate of him since it is cold as all hell outside.

He smirks as he plops the clothing on the bed and sits at my desk. I grumble under my breath, saying nothing in response to him as I pull a shirt over my head.

As my head peaks through the shirt's opening, I see the humor has fallen away from his face. His eyes linger where I failed to cover my chest while I pulled on the shirt. Slowly, his eyes trail up to lock with mine.

I avert my eyes from his heated gaze and pull on soft cotton underwear under the covers. Clothed enough for some feeling of security to settle in my bones, I sit up from the bed and walk over to Malachai, where he is sitting. I stop a few inches away from him and look over his face. The circles under his eyes are more profound than this morning, and his skin has taken on a pale hue.

I instinctively lift my hand to caress the paleness of his face, but he catches my hand before it makes contact and stares at my hand clasped in his as if it were the most foreign thing in the world.

"I'm sorry, I just...." I apologize while trying to pull my hand from his grasp.

He looks up from our hands to my face, and I lose myself momentarily in his dark gaze.

"For what?" He asks as he slowly pulls my hand towards him, allowing it to make contact with his smooth face.

I trace my fingers along his dark eyebrows, down his temple and cheekbones, until I meet the curve of his jaw. I bring my other hand up to the other side of his jaw so that I am lightly cupping his face in my hands. I slowly lean forward so that he can stop me at any point if he would like until I graze my lips softly against his cheek.

Malachai groans and reaches to grab me by the hips, pulling my body flush with his. I lose my balance and fall into him. I try to pull myself away from him, but he adjusts me so that I am straddling his waist, with our chests pressed firmly against each other. He buries his face in the crook of my neck and inhales deeply.

"Kiss me more," he whispers against my neck, sending pleasant chills down my spine.

I kiss his cheek again and leave a trail of kisses from his jaw down to his collarbone, where I pause before pulling him to me tighter in a full embrace. Malachai hesitates slightly before embracing me.

We stay like this in silence before Malachai pulls back and looks over my face as if to take in every micro-expression I might be making.

I get up from his lap and turn to put on my pants, trying to ignore Malachai, casually adjusting himself after our embrace. "When was the last time you slept?"

Malachai shrugs and props his head on his arm as he leans forward to watch me get dressed.

"You need rest. You look exhausted."

"I look devilishly handsome," he murmurs playfully.

I roll my eyes. "True, but you still need sleep, food, and probably an iron supplement after painting with so much...red."

Malachai chuckles and doesn't answer me.

"I am serious. If you need it, I have an excellent bed right there. You use it, and I can get us some food in the kitchen while you sleep."

Malachai glances from me and looks longingly at my bed before shaking his head no and sitting up straighter.

"Oh, for fucks sake," I grumble, walking back over to Malachai, grasping his hands firmly, and pulling him to his feet.

I pivot with him and lightly shove him onto the bed before kneeling to untie his dress shoes and slip them from his feet.

"I like you on your knees," he states.

"Shut it," I grumble, trying to hide my smirk by bowing closer to the ground.

Once his feet are accessible from the confines of his shiny shoes, I stand up and gesture for him to lie down. Malachai rolls his eyes and moves toward the window with his back towards me while closing his eyes. He pulls his legs up closer to his chest since the bed is a bit small for the entire length of his body. I stand there momentarily as I watch his breathing slow within seconds. I remember his almost comical ability to fall asleep anywhere and at the drop of a hat and smile to myself.

I pull on the rest of the warm clothes that Malachai had set out earlier since I am starting to feel the chill of the apartment. I quietly make my way into the living room and kitchen, where I see Riley sound asleep on the couch, still curled up, just like Malachai is in the other room.

As quietly as possible, I clean the apartment before getting out the ingredients to make beef stew for us since Malachai and Riley look anemic.

Once I start the stew, I am soon filled with the anxiety that only comes with trying to be quiet in the kitchen while the rest of the household sleeps. Every chop of the knife or fridge opening causes me to cringe and check if Riley is stirring from her spot.

When I am well into my meal, with the stew simmering satisfactorily on the stove, Riley finally sits up from the couch and rubs her sleepy eyes at me.

"Hey. I'm making dinner before I go back to work later."

Riley yawns while nodding and stands up. After stretching like a cat, she drags her feet over to the kitchen island, plops down, and rests her forehead on the counter.

"Just to let you know, Malachai brought my stuff from work earlier and is currently crashing in my room," I tell Riley as I stir the stew.

Riley's head pops up, and she stares at me, eyebrows almost to her hairline. I quickly let her in on Malachai's casual breaking-and-entering endeavors. There is no point in lying to her about it. If he did it once, he most likely will again.

"Creep," is all Riley says on the matter,

I chuckle at her. "Yeah, do you think I should be worried?"

Riley shrugs and reaches out to snatch the spoon from my hands so she can sample the stew. After blowing on it so her tongue does not burn, she sips it and hands me the spoon.

"Needs more salt."

I nod and add salt as Malachai emerges from my room, yawning and rubbing at his eyes like Riley had been a few minutes prior.

"You should still be sleeping," I tell him as I return to work preparing our dinner by finding three matching bowls and spoons, which is a near-impossible task.

Malachai and Riley offer each other curt nods in greeting as Malachai takes the seat next to her at the island. "So should you. And besides, Ava and I have a meeting with an investor."

I nod as I start serving the stew. I pass the first bowl to Riley and the second to Malachai. Both dig in while I grab us all some water to wash it down with. I am not the worst cook, but I am well out of practice with most, if not all, life skills.

"Does it taste ok?" I ask while eating at the counter across from them.

They both nod and eat as if they are starving. I stand in silence, watching both of them. My mind keeps returning to the moment Malachai and I shared in my room. I want to pretend things are like they once were between us, minus all the chaos that being the wards of Penny and Michael came with. I want to go back to the easy smiles and being able to reach out and touch him whenever I want. I want to hold his hand and caress his cheek. I want him to fall asleep next to me tonight so that I can know he is resting and safe next to me.

I force myself to eat, but I notice Malachai is watching me just as intently as I watch him and Riley. He used to know me so well that sometimes I would wonder if he could secretly read my mind by the way he could say and do the right things at precisely the right moment. Now, with how he gazes at me,

I can almost pretend nothing has changed between us—even though the tension in the air is nearly palpable.

Once Malachai finishes eating and slamming down water in one go, he takes his dishes to the sink. He washes them before setting them on the drying rack by the sink without saying anything to Riley and me.

After completing his task, Malachai walks up to me, pulls my phone from his pocket, and passes it to me. When I reach out to grab it, his fingers lightly graze my wrist, causing the hairs on my arm to stand on end.

"I will see you tonight," is all he says before exiting the apartment, leaving Riley and me staring after him.

A few moments pass before I notice the door magically decide to behave for once and let him pass through it seamlessly, making his exit nothing more than a deafening silence.

Hours later, I stare at the door, wondering how the hell Malachai had gotten it open.

"Son of a bitch!" I screech at the front door and try to pry it open so I am not late for work.

Riley hides her giggles from the couch as I force myself through the door and slam it out of frustration, causing my phone to do cartwheels down the hall.

Cursing once more, I shuffle after it on unsteady feet. The lack of sleep was starting to take its toll, and after Malachai left, I was so anxious that I could not fall back asleep for more than thirty minutes.

Sighing, I pick up my phone and make my way to the elevator solo.

Riley has something to do this evening, so she asked me if I wouldn't mind taking an Uber to work. I have no issue with this, but I need to hustle now because it is two minutes out.

I press the elevator button impatiently a few times and resist the urge to tap my foot while waiting. Movement catches my attention to the right of me, and I see a man well into his fifties walk up to me slowly and pause just a few feet away. I have yet to see him, but he might live here or be visiting one of the tenets. We all keep to ourselves here, so I wouldn't know.

I focus my vision on the numbers above the elevator, signaling that it is well on its way, but the man clears his throat, causing me to glance his way.

"Hey there," he says.

I force a friendly half smile, continue looking at the elevator numbers, and murmur a flat "Hi."

"Crazy weather we are having, huh?"

"Yup."

"You new around here? I haven't seen you before," he states as the elevator dings. I have half a mind to wait for the next one, but my Uber should be downstairs now.

I inhale, brace for an awkward elevator ride, and lie through my teeth, "Nope. Lived here for a while."

"Oh, so you must know, Riley," he says as the elevator clicks shut.

Something about how he said Riley's name has the hairs rising on the back of my neck, so I take a second to look him over as we descend. He has light blue eyes, but not the pretty kind. They remind me of stagnant water sitting outside for a while, murky and like the light can't fully reflect from them. His hair is graying and is cropped short in a military style that matches his too-straight posture. He has his hands in his pockets and leans against the elevator wall opposite me as if trying to look relaxed.

I turn back to the elevator doors and lie once more. "Who?"

He chuckles and straightens up, stepping towards me in the confined space. "Short, dark-haired, pale, sullen type? Wears way too much black?"

"Never heard of them," I state as the doors open.

"Are you sure about that?" He asks, walking too close as I

look around the garage for my Uber. The man has at least five inches of height on me, so I can't help but start to feel intimidated by his presence.

I pause where I am walking and turn to face him, ready to tell him to fuck off, when I hear a familiar voice calling our way.

"I've been waiting for you."

Malachai walks over from a black BMW parked a few spaces away and reaches us with a few long strides. He gives me an agitated glare and places his arm around my shoulders.

"Hurry up," he says, turning me away from the man.

The man's facade falls, and for a split second, he looks pissed that his conversation was interrupted by Malachai. I watch him over my shoulder as Malachai ushers me into his vehicle and closes the door firmly. I watch the man rub his face in frustration as he walks out of the parking garage down the street.

Malachai slides into the driver's side, slams the door, and locks us in the car. His gaze follows mine as the man walks out of sight down the road. "Who was that?"

"Hold on..." I tell him as I pull out my phone and immediately call Riley.

She answers within a few short rings. She doesn't say anything in her usual manner, but the pause in the rings tells me she has responded to the phone. "Hey, Riley? Do you have a second?"

I recap the creepy event and wait for Riley to say anything, but she is silent on the other end.

"Riley?"

"I'm ok. Just go to work. I'll be fine," she says quickly and then hangs up, offering no further explanation.

I stare at my phone, ready to get out of the car and go back upstairs to check on her, but Malachai reaches over and grasps my thigh lightly to get my attention.

"Are you ok?" He asks, with genuine concern in his eyes.

"Yeah...I just..that was weird. Riley said she was okay, though. I'll check up on her during my break at work. Thanks for the save, but I need to catch my Uber before it drives off," I say before trying to open the door.

Malachai shakes his head. "I'll drive you."

I try to unlock the door, but the passenger lock is broken. "That's nice, but I can't waste the money right now."

Malachai reaches over to the seat belt and buckles me in. "I will pay you back for it."

I shake my head and go to try to open the door again. "I don't want your money."

"Lake, you are going to make us both late," Malachai grumbles as he turns on the vehicle and reverses out of the parking spot.

I sigh and lean back into the seat as we silently drive to the gallery. The drive seems short and hellaciously long all at the same time. I do my best just to stare out the passenger window, but Malachai's presence is palpable in the car, and the smell of his cologne is intoxicating. I want to lean over and rest my head on his shoulder...

"What are you thinking?" He asks.

I inhale deeply as I decide to be honest with him. "I don't know what to say to you. You are familiar to me, so I want to pick up where things left off with us."

Malachai pauses in thought before answering. "And where did we leave off?"

I chuckle without humor, "That is a really tough question to answer."

"How so?"

"Well, what has Ava told you?" I ask.

"She told me you and I loved each other and were practically inseparable," he says.

"What else did she tell you?"

"She said my parents were abusive pieces of shit. They brought in Gage and Ava before they brought you in, and they were sick bastards to all of us."

I nod. "They were."

"She said that all of that escalated until the night of the fire," he says while looking over at me.

"What did she tell you about that night?"

"We got in a fight with Michael and Penny. Michael shot me, and you killed them and then burned the house down because you thought I was dead," Malachai states like he is recapping what happened on a TV drama and not something that happened directly to him.

"Did Ava tell you what the fight was about?"

Malachai shakes his head. "No, was it important?"

I look out the passenger window and lie through my teeth. "No."

Malachai reaches over and grasps my thigh again. I look down where his fingers are meeting the fabric of my pants and resist the urge to reach out and hold his hand for support.

"Are you lying to me?" Malachai asks as we stop at a light.

"Malachai, if Ava didn't tell you what it was about, then I think it is best we leave that in the past. I'll carry that weight for both of us anyway," I tell him, looking out the window.

I expected him to push the subject further, but he nods and pulls his hand away. The heat of his hand is gone, and my leg feels cold, which hurts my chest.

"Tell me. Not now, but one day when you're ready. Okay?" He asks. "You'll have to be the one to tell me everything I don't remember."

"Okay," I say softly.

"Okay." He murmurs while placing his hand back on my thigh.

"Is this hard for you?" I ask him.

"What do you mean?"

"Not remembering. Is it hard for you?"

"It is not so much the lack of remembering. There are bits and pieces there that make me know that what Ava has told me is true, but the rest is a fog that only comes out in fucked up dreams. Even then, I'm unsure what is real and what my brain has just imagined as a coping mechanism. I also remember the feelings. The fear, the pain, the rage, but there isn't a specific moment to place it with. Just random images or impressions."

"Is that why you started painting more?" I ask.

Malachai looks over at me. "More?"

I nod, "Yeah, we used to paint together. You were always way better at it than I was. I could only do landscapes, but never people. I could never get the dimensions right, and they ended up looking like aliens more often than not."

"No one ever told me I painted before," Malachai states.

"I don't think they knew. It was more of a me-and-you thing. We would paint during lunches at school and sometimes when it was just us in the cellar."

We sit in silence for a moment before Malachai speaks again

"It's a relief to know I kept some part of myself."

"You seem like yourself, just a bit muted and off. But still you, which makes it a bit difficult not to be all over you again."

Malachai laughs. "Oh?"

I blush. "Like holding your hand and whatnot."

"If you wanted to hold my hand, you could have just asked," he says while causally offering me his right hand.

I look down at where my hands are laced in my lap. "No, it wouldn't mean the same to you as to me."

"What if it did?" He asks.

I shake my head. "It wouldn't."

More silence envelops us as Malachai parks in the garage

80

parking across from the gallery. He turns off the car, walks over to my side of the vehicle, and opens the door for me.

I nod my thanks and wrap my arms around myself to brace against the cold as we make our way to the gallery with Malachai in step beside me. I am about to open the front door for us when Malachai reaches past me and stops me from opening the door with a firm hand on the glass. I look up at his intense gaze, unable to move.

"I've dreamt about you this whole time, you know. Your face, your scent, your smile. Everything may not be linear in my head, but I could never forget you. You have haunted me this whole time."

I reach up and gently remove Malachai's hand from the door and continue inside. I hope to find the right words to tell him as we step through the doors, but our conversation is interrupted by a perky hostess that I have not seen before.

"Mr. Rosemond, how nice to see you!" She gushes while clasping her hands together in excitement over her chest. She is your classic blonde-haired, blue-eyed girl. Pretty.

Malachai spares her a polite hello, but his gaze falls back on mine for an answer. I open my mouth, but the hostess interrupts us once more.

"Ava told me to tell you she is waiting in your office with your mother."

I stiffen at the word mother but quickly realize the host isn't talking about Penny. Old habits die hard, I guess. I lightly nudge Malachai forward.

"Go on...Don't keep everyone waiting. I have work to do," I say while letting my hand drop.

Malachai lingers a moment longer before sighing and walking off towards the stairs. I watch him go before clocking in, but the hostess steps in my path.

"The trash for the installed fixtures must be recycled and

thrown out," she says, all cheeriness reserved for Malachai only.

"Ok, thanks for letting me know," I say while smiling at her.

She doesn't smile back and just walks off back to her post. I sigh to myself. Over the past few days, I have noticed unusual behavior towards me from the front-of-house staff, almost as if my presence to them is negligible. I am glad I work at night, so I only have to deal with their bullshit for a few hours until closing.

I clock in and then pick up my list of extra activities Ruby would like me to do. A few special events are planned for this week, one of which is a significant benefit that requires some setting up over the next few days. I keep the list and drop my stuff off in the employee lounge.

I slowly work down the list until I am to the parts that go over the setup for the benefit. They want me to rearrange some lights and decorative fixtures to make room for some tables they will set up on the day of. I memorize the setup and get to work yanking and pulling things into place. I soon learned that my years at Willow Creek have left me more atrophied than the average person, and I feel my muscles scream at me as I work to get everything into place.

After that task, I make a quick trip to the bathroom to clean up some of my sweat. I peek at my reflection and cringe as I see my hair plastered to my face. I rinse my face in the sink and pull my hair back into a new ponytail to look more put together. Satisfied with my work, I leave the restroom.

I lock up the front doors since all front-of-house staff have left a little after closing time. While setting the alarm, I hear some shouting from upstairs. I jump a bit and start to make my way to the noise. I follow the shouts to Malachai's studio. I linger outside the door but cannot make out any clear words. It sounds like there are three voices.

I turn and hurry to the ladder that leads up to the catwalk. I make my way up and over Malachai's studio and stop right on the edge, out of view of the people shouting. It is Ava, Malachai, and a woman well into her fifties or sixties. Ava looks pissed as hell as she stares down the older woman.

The woman reminds me of an older version of Penny: prim and proper, adorned in the finest clothing and jewelry. She screams old money, and I immediately distrust her based on that fact alone. I look over and see Malachai glaring at the woman silently, his arms and legs crossed, as he leans against the wall adjacent to Ava and the women. If looks could kill...

"You had no fucking right!" Ava screams at the woman.

The older woman throws her arms up in the air. "I was trying to protect you from her! She committed murder, for Christ's sake. I cannot believe you two can casually forget that fact and act as if that is nothing to blanch at. She is dangerous, and I want you all safe."

"Where are her letters?" Malachai asks in a deadly, even tone.

The woman sighs and opens her purse. She pulls out a stack of at least twenty letters. "I have the others in our office at home. These were the first few that she sent."

Malachai approaches her, snatches the letters from the woman's hands, and then walks back to his spot along the wall. "I want all of them by tomorrow morning."

The woman rolls her eyes. "Why? She is a criminal!"

"She is our sister!" Ava yells at her. "I can't believe you let me think for the last eleven years that she didn't give a fuck about us. Did she ever get any of my letters? What about Gage's? Or did you steal those, too?"

The woman reaches into her purse, pulls out another stack of letters, and hands them to Ava. "Here. Do what you must with these, but I highly suggest you do not contact her. You two need to move on and look out for yourselves. You both have grown so much since I met you, and you have worked so hard to leave your past behind and recover. I do not want to see you both relive any of that."

Malachai glances up in my direction and then looks at the woman. "I already reached out to her, and she is not anything to worry about."

The woman turns back to Malachai. "You what?!"

Malachai shrugs. "She is nothing like what the press or anyone else has said. She is nothing to worry about."

The woman looks exasperated and shakes her head. "Malachai...I love you like you are my flesh and blood. And you too, Ava. But Malachai, sweety, you do not know the full extent of everything that transpired. So that is why I'm begging you, leave the past behind."

Ava stares down at the letters in her hand. A moment passes before she shakes her head and storms off past Malachai and the woman, whom I assume is their adoptive mother, into Malachai's office, slamming the door behind her.

Malachai opens the first letter of the stack without looking up at his mother. "I will see you tomorrow with the other letters."

Sighing again, the woman turns on her heels and leaves the studio. Malachai looks up at me from where he is standing.

"I want those letters from Ava and Gage," I say down to him.

He nods, slides down the wall into a sitting position, and continues reading. I stand up from my spot and go down the catwalk to finish my work for the night. I would be lying if I said I didn't slam a few things a bit too hard or aggressively scrub at the bathroom toilets with more vigor than needed due to the simmering rage that is boiling beneath my skin at the revelation that that woman tried to keep my family and me apart for so long.

All those nights, all those fucking nights I stayed up, unable to sleep, wondering if Malachai was dead or alive because there was no way if he was alive by any chance, that he wouldn't have tried to find me. All those nights where I was worried about Ava and Gage and where they ended up, I had no fucking clue and just hoped that they met a better outcome than I did and that they were safe.

I slam the door of the cleaning supplies room one final time and glare at it, breathing heavily as my anger reaches new heights. I want to hit something, break things, and scream, but I cannot move from where I stand, staring at the gray door.

I hear someone clear their throat and see Malachai standing off to my right with a stack of letters. I walk over to him as he extends the letters to me. I reach up and take them from him gently.

Feeling them in my hands now, the weight of loneliness from all these years weighs on me and threatens to drown me. My breathing quickens as I look down at Ava's handwriting and see she wrote a heart next to my name from where she addressed the letter. I opened the first letter and started to read the first few lines.

Lake,
I buried them under the willow tree by the pond. I am so sorry...

I stare at the words, unable to read further, until my eyes blur with tears. I look up at Malachai and clutch the letters in shaking hands. He reaches to me, pulling me into his chest, where I bury my face. I crumple the letter in my fist, obscuring the words from his view before leaning further into him and holding him to me.

I clutch his black dress shirt like a lifeline. It has been years, and every time I think of that night, the horror and sorrow never fail to drown me. I try to ease the trembling and hold in my tears because I know deep down this is a wound that will not heal, and if I start to cry about it, I will never stop.

Malachai holds me silently, unaware of the cause for my grief—blissfully so—but he holds me nonetheless. This is the Malachai that I remember—the one who would rescue me at the very second I needed it without question.

I pull away from Malachai and inhale deeply to steady myself. "Where is Ava?"

"She left," he states.

I try to hide my disappointment. "Oh, is she ok?"

Malachai shrugs lightly. "I think she was holding onto anger towards you this whole time to hide her grief for everything that happened. Now she knows it's been misplaced, and she feels bad about her reaction to seeing you."

I hold up the stack of letters and laugh without humor. "Well, this explains a lot. It's not her fault, and neither of us knew."

Malachai nods. "I think she needs some time to process everything."

"Okay. I am always here when she is ready. If she needs space, I get that, too. She can have whatever she needs," I say in a shaky voice.

Malachai nods slowly again, still looking me over.

I clear my throat and hold his gaze evenly. "Is there anything else you guys need me to do for the benefit? I think I got most things exactly how Ruby wanted them."

Malachai shakes his head. "I don't give a fuck about the benefit right now, Lake."

"I know...But there is nothing else to say about everything at this point. I'm at a loss," I say while wrapping my arms around myself.

"I read a few of your letters...You loved me a lot," he says, observing me more intently.

I give him a sad smile. "I never stopped."

With that admission, I walk past him and again head to the employee lounge to gather my things. Malachai follows behind me, giving me the company I need. I clock out next and then look back to Malachai.

"Can I catch a ride home with you? I haven't heard much from Riley, so I assume she is still asleep, and I don't want to wake her to bum a ride," I ask.

"Of course."

I follow Malachai to his car and am again met with the early morning chill. The bite of the air is enough to calm my nerves so I can settle into my skin. I lean back in the passenger seat as Malachai drives me home in comfortable silence. Every once in a while, I glance in his direction and see that he looks troubled.

All too soon, Malachai pulls into my apartment's parking garage. I go to get out of the car, but Malachai keeps my door locked as he gets out of the driver's side and walks over to open it from the outside. I step out of the car and look up at him from where he is still blocking my path to the point that I can feel the heat of his skin through his clothing.

"Thank you for the ride home," I say as I try to step around him.

Malachai reaches down and gently places my hand in his warm grasp. "I will walk you upstairs."

"You don't have to."

Malachai closes the door behind us and pulls me along with him, giving me no other chance to argue with him. I follow him almost mindlessly because my gaze is transfixed on where my hand is buried in his.

There are points in your life when you receive something you have wanted so badly, and once you have it, you are almost in disbelief that it's real. Gazing at our intertwined fingers, something so gentle and innocent is one of those times.

Malachai leads us to the elevator, and I almost miss the man from earlier lingering on the outskirts of the garage, pacing back and forth. My stomach drops as we lock gazes, and he starts to take a step in our direction. Malachai immediately notices this and maneuvers me so that I am behind him fully, blocked from the other man's view. The man pauses in his steps as he sees Malachai's hostile gaze.

The elevator dings and Malachai pushes me into it before blocking me behind him. The elevator doors close, and we both stand in stunned silence. Once the doors open again, I step around Malachai, rush to my apartment, and open the door while shoving my shoulder into it.

The door creaks open, and I look back and see Malachai is hot on my heels, his gaze turned behind us to watch our backs. I grab his dress shirt, pull him into the apartment, and lock the door behind us.

Sighing with relief, I turn and am met with an apartment that looks like a tornado has come through it. Drawers are left haphazardly open, and random books and nicknacks are strewn about. I rush forward and start looking for Riley.

"Riley!" I call out.

I go to her room and try to turn the knob which is locked, and I bang on the door.

"Riley? Riley, please open the door!" I call in a choked voice.

Please, please, please let her be ok...

The door suddenly opens, and I meet Riley's panicked gaze. I look her up and down to see if any harm has occurred, but she looks put together. The only thing out of place is the steak knife she is once more wielding.

Malachai places a hand on my shoulder to pull me behind him again once he sees the knife. I put my hand over his in

88

reassurance and looked around the room. I noticed Riley had random trash bags, a suitcase full of items, and clothing sprawled on the floor.

"Riley, what the hell? Who is that man?" I ask her as I take in more of the scene.

Riley turns and starts packing items into the suitcase with no apparent order.

"My stepdad," she says in a shaky whisper. "He won't leave me alone."

I kneel before her and gently place my hand over hers to slow her frazzled movement. "Hey, hey, hey...We can work through this. Just tell me what is going on."

Riley looks up at me with tears and lets out a choked sob. "He...He hurt me—a lot. No one believed me. And then my mom...sent me away."

Cold starts to creep down my spine in understanding. I look over my shoulder to Malachai, who has a murderous look on his face. I turn back to Riley as she starts packing again and then pauses.

"I need to leave. I need to leave, but...but...I have nowhere to go," she sobs.

"You can stay with me," Malachai states simply. "You will be safe."

Riley and I both look back at him, and he starts grabbing things from Riley's closet and tossing them our way. I have no other solution, so I just catch items and place them into the suitcase and a random backpack.

Riley looks at Malachai as if he is her savior, nods to herself, and starts packing alongside me again. Within ten minutes, the essentials are in the suitcase and backpack, and I can bring her the rest later.

Malachai turns to me. "How do we get her out without him noticing?"

"I have a fire escape out my window," I tell him.

He nods. "Okay, I will bring my car around and give you guys the all-clear. I programmed my number into your phone already."

I pull my phone out of my pocket and scroll through my contacts, and sure enough, there is a new contact labeled *M*.

Malachai walks out of the apartment while I help Riley wrangle the suitcase onto my bed and open the window, ready for her to make her escape.

Riley looks at me from where she is perched, standing on my bed, backpack thrown over her shoulder. "Are you coming with me?"

"I will hang here in case Shelly shows up randomly to check on us so I can give an alibi to where you are and keep an eye on things. Malachai will take care of you, and I will be in touch. Just be safe, and don't worry, we will get this all figured out," I tell her.

Just then, my phone rings. I see it is Malachai, and I answer it.

"He is lingering by the elevator again, so I think you guys are good to come down," Malachai says.

"Ok, Riley will be down in a second."

"You are coming too," Malachai tells me.

"I need to clean up here and get things situated in case our case worker shows up. I just can't leave."

"It's not safe," Malachai protests.

"I will be careful. Just take care of Riley for me, please," I tell him.

Malachai is silent momentarily before continuing, "Once Riley is set up, I will come to get you."

I smile at that. "I can't thank you enough for this Malachai."

I hang up the phone and meet Riley's sorrowful gaze.

"Go. I will be ok," I tell her.

Riley nods and makes her way down the fire escape. I watch her make it down safely and into Malachai's car. As they drive off into the distance, I have a sick feeling that the last thing I told Riley was nothing short of famous last words.

Chapter Eleven

LAKE

"You look so beautiful today, Lake."

I shiver and lock eyes with Malachai as Michael runs his index finger along my bare shoulder. I try to hold my breath and concentrate on Malachai, who is chained to the cellar wall by his throat like a dog, trapped and out of arm's reach.

Fresh bruises cover his cheeks, and a look of absolute horror is on his face, but he, too, keeps quiet and doesn't dare break eye contact with me. If we were to look away for one second, we would both be lost in the terror we both feel.

"You look cold," Michael says in a tone that is too smooth, too even. He only uses that tone before he causes pain.

I force myself to hold still from where I am standing on the cold stone floor, trying to ignore Michael and the warmth of his body that I can feel against my back. I swallow and resist the urge to vomit at the scent of his cologne.

"Where is your clothing, Lake?"

"Penny took them," I state emotionlessly.

"Ah, and what did you do to deserve that?"

"I got blood on them at school," I whisper.

"She said you were acting out to get back at me for always being gone. Is that true?"

I clear my throat before answering, "No."

"Ah, poor Lake. Are you playing hard to get? Am I not giving you enough attention? Have I been that much of an absent father to you?" Michael murmurs against my hair as he runs a finger down my spine.

I repeatedly chant in my head not to move or breathe, just focus on Malachai. Everything will be okay if I focus on him, and nothing can hurt me. It is just me and him in the room, and no one else...

"I could be around more if you want me to. All you have to do is ask me. Do you want me around more? Or am I enough for you?" Michael asks while slowly pulling me firmly against his chest. I can feel the cold bite of the buttons on his blazer, leaving impressions of themselves on my back as his nails dig into the soft flesh of my hips.

Say nothing, do nothing, doing anything will just make it worse...

Suddenly, Michael yanks me around to face him, and he grasps me by my throat. I hear Malachai strain against the chains on the wall.

"FUCKING ANSWER ME," Michael growls, losing all pretense of calmness.

I weakly grab his hands and gasp, "Enough...you're enough...."

As quickly as he grabbed me, Michael lets me go. I crumple to the floor and crawl away from him until I am pressed against the cellar wall adjacent to Malachai.

Michael stares down at me, unmoving, as if he is deciding his next move. Finally, his gaze travels over to Malachai and then back to me. He crouches down slowly, grips me by the chin, and forces me to look him in the eyes. "Remember, you are mine. All of you here are mine to do whatever the fuck I want with. Understand?"

I nod as Michael releases my face and stands up from his crouching position. He takes a moment to straighten his suit and then turns to walk out of the cellar, slamming the door behind him.

Once the lock clicks, signaling that we are trapped here, Gage and Ava crawl out from hiding behind a wine barrel and run over to me as tremors shake my body. Gage pulls off his gray hoodie and hands it to me. With shaking hands, I pull it over my head and shove my hands through before crawling over to Malachai.

He pulls me close to him and lightly rocks me back and forth while I try to gain control of the uncontrollable tremors of terror that are wracking my body. Soon I feel Ava and Gage wrap their arms around me as well.

After a few minutes, I look up at Malachai, who stares at the closed cellar door with hate and disdain.

"I am going to kill him."

I roll onto my side on the couch and gasp for air as I try to shake the memory. I rub my eyes and force myself into a sitting position. I can still feel the phantom touch of Michael against my shoulder, and I subconsciously reach back to dig my nails into the skin to block out the feeling with pain.

Looking around the room, I see my phone on the coffee table. After Riley left, I spent the next few hours straightening the apartment to make it look like Riley still lived here, minus a few of her items.

When Riley made it to Malachai's, I got a call from both of them, and I reassured them that I was okay and safe in the apartment. Malachai finally agreed to let me stay but told me he would be back to pick me up again for work later that evening and that he didn't want me stepping foot outside of the apartment without him. I agreed and even went as far as to pack a small backpack if I needed to leave in a hurry.

I reach out and pick up my phone from the coffee table. I see a few missed calls from Malachai. Fuck, I forgot to tell him I was napping. He must be so worried...

Right then, a loud crack, like that of wood giving in on itself, sounds from the front door. I immediately jump to my feet and back up a few paces as I look over to see the front door swing in on itself.

"Malachai?" I call out hopefully.

But it is not Malachai that I see step through the front door. Riley's stepdad stares at me blankly as he advances toward me. I run to the kitchen to grab a knife from the knife block, but once my hand wraps around the handle, he grabs me by the hair and slams my head down onto the counter with such force that my vision goes black for a moment.

My grip releases on the knife as I slump to the ground. Fear chokes me while I try to mindlessly crawl away from him as I feel his calloused grasp around my ankle, pulling me back toward him.

I kick at him as my vision clears and let out a scream, hoping that one of my neighbors will hear. Riley's stepdad cocks back his fist and slams it into my mouth, silencing me as I feel blood burst from my lips where my teeth cut into them.

He grabs me by the throat and lifts me off the ground enough so that I am looking him in the eye as he leans over me.

"Where the fuck is she?" He growls.

"Not...here..." I gasp while trying to pry his hands from

TERRAN FERNIZA VALENZUELA

my throat. My vision starts to blur, and for a second, I swear I am looking into Micheal's cold, dark gaze again.

He releases me abruptly, causing me to fall back and hit my head on the kitchen's tiled floor. I see stars again and feel the urge to vomit as I roll onto my side and try again to maneuver away from him.

He looms over me, and a slow, evil grin forms on his face. "Well, since you let her go, I guess it is only fair that I have fun with you instead."

He grabs me again by the ankles, and I feel my elbows cut open on the hard tile as he drags me across it to pin me beneath him. He shoves an elbow into my spine painfully as he knots his fist into my hair and shoves my face into the floor. I let out another scream as he starts to rip at my clothing.

"Please stop! Stop, stop, STOP!"

As abruptly as his weight was upon me, it is gone. I take the opportunity to roll onto my back while pulling my torn clothing closer to my body. Tears stream down my face while I try to look for my attacker, but I am met with the beautiful sight of Malachai kneeling above Riley's stepdad. Malachai has him pinned under him as he straddles his chest.

Malachai raises his arm, and I see the gleam of the kitchen knife I had dropped, which is held firmly in his closed fist. I crawl into a sitting position with my back against the wall as I repeatedly watch Malachai bring the knife down.

Whether from the sight of Malachai stabbing the man or from a probable concussion, I turn my head and vomit onto the floor. I retch until my stomach is empty before I can sit against the wall.

Looking over at Malachai, who is still stabbing the man with more and more force with each thrust, I use the wall to guide myself to my feet. I slowly approach him, using any surface to balance myself as I get within a few inches.

"Malachai…" I call to him as time slows, but he doesn't stop, lost in the frenzy of his kill. "Malachai…He is dead."

Malachai starts to slow his thrusts until he buries the knife into the man's chest again. I watch with abstract horror as Malachai slowly drags the knife down the man's chest, as if relishing in the feel of the blade's pressure buried in flesh. I look at his face and see his unblinking gaze locked on his kill.

The world goes black.

Chapter Twelve

MALACHAI

"Malachai...He is dead," Lake's weak voice sounds from behind me.

I know...I fucking know. I know, but I can't stop.

He had her...He was going to...

This isn't enough. He can't be dead. He needs to suffer for what he did to Lake, for what he did to Riley. For years...for fucking years, he hurt Riley.

When I walked in and saw her beneath him, I thought I was too late. There was already blood on the floor—Lake's blood.

Lake's blood, the blood that I dream about nightly. She has spilled more than anyone should have to in a thousand lifetimes. I can't get the images out of my head. That's why I need so much red now. I need it from strangers, from friends, from anyone who I can fucking get it from, just to make up for every drop that has spilled from her veins.

My thrusts slow, and I slowly drag the knife that is buried

in...No, he doesn't deserve a name. Monsters don't deserve names.

I start to see all the red now. It is on my hands, his chest, the floor, the cabinets, the ceiling...I feel like I'm showered in it.

His face is carved inward, his throat nothing but a bloody pulp. His chest...Fuck I wish there was more of him so I can keep cutting. I need more. I need more than what he can give me for what he has done.

My breath hitches as images of Lake covered in red like this flood my vision. No, not now...I can't break. I need to save Lake and...And who? Who else do I need to save?

Who else couldn't I save then?

I drop the knife and clutch my head as more images flood my brain.

A dull thud behind me rips me out of the spiral of chaos that has become my mind.

I turn slowly and see Lake crumpled on the floor, curled in on herself.

Just like then...Just like when I couldn't save...

"Lake?" I whisper in fear.

I crawl off of Riley's stepdad and pull her into my arms. Her body is limp, and I watch in horror as blood drips from her nose and lips in a steady stream as her head lulls to the side.

"Lake?..Lake? Lake, please wake up, love...Lake, please!"

My voice is lost to my ears as I pick her up in my arms and start running with her clutched to my chest. She feels too tiny in my arms. So delicate. How could anyone hurt someone so innocent?

I slam my hand into the elevator button and look Lake over as we descend into the parking lot.

"Come on, Lake, wake up..."

I check her pulse, which is fast but present. I lean her head towards my chest more so she doesn't choke on her blood as I try to stabilize her neck in case it is hurt.

The elevator dings our arrival at the parking garage, and I do my best to run without jostling her. As we get to the car, I adjust her in my arms and place her delicate body in the passenger's seat, making sure she is buckled in safely.

Seconds later, I am driving at illegal speeds to the nearest trauma hospital. My hands shake as I fidget with the Bluetooth on the car to call Ava.

She answers on the second ring. "Malachai?"

"Ava, I need your help." I choke out.

"What happened?"

"He was there, and he was trying to...He hurt Lake badly. And she isn't waking up. I am taking her to the hospital now."

"What do you mean she isn't waking up? Is she alive?" Ava asks in a choked whisper to match my own.

"She is alive, but she is bleeding from her head. I need to get her help..."

"Where the fuck is he?" Ava asks, anger filling her voice. I hear rustling in the background as she gathers herself.

"Dead. I killed him, Ava."

"Fuck...Malachai, where is the body?"

"What happened?" I hear Riley ask from the other side of the phone. Panic fills her voice.

"I need you to go to Lake's apartment. It's a mess. I don't know who heard what, and I don't know if anyone saw me leave with Lake...I don't even know if I closed the door; I just ran with her. I need you to make this go away, Ava."

"I will Malachai. Text me what hospital you are at, but do not say anything to anyone. I will call Mom and have her and Dad make a few calls to wherever you are."

"I need clothes."

"I'll have Mom send a new suit."

"I love you, sister."

"I love you, brother."

The line goes dead as I arrive at Memorial West with Lake. She groans slightly and slumps over against my right arm as we park. I lift her head gently as I slip out of my seat and retrieve her from her side of the vehicle, once more doing my best not to jostle her too much as I run for the emergency room entrance.

"Help! I need help!!" I yell to the staff.

Immediately, I am surrounded by security as staff runs up to me and takes Lake from my arms. I reach out to her as they place her on a gurney and ask hurried questions about what happened to her, but I hold my head high and keep my gaze on Lake.

She stirs once more as they start to wheel her away from me. I step to follow her, but I feel a firm grip on my arm. "Sir, are you injured?"

I look down at my blood-covered hands and clothes. "No."

"Then we will need you to come with us."

"I need to be with her," I tell the security guards and a nurse as they take Lake behind a secured door. I watch the door swing shut, and panic consumes me as soon as she is out of my sight.

"I need to be with her," I tell the nurse again, allowing my face to show the panic in which I feel.

Her eyes and posture soften slightly, but she shakes her head almost apologetically. "I'm sorry, sir. She needs to be treated before we can let you back."

Bullshit. They think I did this.

"You need to come with us." The head security officer tells me as his grip tightens around my arm.

I ball my fists at my side, allowing him to guide me through doors opposite where they took Lake.

Five minutes later, I am handcuffed to a desk in the securities office as we wait for the police to arrive. I stare off at the wall as time ticks on.

I hear the door behind me open, and the security guard sitting by my side looks up. His eyes widen in surprise.

"John, there seems to be a misunderstanding here." A deep male voice says from behind me.

The security guard jumps to his feet, and I slowly turn to look at an old doctor who is well into his fifties and has a police sergeant by his side.

The security guard looks to the police sergeant for confirmation, to which he nods with a deep scowl.

"Dr. Roberts?" The security officer asks in confusion.

Dr. Roberts gestures to me. "Release our friend here. We will take it from here. You are dismissed."

The security guard nods and hurriedly unlocks the handcuff, securing me to the desk before leaving the room. The sergeant glares at me with agitation before he hands a black suit to Dr. Roberts and follows the security guard out as well.

I watch silently as the door closes behind him before glancing at Dr. Roberts.

"You are Malachai, I presume?"

I nod silently.

Dr. Roberts sets the suit down on the desk by me and takes a few steps back, ensuring he is out of arm's reach.

"I am on the board with your mother. She called me and let me know there was a...situation."

I stare at him, revealing nothing.

Dr. Roberts chuckles nervously. "Well...I guess that is for the best. Plausible deniability is a beautiful thing, no?"

"How much?" I ask him, deadpan.

Dr. Roberts fakes confusion. "Pardon?"

I fight the urge to grab him by the throat. "How much do you want?"

"I don't know what you are talking about."

I sigh as I give him a bored look. "I'll double whatever my mother promised you if you erase all the footage and records we were ever here."

"It's already done."

I nod. "How is she?"

"Alive and well. She has quite a few lacerations and bruises, a concussion to her frontal lobe."

I stand up and start to unzip the suit to look it over. "Do you have a shower I can use?"

Dr. Roberts smiles. "Yes, of course."

"Good. Take me to her after."

"Of course, Mr. Rosemond."

Chapter Thirteen

LAKE

C old...It is always so cold now.

How long have we been left here?

I lean my head against the cellar's cement while pulling Gage's hoodie close to me. My eyes drift to Malachai, asleep on the cold floor next to Ava. They are a few paces away from Gage and me, cuddled together on the ground. Their soft snores indicate they are well into sleep.

I rest my head on my knees as blood drips from Malachai's lips onto the floor. I try to force myself to my feet, but my limbs don't seem to work as they used to, and I feel tired all the time... and cold...so cold no matter what I do. But Malachai is the only thing that seems to make the cold less.

Malachai shifts his unconscious face towards me, and I remember how it feels when he pulls me into his arms in a tight embrace. I love to bury my face in his neck and inhale his sweet scent. He smells so lovely. The scent is what I imagine heaven might smell like.

I reach over to him and wipe the blood from his lip with my thumb. I stare at where the red stains my pale skin. So pretty. It might be one of my favorite colors.

I gently guide my thumb toward my lips and smear the red against them. I instinctively run my tongue over my lips and taste the saltiness of his blood. I want more.

I have wanted more for a while now, and I think I have been too afraid to admit that to myself or him. I see Malachai's soft features, knowing he has wanted more as much as I have.

I have been with him for years, and slowly, over time, he has become an integrated part of myself. When he hurts, I hurt. What he wants, I want. Whether this is some fucked up trauma bond or true love, I don't care. I love him. And I hate him. I hate him for all he has to endure for us because that makes me love him even more.

I love the way Malachai holds me against him and uses his free hand to brush my hair out of my face. I love how it feels to lean into his touch and close my eyes as I feel his hands shakily trail down my neck, where he hesitates before placing his hand gently to cup the back of my head so I can look up at him.

I resist the urge to laugh at myself. I should be focusing on a way to get us out of here, but the truth is, I have given up escaping this hell. But as long as I have Malachai and my siblings, I can endure every moment of this, as long as I get to be with them.

I roll my head away from Malachai and Ava and look at Gage, "Thank you."

Gage looks at me with his crystal blue eyes, from where he traces random images into the dust of the floor in the wine cellar. "For what?"

"The hoodie. I know it is cold. Thank you," *I tell him as I pull the clothing closer to my body to keep out the chill.*

Gage looks over at me before scooting closer to me. I reach out my arms to him and envelope him in a hug, covering his bare arms as much as possible. He still shivers slightly, and I notice his lips are starting to take on a blue hue.

"Want to share this?" I ask while pointing to the hoodie.

It hangs loosely from my body, making it big enough for the both of us.

Gage hesitates for a moment before nodding. We situate ourselves closer to Malachai and Ava to get as much heat from them as possible before Gage sits with his back against the wall. He has grown over the last few months, and now we are about the same height and weight. It's odd to notice the change as I sit between his legs.

I pull my arms out of the sleeves and wrap my arms around my legs inside the clothing as Gage slips his arms into the sleeves. His head and torso follow suit. Gage pulls me against his chest, and I rest my head on his shoulder as he wraps his arms around my bare waist to keep me close.

We sit in silence until Gage's shivers stop, and he rests his chin lightly on my shoulder.

"This is comfortable," he states playfully.

I snicker. "Yeah. The comfiest."

Gage chuckles as well before growing silent with thought. I almost think he fell asleep until he nudges me.

"You don't have to be scared of Michael anymore. Malachai will do everything he can to protect you from him, and I will, too."

Wide awake now, I turn to him as much as possible in our position.

"I know Gage. Sleep now, okay?"

He rests his head against my shoulder once more. "Okay, Lake."

. . .

I wake up in a dimly lit room. I expect to open my eyes to the gruesome sight of the kitchen but am met with pristine white walls. I sit up and see that I am in a hospital bed with an IV in the crevice of my elbow. I follow the IV tubing and see that some opiates are hanging above me from an IV pole.

I immediately pull out the IV and press firmly from where the blood starts to pool from the wound. I look around the room for any familiar faces but see none. I try to get up out of bed, but movement from me causes the alarm to sound from the monitor above me. I frown and start pulling the wires from my chest to silence the constant beeping, but the machine that the IV was attached to also starts to alarm.

Giving up on the idea of a semi-stealthy escape, I cover my ears and lay back down as the pounding in my head increases.

"Mrs. Rosemond?" I hear someone call off to my left.

I scrunch my eyes open and see a nurse in deep blue scrubs walk into the room. She immediately walks over to the monitor and silences both machines by pressing a few buttons. She sees my freshly ripped-out IV and looks at me disapprovingly.

"No opiates," I tell her.

She frowns more but nods. "You could have asked me to take it out for you."

"I didn't know you were close by," I state, trying to sit up again, causing the world to spin slightly. "Where am I?"

"Your husband brought you in after you fell down some stairs," she says.

The look on her face says she thinks that story is complete bullshit. Wise of her. She goes to fluff my pillow for me and leans in close.

"If you feel unsafe at home, please inform any staff here, and we can get you away from him," she says in my ear.

I am about to tell her I am safe, but I think back to the events with Riley's stepdad and Malachai. Am I safe? I sure wasn't earlier in the day...or was that yesterday? How long have I been here?

Right then, Malachai walks in with an older man in a white coat.

The man looks over to my nurse. "We will take it from here, Nancy."

Nancy glares at him and Malachai but steps away from me and makes her way to the door. "Sure thing, Dr. Roberts. Whatever you say."

Nancy shoots me one more look of concern before exiting the room. Dr. Roberts slowly approaches me with Malachai, only a pace behind him. I try not to make eye contact with Malachai, but I'm scared of what my face may betray now.

"So, Mrs. Rosemond, how are you feeling?" The doctor asks me.

Ignoring my confusion about why he is calling me Mrs. Rosemond, I answer, "Dizzy and nauseous."

"You are going to feel that way for a while. Your CT and MRI came back clear of any bleeds or fractures, so it looks like you have a concussion from...." The doctor trails off and glances at Malachai to fill in the rest.

"Your fall," Malachai states firmly.

"Ah yes, your fall," the doctor finishes. Your face should start to heal in a few days, but you will have some bruising for a few weeks. Rest up and take it easy. If you need any medication stronger than over-the-counter, just contact me directly, and I can get you a script."

I nod and sit, waiting for him to continue.

"If you feel up to it, we can get you on your way. Your husband already has all of your discharge paperwork."

Finally, I glance at Malachai, and he holds my gaze with such tender concern that it makes my heart ache.

I look back to the doctor while blinking back tears. "Yeah, I want to leave."

"Ok. I will leave you and your husband to it then." The doctor turns to leave, and as he does, Malachai goes to shake the doctor's hand.

"I appreciate you and your staff's discretion," Malachai tells him.

I watch as the doctor puts a wad of hundred-dollar bills into his pocket. "Any time, Mr. Rosemond."

And with that, the doctor leaves me alone with Malachai. Malachai takes a few steps toward me, and I scoot back in bed, away from him.

Malachai pauses. "Are you afraid of me now?"

I shake my head and instantly regret it as pain blurs my vision. "That was disgusting."

"What happened earlier?" He asks with a slight head tilt.

"No, the bribery. You looked like your father just then."

Malachai steps towards me again and sighs. "A necessary evil."

"I'm sure he used to think that, too," I state while looking up at Malachai.

He reaches out a hand to help me to my feet. "Probably."

I grasp his hand lightly and let him pull me to my feet. It takes me a few seconds to steady myself, but I soon find my footing. Malachai keeps my hand firmly tucked in his as he helps guide me out of the room and into the hospital hallway. As we pass the nurses' station, I see Nancy and a few other nurses talking in hushed voices, all visibly concerned.

I turn away from them and concentrate on putting one foot in front of the other and swallowing the nausea threatening to make me leave my stomach contents in the hall. Soon, we are out in the brisk nighttime air.

Malachai takes off his black peacoat and drapes it over my

shoulders. I put my arms through the sleeves and then grab his hand again.

I follow Malachai to where his car is parked. He opens the passenger side for me, and I slide in and bury myself in his coat as he closes the door and makes his way to the driver's side. I inhale deeply and allow myself to enjoy his scent momentarily before Malachai takes his place in the car and speeds off down the road.

After a few minutes of gut-wrenching silence, I ask him, "So what are we going to tell the police?"

Malachai glances at me in confusion. "The police? Why would we tell them anything?"

"Because there is a dead body in my apartment, and we can't just leave it there," I state incredulously.

"Oh, that is not an issue," Malachai states calmly.

"What do you mean?" I ask slowly, anxiety starting to build.

"While you were in the emergency room, Ava, Riley, and I cleaned up a bit. Ava is there now doing some more detailing as we speak. If the police stop by, they won't be able to see any blood, even if they use luminol."

"Malachai, why didn't you just call the police? Oh my God, where is the body?" I am starting to panic now.

Malachai glances at me briefly and then back to the road without answering. It takes a moment for the realization to hit me.

"Um...Malachai?" I ask quietly.

"Hmm?"

"Is the body in the trunk?" I ask him.

"....Yes."

"FUCK!" I yell and wince as the movement causes a fresh wave of pain to accumulate behind my eyes.

"Lake, I couldn't have just left it there. Ava had to bring in some workers to replace the flooring and cabinets in the kitchen, and I don't think they would have wanted to do their job with an additional guest on the floor," Malachai states like this is all common sense.

"How long was I out?" I ask while trying to slow my rapid breathing.

"You were in and out of it for a few hours," Malachai says.

"So you're telling me you cleaned up a crime scene, packed a body into the trunk, called up Ava and had her bring in workers to rip out flooring and cabinets, and finished that all out by bribing a doctor to keep my injuries under wraps, all over a few hours?" I recap while staring him down.

"...Yes," he answers again emotionlessly.

"Where are we going now? Is Riley okay? Does she know what happened?" I ask him as I grab the door handle to steady myself.

"I wouldn't do that if I were you," he states while side-eyeing my hand.

I swallow. "Why not?"

"It won't open, and I have the locks all disabled," he says, once again, in an emotionless voice.

"Why?"

Malachai shrugs. "In case I need them that way."

I lean back in the seat and stare ahead. "I need to talk with Ava. Please."

"We are almost to my house. She said she would meet us there once she is done at your apartment."

I nod, trying to force myself to relax into the seat.

We drive in silence. I inhale and exhale slowly to calm my frayed nerves, but I am drowning in the scent of blood. The metallic scent makes me crawl out of my skin as the drive continues.

Once we pull into Malachai's driveway, he opens the four-car garage. We drive into it slowly, and an overhead light greets us in the dimly lit space. Malachai turns off the engine and walks over to my side of the vehicle. He doesn't let me out until the garage door shuts completely, locking us in together.

Malachai opens the door for me and steps to the side, allowing me to walk past him swiftly so that my back is to the wall, and I am facing him and the car. I cross my arms before myself, trying to make myself smaller in this vast space.

Malachai looks me up and down and shakes his head as he opens his car's trunk. He then reaches down past the car's tires and opens two metal doors. I walk forward slowly to better see what he is doing and see that the doors open to cement steps that lead into a basement. There are no lights, so it looks like a black void.

Malachai glances at me hesitantly as he reaches into the trunk. With one swift movement, Malachai pulls the body, which is wrapped in plastic, onto the stairs. With a firm shove, the body rolls down the stairs and stops with a sickening squelch.

I watch Malachai reach up and close the trunk when I hear a door open in front of the car. I step to the side to see who it is when I see Ava and Riley standing side by side at the top of some stairs that look like they may lead to the central part of the house.

Riley takes one look at me and hurries to my side. She immediately reaches up to touch my face, which I am sure looks bruised and battered.

"I'm ok. I've had worse," I tell her, gently removing her worried hands from my face.

This doesn't reassure her in the least, and tears start forming in her eyes. My heart squeezes at the sight of her, and I pull her into a strained hug.

"Hey, it's not your fault. None of this is. I decided to stay behind, and I'm just glad you are safe," I tell Riley as I let go of her.

She finally nods while releasing me and then turns to

follow Malachai, who is already making his way down the stairs. I look over to Ava, who is watching them descend with an unreadable expression. Once they are out of sight, she finally meets my gaze. Her face crumples when she takes in the sight of me.

"Ava?" I ask in a shaky voice.

She runs down the steps and throws her arms around my neck in a crushing embrace. I hold her to me and try to swallow the sob that is about to escape me. I can't break now. I can't. If I do, I might not be able to put back the pieces again.

I hold Ava to my chest and run my hands over her back and neck until I bury my hands in her hair. She feels so healthy. She isn't the tiny teenager that I left behind anymore. She is healthy and safe. It was worth it...to have her here and safe.

We finally managed to untangle ourselves before I gestured towards Malachai, who had disappeared from the floor. "How long has this been going on?"

Ava looks away from me. "He never got better, you know. He was never the same after that night. I think it broke him."

We both jump as we hear the sound of metal clanking from below us and then the sound of something ripping. I swallow and look away from her, waiting for her to continue.

"After you got out of the hospital and were placed into police custody, he just wouldn't wake up. They thought he was brain-dead, and Gage and I were placed into emergency custody with the Saavedras. Do you remember them? They used to work with Michael in DC."

"Yeah, I only saw them once, at my trial..." I trail off while running a frustrated hand through my hair.

"They kept us after discovering everything Michael and Penny had done to us, especially you and Malachai. But after a few months, they started talking about taking Malachai off of life support, and he just woke up.

113

"He suffered. He had to relearn everything. Walking, talking, eating...the Saavedra's, Carrie and Jack, they spared no expense with all the rehabilitation he had to do. After he got better, though, he was just off. And not just the memory stuff. He just wouldn't react the same or smile anymore. I thought it was maybe because he subconsciously missed you, and that's why I kept writing, but...."

"Carrie saw fit to keep you all away from me?" I interrupt.

Ava shrugs. "She didn't know everything, Lake. She thought she was protecting us. Especially after a few incidents with Malachai, she thought you would be a bad influence on him."

"What happened?" I ask.

"It started when Malachai went away to college. He would get into a lot of fights. He would hurt people over the smallest things; you know him–he wasn't like that before. He wouldn't have hurt a fly."

I nod in agreement, remembering.

"Carrie and Jack brought him home after, and they got him into therapy. That didn't go so well...they said he was showing psychopathic tendencies, and Carrie didn't want to believe that, so she stopped the therapy and tried some art classes instead...and that seemed to work out."

"How many have there been?" I ask while looking around the garage more.

"I've lost count," she states while looking at the ground.

"Who knows?"

"Just Carrie and I...and Gage."

"Where is Gage? I want to see him," I tell her as I walk closer to the opening in the basement. "Is he here?"

"He's coming home soon," Ava states, following close behind me.

I glance over at her. "Where is Gage, Ava? Both of you have hardly mentioned him at all. What happened to him?"

"He's in rehab," Malachai calls up to us. A light flickers on, and I see Riley sitting at the bottom of the steps, staring at her stepfather's partially dismembered body, lying on top of plastic wrap in the center of the cement basement.

Malachai walks into view wearing a transparent raincoat with a saw in one hand and a severed arm in the other. I hold his gaze evenly as I descend the steps to stand eye-to-eye with him.

I look him over and take in his hauntingly familiar features. I see the familiar lines of exhaustion beneath his eyes and the light pull of his lips to show he is upset. I reach up and trace the curve of his jaw until I let my fingers run over the smoothness of his neck. He closes his eyes and leans into my touch with a relieved breath.

"Did they deserve it?" I ask him.

"Yes," he answers without hesitation.

"Okay," I say as I reach for the saw to help him.

"What are you doing, Lake?" he asks, holding the saw from me.

Unable to voice my intended actions, I stare up at him silently.

Malachai drops the saw to the floor and gently cups my face. "No, you need to rest."

I shake my head at him and hold onto his sleeve. "I am not leaving you."

"He won't be alone," Ava says as she slips on a raincoat on the other side of the room. I force myself to stare at her so my gaze is not lowered to the floor.

Malachai looks over to Ava. "She is hurt and is still recovering. She shouldn't be here. You should take her upstairs."

I tighten my grip on Malachai to bring his attention back to me. I offer him a forced smile that I hope is reassuring before I let go of his arm.

"I am fine. You guys stay here. I'll go rest for a bit."

"Are you sure?" Ava asks.

I nod before looking over to Riley. She stares down at the saw on the floor and then back to her stepdad.

"Riley? Do you want to go with Lake?" Malachai asks over his shoulder.

Without looking at either of us, she walks over to the saw and picks it up. Following the path of her hand, I cannot help but look at the disarticulated body of Riley's stepdad and where blood is slowly starting to ooze from the severed ligaments at the joint.

Malachai grabs my chin and forces my gaze back to him. "I'll come find you in a bit, okay?"

I nod as I swallow the bile that rises in my throat and turn to walk up the stairs. It's a slow ascent to the central part of the house. Halfway up the steps, my anxiety is replaced by overwhelming fatigue, and I struggle to make it up the last few steps.

After opening the main house door, I take a minute to walk around and familiarize myself with my surroundings. The modern design of the gallery's gold and glass fixtures is very much reflected in the style of Malachai's home. Everything is pristine and brand new. It is a different kind of wealth than what we grew up with, which I am glad for. If I were to see another Victorian doily right now, I would throw myself headfirst off the roof.

I go through the living room, into the adjacent kitchen and examine all the appliances. It looks like no one has ever used this kitchen before. My stomach growls a bit, but I decide against scavenging for food. After exploring the rest of the first floor–which included an office, dining room, and a simple half bathroom–I am again left at another set of stairs leading to the upper floor.

"Fuck..."

Grumbling to myself and trying to ignore the aching in

my bones from the last hours of trauma, I finally make it up and limp my way through a hallway with multiple bedrooms and bathrooms attached. At the end of the hall, away from the others, is a more oversized bedroom with monochrome fixtures. It looks like something that a man would call his bedroom if he were Patrick Bateman.

I shudder at the thought, remembering what Malachai is currently doing a few floors beneath my feet, and step further into the room. I stumble into the large bathroom to the right of his California king-sized bed and feel around on the wall for a light switch but feel none. I step in further, and lights turn on above me automatically to illuminate the bathroom, which matches the aesthetic of the rest of the house. My eyes drift to the large bathtub, which calls to my soul.

Walking towards the tub, I glimpse my reflection in the mirror and cringe when I see myself fully for the first time. Dark purple bruises trail across my forehead, and my lip is busted, with dry blood coating my chin and throat. I look closer and see that the blood vessels in my dark eyes are also broken, making me look like something from a zombie movie.

How am I going to go to work this week?

Bracing my hands against the sink, I inhale deeply and meet my gaze in my reflection. I sniffle and rub at my nose as I see a drizzle of blood leak from it. I pull up my shirt to wipe it and turn away from the mirror to the tub. After some fidgeting with the fancy faucet, I manage to turn on the hot water. Stripping out of my clothing, I slide into the scalding water that immediately starts to soothe my aching muscles.

I groan at the feeling and curl in on myself as the water rises to cover my body. I pull my knees tighter to my chest and press my fist into my mouth to silence any other noise threatening to escape me.

"You're going to hurt yourself doing that."

I look up from the water and see Malachai leaning against

the wall, watching me. His hair is wild, and his clothes are ruffled, but he looks like himself–especially since he ditched the raincoat. I immediately drop my hand into the water and look away from him.

"Turn around," he says as he strolls towards the tub.

I close my eyes and turn around so that my back is facing him. As I listened to his clothing hit the floor, I could almost pretend this was like that moment we shared all those years ago. I hear him slip into the water, but instead of feeling his back press against mine as it had, I feel his hands work through my hair to untangle it.

I pull lightly away from his touch. "What are you doing, Malachai?"

Malachai grasps my shoulders firmly and pulls me against his chest.

"I want to take care of you..." he murmurs while trailing his fingers gently along the crook of my neck.

I feel burning in my throat as I ask, "Why?"

Malachai deepens the pressure on my neck, and I can feel him massage the tender flesh there. "Because you've seen me... You've seen me and didn't turn away. You stayed. You must love me."

I open my eyes and look down to see where my dried blood is starting to dissolve into the water around us. As the water rises, it slowly turns from red to pink and then to nothing.

"More than you know."

Malachai lifts his fingers from my neck and returns to untangling my hair. His hands are gentle in their movements, and he is careful not to tug on my tender scalp. I lean forward to rest my head against my knees and close my eyes.

"Stay with me," he says, pausing his movements.

"Why?" I ask again while staring into the blackness behind my eyelids, exhaustion from the day's events taking hold.

"Stay because I want you with me."

I pull away from him again and fully turn to face him in the water. I watch his eyes lightly trail down my bare body and then back up to hold my gaze. I try to resist an amused smile as I see a light pink start to cover his cheeks.

"I could try to be like I was for you," he states with a slight pleading undertone while pulling my hair over my shoulder to continue his work.

I gently reach up and place my hand over his to pause his movements. Malachai opens his mouth to speak, but I cut him off while trying to fight the tightness in my throat that threatens to strangle me.

"I remember when I first knew I loved you. I was scared because of the world we lived in, but you made loving you worth every moment of it. I told myself then that no matter what, I would love you. And meeting you again after all this time, it's as true for me now as it was then. So, I don't want you to try Malachai. I'll love any form of you."

Without a further statement, I lean back in the tub so that my head is resting against the cool marble. Malachai mirrors my actions, causing our legs to entwine lightly. I try to ignore his naked body as he begins to speak.

"Stay with me. You are my family. Stay, at least for the night," he asks gently.

I stare at him for a moment before nodding. I know the truth is that I don't want to leave. Regardless of what Malachai has done in the past or what he did to save me today, I want to stay with him so badly it feels as if I would be peeling off parts of my soul to be separated from him for another moment, and I don't think I could bear it.

Malachai breathes a sigh of relief and leans back again, resting his head along the tub's edge and gazing up at the ceiling—this time, I allow myself to take in his appearance selfishly.

Sweat drips down his temple, causing his hair to curl even more at the tips than usual. I follow the sweat dripping down his strong throat to his broad shoulders and chest. I can see the definition of toned muscle under his skin. I swallow as my gaze trails further down his chest to his abs. They end in a strong v-shape, leading to a trail of curly black hair....

"Like what you see?" Malachai asks.

Heat rushes to my cheeks, and my gaze shoots up to his face, where I lock my eyes with his. He looks at me with heavy regard from under hooded eyes. I watch with curiosity as his eyes leave mine and slowly wander south. Does he like what he sees as well?

I fight the urge to cover myself and relax further into the water. I look away from him and start slowly scrubbing away dried specks of blood on my body. Malachai's eyes soften as he looks past his lust-filled gaze and sees the extent of the damage I have sustained.

Malachai moves from his position and kneels before me in the water. He caresses my face lightly as he grabs a washcloth from a nearby towel rack and gently wipes blood from my face.

"I am so sorry, Lake. I should never have left you," he murmurs, barely above a whisper.

He sounds so much like he used to at this moment. My heart clenches as I reach out to him, and he doesn't hesitate to pull me close to his chest as I cling to him. I bury my face in the crook of his neck as he moves us to a more comfortable position, with me curled against his chest while resting my weight against his thighs. He doesn't attempt to tell me that it is okay or to try to soothe me. He lets me cling to him and feel what I need to, which I have missed most all these years.

Malachai holds me until I release my grip on him. After we separate, we quickly finish our bath, and then he helps me to my feet and guides me out of the tub, ensuring I don't slip on the marble floors.

Malachai releases me, and I cover my naked body with my arms, all bravery gone now as I watch Malachai wrap a white towel around his waist. He turns to face me with another towel in his hands. He kneels before me once more and slowly dries me off from my feet to my face.

After I am thoroughly dry, Malachai walks over to a cabinet, pulls out a few essential toiletries, and gives them to me. I use his deodorant and toothbrush quickly, and I am grateful for his generosity so I don't have to taste blood in my mouth anymore. I glance at Malachai in the reflection of the bathroom mirror and watch as he lathers a substance in his hands that I am assuming is lotion, and then he begins to rub it into my skin. As he does this, he traces the outline of my bruises and scrapes with a soft touch, leaving a trail of tingles along my skin as he finishes his work.

Once he stands at full height before me, I fake a pout and murmur, "I liked you on your knees."

Malachai looks down at me and gives me a faint grin. "Come on; you're going to get cold," he says.

Malachai takes me by the hand, and I follow him silently, still trying to use my free arm to cover myself. Malachai leads us into his room, over to a sleek black dresser. He drops my hand and rummages through his neatly folded clothing until he finds a black long-sleeve shirt and gray plaid boxer briefs. While keeping his back to me, he gives me the clothing items, and I quickly pull them on and clear my throat to signal I am done.

Malachai turns around and looks me up and down once more. He gives an approving hum at the sight of me in his clothing before gesturing to the bed. I follow him as he pulls back the dark silk sheets and pats the mattress.

I hesitantly sit down and immediately want to sink into

the sheets and lose myself in them for hours, maybe even days. They feel like feathers caressing my skin. I mirror Malachai's previous hum of approval as I adjust myself further into the sheets.

Malachai reaches into the bedside table to pull out a remote and presses a few buttons, and I immediately notice the lights dim as the bed begins to warm up beneath me. He presses a few more buttons, and soft piano music surrounds us in a calm embrace.

Malachai sets the remote down and then gently presses a hand to my chest to guide me into a more restful position. I lay my head back against the pillows and gaze up at him. He holds my gaze before pulling the covers around me and then turning to leave.

"Rest," he says over his shoulder before exiting the room.

I roll onto my side and curl in on myself as I watch him go, resisting the urge to beg him to stay with me until I fall asleep. Instead, I let his soft footfalls lull me into the abyss.

Chapter Fourteen

MALACHAI

I sit with Lake under the Willow tree by the pond at our estate. The sun illuminates her eyes and makes them look like glowing amber. I feel my breath get caught in my throat as she offers me a soft smile while she rests her head on her knees.

It is astonishing how she could smile and show me such kindness after being humiliated in every way a human can be. She is astonishing. I want to stay with her forever and hear every word on her lips.

I want her.

I glance away from her to look out onto the pond where dragonflies flutter about. I shouldn't want her. She is so young and innocent. She probably sees me as nothing more than a confidant, a friend.

I have a responsibility to her.

Over the last four years, though, she has become my world. My day begins and ends with her soft smiles and soft words.

When I wake, she is the first person I look forward to laying my eyes on.

On my worst days, she is the only person who grounds me. Without her, I am weightless and adrift.

I've tried to distract myself, but my gaze always drifts back to her. I can't escape her.

"Malachai?"

I turn to her and lose myself in her endless gaze. "Hmm?"

A light blush creeps up on her cheeks. "You seem distracted today."

I sigh and lean back against the tree.

"I am."

"By what?"

I let my head lull to the side and hold her gaze. "By you."

Lake looks away from me and fidgets with the edge of her school uniform. Her pale thigh sticks out against the contrast of the navy and red skirt. My throat tightens at the sight.

"Oh? How so?"

I swallow. "I don't want to be like my father."

"You are nothing like him." She states firmly.

I shake my head. "I am."

Lake sits up and kneels in front of me. "Why would you think such a terrible thing?"

I let silence envelop us as anxiety twists my stomach to the point I feel like I might be sick on the grass beside us.

"Malachai?"

"Because...I think of you. I think of you when I shouldn't. When I should be protecting you from people who think about you like I do."

Lake's blush deepens. "How do you think of me?"

"Lake...I...can't." I choke out.

Lake holds my gaze before nodding to herself. "I...Love you Malachai."

"I know," I say with a forced smile.

I exhale as I push myself to my feet, planning on distancing myself from her further, as I feel her grasp my wrist with a strength I did not know she possessed in her frail state. I look down to where she is still kneeling in the grass and hold her intense gaze.

"I love you...In a way that I shouldn't." She says barely above a whisper.

I feel my heart drop into my stomach at her admission and pull her to her feet. Over the last year, I have grown more than her, causing her head to barely reach my collarbone. I stare into her eyes before planting a chaste kiss on her forehead.

"I love you in a way I shouldn't," I admit.

M y eyes slowly open, and I sit up in my chair from where I had been resting my head by Lake's side while she slept. I look down with heavy eyes to where our fingers are still entwined, even after being in this position for hours. I start to untangle my fingers, but her grip instinctively tightens.

She needs me. She wants me near her even though she shouldn't.

I'm a monster.

I feel a pang in my chest as I take in the sight of her. My beautiful Lake. So soft and delicate. Still so innocent. I want to run my hands through her hair and feel every inch of her skin.

I think back to the dream I just awoke from. Even then, I knew what I was and what I would turn into after everything they did to me. But yet, Lake still loved me. She wanted me then, and she came to me now. She sought me out.

But I'm a monster.

I'm a monster, and I'm...

I am broken...

I wish things were different for us. I wish I were different for her. She deserves to be with someone who has their whole mind intact and isn't constantly fighting against their more based urges to hurt others.

I look at her now and want to bear my soul to her. I want to tell her that I've tried. For years, I have tried to be different, but something is missing from me, which was taken all of those years ago, and I have been struggling to find it again. I want to tell her that I am sorry.

I want to tell her I am sorry for every life I have taken, even though I know the world is better off without those lives.

I am sorry because I know every life is just one more wedge I have shoved between us that will forever keep her from me.

I shouldn't have asked her to stay with me. No, I know I shouldn't have, but I also know that I am weak.

I ascended the stairs earlier with every intention of pushing her away after seeing her unconditional love for me, knowing that it would one day be what caused her downfall. But when I saw her naked and hurting, I couldn't bear it. I wanted to bury her in my arms and never let her go. I wanted to lock her away in this very room to keep her to myself for all of eternity.

This is just another reason why she is better off without me. I am selfish and impulsive, and she doesn't deserve to be with a broken thing like me.

But I want her. I have wanted her for so long, and now that she is here, I cannot let go. I don't think I will ever be able to.

I sigh to myself as I lay my head back down on the bed and begin to count her breaths again, just to remind myself that she is safe and alive while I wait for her to wake. When she does, she won't know my thoughts and my regrets. Those are mine and mine alone to bear.

Chapter Fifteen

LAKE

"I had a dream last night," I murmur while looking at the stars above us.

"What about?" Malachai asks while rolling on his side to face me.

I spare him a glance as I feel the wet grass beneath my fingers. We snuck out to the large park at the end of our neighborhood tonight. I know I should feel fear or anxiety about the repercussions awaiting us at home if we were caught, but lying here now, with nothing but the warmth of Malachai's body heat, this moment is worth any possible punishment.

"It was about you," I state as I gaze back at the nearly cloudless sky.

Malachai rests his head on his arm and casually inches closer to me. I pretend I don't notice as I continue.

"Do you dream of me often?" he asks.

"Every night, Malachai."

"Do you believe in soulmates?" Malachai asks while tracing

his fingers from my jaw, down my neck, and finally to the edge of my shirt on my chest, where he lets his fingers slowly stop.

"Yes," I state a bit breathlessly.

Malachai looks up from my chest to hold my gaze. "Am I your soulmate, Lake?"

"Yes."

Malachai is silent for a moment as he continues to take in the shape of my body with his hand. He gently trails from my chest to my stomach, hesitating briefly before sliding his hand under my shirt. I stop breathing entirely until he rests his hand against my bare ribcage.

"I never believed in soulmates. But after meeting you, if there is such a thing, it would be you," he says softly.

Malachai tightens his grip on my ribs as he pulls me to him. I hold onto his neck as I brush my lips against his. His lips are soft and welcoming. I get lost in the feel of them.

My eyes flutter shut as he deepens the kiss and pushes his tongue into my mouth, causing me to let out a light moan at the contact.

Malachai breaks the heated kiss and brushes a few stray hairs from my forehead as he murmurs, "I love you."

I crush my lips against his again, and he grabs me by the hips to roll me on top of him. Malachai places his hand under my shirt again and trails up to where he is cupping my breasts. He hasn't touched me like this before, but it feels nice, and I want more...

I gasp as I feel him hard against me. Anxiety suddenly burns in my chest, but I try to ignore it. This is Malachai, and there is no one in this world I am safer with, and I know he would never hurt me. Not like them...

Even still...

Malachai feels me tense up, and he breaks our kiss once more. I protest, embarrassed at my hesitation, but Malachai shakes his head with a gentle smile.

"There is no rush, my love. Come here," he says while shifting me to sit higher up on his stomach and guiding my head into the nook of his shoulder.

I tuck my arms between our chests and lose myself in the comfort of his scent.

"I love you, Malachai."

I wake up to the smell of peanut butter adjacent to my face. My eyes flutter open, and I gaze at the PB and J on a shiny white plate as I feel a knot form in my throat at the sight of it. I hear my stomach growl, but I fail to reach out and grasp the food. Instead, I curl in on myself, burying deeper into the soft sheets.

"You need to eat."

I roll onto my back to see Malachai lounging in a black chair within arm's reach. He has one leg propped up with his knee while holding up his chin leisurely, his arm resting against the chair at his elbow. His head is tilted slightly in a carefree manner as he watches me.

I let my gaze linger on his casual appearance. I haven't seen him wear anything except a black button-down and dress pants. Well, except for our bath last night.

Now, he wears a black v-neck tee and gray cotton sweats. His feet are bare. I feel a smile pull at my lips at his casual appearance, primarily his messy, curly black hair.

"How long have you been here?" I ask while forcing myself into a sitting position.

The movement makes the muscles in my body scream, and I do my best to resist a wince as I scoot back into the bed until I am flush against the headboard. Malachai waits for me to situate myself before he answers.

"On and off for the last day."

I glance around, looking for a clock. "Have I really been asleep for that long?"

"Just about."

I look back over to him. "What day is today?"

"Thursday."

"Fuck, the banquet!" I curse while trying and failing to jump out of bed by getting tangled in the sheets.

Malachai stands to his feet in one smooth motion. "Everything is already complete. Ava and Riley took over your duties last night and finished up all of the preparations."

I relax against the headboard once more. "Oh, good. I'll need to thank them for that."

Malachai nods once as he sits on the edge of the bed and gazes at me. He caresses my cheek before letting his hands trail down from my face and throat. His fingers and eyes linger as he traces the artery back and forth. The motion makes shivers run down my spine and my heart races.

Malachai feels my pulse quicken under his touch, and his pupils dilate in reaction. He looks up from my throat to my eyes before looking back down to his fingers and allowing them to trail lower to my collarbone, where he pauses once more to gauge my reaction.

He grins as he feels my pulse quicken even further. "I wonder how fast your heart will beat once I'm inside you."

My eyes widen, and I feel my face go red. Malachai notices and lets out a soft chuckle before standing from the bed, leaving me breathless and flushed.

I watch silently as Malachai walks over to his walk-in closet across from the bed and starts to pull clothing wrapped in plastic out as if they had just come fresh from the store. He walks back and forth from the bed to the closet as he plops down more and more clothing items. He has gathered a black-on-black suit, which fits his aesthetic.

134

"Does Ruby still need me to come in tonight?" I ask him as he walks into the closet one final time.

Malachai exits the closet with a bundle of clothing and a small red box stacked on a shoe box. He sets them down on the bed at my feet, next to his clothing.

"No. We have enough staff to cover tonight's events."

I watch him closely as he pulls his shirt over his head, revealing his smooth chest and abs. It has to be a sin to have that many abs. When does he even have time to work out?

I look back down at the clothing at my feet to distract myself from him.

"Then what are those?" I ask curiously.

"They are for you. You are coming with us tonight."

I feel the blood drain from my face. "I can't go, Malachai. Look at me."

Malachai shrugs on a black button-up shirt and walks over to me as he works on the buttons. He leans close to my face, observing the damage from days prior. Once the shirt is buttoned up, he gently grasps my chin, tilting my head from one side to the other. He nods to himself before releasing me and stepping back to continue dressing himself.

"The blood vessels in your eyes have gone back to normal. The only thing to worry about is the bruising, but Ava got some things for that. After we get dressed, she and Riley will help you."

I frown to myself, not fully believing that they will be able to make me look semi-regular for tonight's events.

"Why am I going with you and not just working the event like I should?" I ask him as I make my way out of the tangle of sheets and to my feet.

Malachai looks at me like that is a ridiculous question. "You are one of us."

I hold his gaze evenly. "That doesn't change the fact that I have a job, an obligation."

"Your only obligation is to me," he mutters as he buttons up his dress pants, "If you want it to be."

"I don't want to let anyone down." I state in protest.

"You aren't because I need you to help the family," he retorts.

"And what do you need me to do for the family?" I ask as I open the boxes to see what Malachai has put together for me. I have a pair of black stilettos and a silver jewelry set to wear. The tags are still attached, and I blanch as I look at the price tags.

I lift the small box and look over at Malachai. "What's with all of this? *Cartier*? Really?"

"I need you to show up and be a united front with the family," he states while putting the finishing touches on his outfit and blatantly ignoring my question about the price. "We have some special guests from the local police force visiting with us this evening at the banquet since we are a significant benefactor of theirs. We need to appear inconspicuous. They also need to see you unharmed after what happened to Riley's dad so that it will make it harder for them to connect you with his disappearance. If anyone asks you about the last forty-eight hours, you were with me, in my home, in my bed, understand?"

"Malachai..." I say while setting the jewelry back down on the bed.

"Hmm?" he murmurs as he trades his glasses for contacts and then begins to fuss with his unruly hair.

I immediately forget what I am about to say and simply nod in agreement to his alibi. He looks stunning as he runs his hands through his locks with some product from a jar on a side table. He sleeks his hair back, and with that, he's ready to go.

Turning away from his distracting appearance, I shuffle along to the bathroom on stiff legs as Malachai follows me and

136

leans casually in the doorway. I keep accidentally locking eyes with him in the mirror's reflection, and I feel my face redden a few shades deeper each time. Malachi smirked and straightened up from his position, where he was watching me, after glancing at his watch.

"I will see you there. I have to be there early after making a stop," he states before walking from the room, leaving me to finish freshening myself up without further explanation.

Once my face and teeth are as pristine as they can be, I walk back over to the bed and make quick work of the PB and J before I unwrap the dress from its packaging. It is a simple black silk dress with a slit on the right leg and delicate straps. I also look at that tag and lose a year off my life from all the zeros.

"Goddamn," I mutter to myself as I slip into it.

I add the shoes and jewelry before I look at myself in a floor-length mirror in Malachai's closet. He got my size perfect, and the dress hugs me in all the right places without making me look too skinny. The shoes and jewelry complement the clothing with their subtle yet timeless elegance. I stand in front of the mirror, staring at my reflection until I hear the door to Malachai's room open.

I leave the closet and see Riley and Ava standing side by side. Riley grins at me as I take in her and Ava's appearance. They are both wearing different styles that complement each other. Both have their hair slicked back out of their faces, similar to Malachai's, but Ava's ends in a tight bun at the nape of her neck.

The style compliments the sleek black dress that covers up to her delicate neck and trails down to the floor behind her in wispy strips. My gaze travels from the edge of the dress to the spiked stilettos that make her almost my height.

On the other hand, Riley is wearing a black suit made of the same materials as Ava's dress. The suit hugs her small body but accentuates her figure, especially with the deep v-cut of the blazer that has nothing underneath it. It is a stark change to how Riley constantly covers almost every inch of her skin. She looks hot. I feel a smile widen on my face as I take in the other small details of them both.

Neither opted for jewelry other than small black and white stud earrings, matching once more. It's a subtle detail, but they look like a pair.

My gaze travels back to Ava as I watch her walk over to Malachai's dresser and place down items. I walk closer to both of them to see better what Ava has brought.

"How are you feeling?" Ava asks over her shoulder as she organizes the makeup and hair products in a specific order from left to right.

I shrug a bit and sit down on the bed, careful not to disturb the fabric of my dress. "I have been worse."

Ava gazes at me from head to toe before mirroring my shrug. "True."

Riley scowls at that before walking over to the bed and maneuvering so that she is sitting behind me. She holds her hand out to Ava, who passes her a brush and hair spray. Riley starts to drench my hair and then passes the brush through it repeatedly as gently as possible.

I relax with the soothing, repetitive motions and look up as Ava walks over to me with some color-correcting concealer in her grasp.

Ava and Riley make small talk with one another while they both make me look presentable. Well, more so, Ava talks to Riley. Ava uses a bit softer tone with her than with me, which is interesting to hear. Riley makes small hums of agreement here and there, encouraging Ava to keep engaging.

I try to listen fully to what they are saying, but my thoughts keep repeating something Malachai had said while we were in the garage. Concern wins out, and I look up at Ava and briefly place my hand over hers to pause her movements.

"What happened to Gage?" I ask.

Ava grimaces as she applies rouge to my cheeks.

"Gage didn't get along with the Saavedra's as we did. They never did anything wrong to him, but after everything we went through, I think he could never trust them. It made him lonely. Especially with Malachai being different after that night...And I was so caught up with helping Malachai that I didn't notice things started to change with him either. I didn't know he was doing drugs until Malachi found him in a bathtub at Thanksgiving last year. He overdosed and had to be hospitalized."

Ava pauses before clearing her throat nervously and continuing, "He has been in and out of rehab for the last year. He comes home tonight, and Malachai is getting him from the airport now before the benefit."

Hope fills my chest at that. "So I will get to see him?"

Ava offers me a small, sad smile. "Yeah, you will."

We are silent for a few more minutes before Ava stops what she is doing. I gaze up at her and see her staring off a bit past Riley and me as she says, "I should have been there for him, too. If you had been here, you wouldn't have let things get that far with him. You would have noticed the change. I fucked up and...I should have been there for him."

I reach up and grasp her hands with my own. "Ava, I couldn't have done better in your shoes. You held everything together the best you could."

Ava nods slightly before dropping my hands. She is silent as she adds the finishing touches to my face and covers the bruising on my neck and arms.

After that is done, Ava gives me a forced triumphant grin. "There. Now let's finish that hair."

Riley and Ava have me move over to the chair Malachai

had been sitting in earlier. We all sit in silence as Ava curls my hair with a large barrel iron. Once that is complete, she adds more product to my hair and then helps me to my feet to look in the mirror.

I gaze at my reflection with wonder. I look at myself from all angles and smile at Riley and Ava. I can't see any of the bruises from the previous days, and my skin looks youthful and pretty without looking like we tried too hard to make me look that way.

Ava opted to leave my hair down in large, flowing curls, which I am glad about since I usually don't like to wear it up. Between the clothing, hair, and makeup, I still feel like myself, just a more refined version.

"You look hot," Riley says while leaning into the view of the mirror.

I grin and look at her. "So do you. Do you want to be my date tonight?"

Ava walks behind Riley and lightly drapes her arms around her shoulders. "Riley is mine tonight. You can have Malachai and Gage."

Riley's face turns red, and I can't hide my laughter. Ava grins while releasing Riley, and we follow her out of Malachai's room and down into the garage. Once there, Ava pulls out keys from a black clutch purse and unlocks a black Model Y Tesla. Riley slides into the passenger's side while Ava takes the wheel. I gingerly get comfortable in the back seat as Ava peels out of the garage.

Chapter Sixteen

MALACHAI

I shove my shoulder repeatedly against the cellar door, blood coating my skin from every inch where Michael decided to inflict his rage. I yell at the top of my lungs and pry at the lock with broken nails.

They took Lake away from me three days ago after we returned from the park. Michael had gone looking for Lake at night, and when he found her absent, he sat on the porch, waiting for us.

I haven't seen her since then but have repeatedly seen Michael. I can usually survive his punishments with sanity by placing the pain and humiliation into a box, a box deep inside me that no one can break open—no one but Lake, and they took her from me. The box is overflowing without her, and I feel like I am losing my mind.

I need Lake.

I need Lake.

I need Lake.

And she needs me. I can only imagine the ways she is being punished by that sick fuck. The thought drives me to the edge of insanity.

"LAKE!"

I scream until my lungs are sore. I scream until tears blur my vision, and my lungs burn with the lack of oxygen. I collapse with exhaustion and try to pry uselessly at the door's hinges. I shiver from the cold, from the emptiness.

"Gage...GAGE!"

I call for him repeatedly for minutes and hours until I finally hear the door start to open, and I crawl away from it as it swings inward.

I brace myself for Michael to come in and silence me again, but I see Gage's beautiful blue gaze staring down at me with a look of deep sorrow.

"Malachai..." he says with a choked sob as he looks me over.

I crawl to him and grasp onto his legs like a lifeline. "Where are they?"

"They left. I don't know when they will be back." Gage tells me softly as he helps me to my feet.

"Where...Where is Lake?"

Gage swallows. "The attic."

I tear off down the hall from him and make the journey through the estate on bleeding feet. I don't even feel the pain of my body anymore. Not when I am running to Lake. Not when I can finally see her again.

Nothing matters now but her.

I pry open the door at the end of the south wing on the third floor that leads me to a hidden white staircase. I take the steps two at a time until I reach the attic door, where I shove my weight into it as I turn the knob.

The door gives away easier than I anticipated, and I fall to my hands and knees as I turn to my left, where I see Lake.

Lake is chained to a white mattress by her left wrist, naked except for a pair of white underwear. She sits up with tears in her eyes and pulls against the bloodied chain.

"I heard you calling for me...I couldn't get free." She cries, pulling against the chain once more.

I stumble to my feet before I fall before her on the mattress and pull her to my bare chest in an embrace. I feel tears stream down my face as I inhale the scent of her hair. I kiss her forehead, then her face, and then down her neck before she pulls away from me.

"Oh god, what did he do to you? You are covered in blood, Malachai...and where are your clothes? You feel like ice." She cries while looking me over and caressing my face with her soft hands.

I shake my head as I continue to hold her to me, embarrassment and shame churning my stomach. I couldn't get away from him. I couldn't get away from all of the pain he inflicted. I can't get away from it now.

"Did he...Did he hurt you?" I ask, barely above a whisper.

Lake shakes her head and pulls herself closer to me. "Not... not as much as what he did to you."

I let out a broken sob and let my head drop to her chest. I feel her wrap her tiny arms around my neck and shoulders to soothe me. The kind touch causes another sob to escape.

"Everything hurts, Lake."

"I know, I know Malachai. I am so sorry," she whispers against my ear.

"I need the pain to stop. I need you to make it stop."

I plead with her as she tightens her grip on me. I don't even know what I am asking of her now, but I am desperate to feel anything other than what I am feeling right now.

"Please...I need it all to go away."

Lake places a soft kiss against my ear before continuing along my jaw and the corner of my mouth. Before she can pull away, I turn my head and crush my lips against hers, the taste of my blood mixing in with the taste of her.

I push Lake against the mattress before covering her body with mine. She lets out a startled gasp, but I keep moving, touching, tasting anything to drown out what I am feeling.

"Lake..." I moan against her mouth as I fist her underwear in my grasp along the sharp edge of her hip.

Lake pulls away from me and looks up with wide eyes. "Malachai?"

I tear the fabric away with a swift pull. She lets out a sound of pain from where the fabric burned her skin. I ignore it as I kiss along her neck and feel my teeth graze along her rapid pulse. I run my tongue along the flesh there, down to the soft muscle of her shoulder, where I bite down hard until I taste blood.

Before I can stop myself, I have her hands pinned under mine while I am pushing deep inside her. She lets out another pained cry as I feel her open to the length of me.

The sound pulls me from my desperation, and I look at her tear-filled gaze.

"Oh fuck Lake...I'm sorry...I'm so sorry." I gasp as I see more blood start to spill on the mattress from where our bodies connect.

"Wait!" Lake grabs me as I begin to pull away.

Our rapid breathing matches as she stares into my eyes. "Lake...I..."

"It's ok Malachai."

I see the sincerity in her eyes and know she means what she says with every ounce of her soul. She would let me take anything that I wanted from her.

I crush my lips against hers again before I take everything.

A sharp tap against the glass wakes me from my dream. I look over to the passenger side of my car and see Gage glaring at me through tinted sunglasses.

Fuck, I need to sleep more. I'm fucking exhausted. I must have crashed out while waiting for him at the passenger pick-up at the airport. I wipe at the moisture in my eyes as Gage opens the door and tosses his duffle bag to the floor before sliding into his seat without a word.

I stare silently out the windshield until he finally glances at me. "Were you crying?"

I clear my throat as I put the car in drive. "No. Just dreaming."

"Liar," Gage murmurs under his breath as he looks out the passenger side window.

I clear my throat and focus on the road ahead. As the minutes drag on between us and our destination, I start to feel something akin to anxiety, with a mixture of guilt in Gage's presence. I want him to say something. Anything.

We haven't spoken much since I found him half dead in the bathroom of Mom's house. I remember that was the first time I can remember feeling fear. True fear. The kind that sucks the air from your lungs and makes you feel like you are drowning in the moment.

Even thinking of it now–how his lips were tinted blue with cold sweat covering his whole body–makes the air in the car feel thinner.

I haven't gotten the image out of my head since it happened. I almost lost a vital part of my life–my best friend, my brother.

I glance at him through my peripherals and remind myself that he is okay. He is safe and here with me. Our family will be whole again.

I clear my throat and ask him, "Have you spoken with Ava recently?"

"I've been ignoring her calls," Gage states.

"She is going to be pissed about that when she sees you."

Gage just shrugs his shoulders and continues not looking at me.

I sigh and decide to rip the bandage off. "Lake is free and living with us. She is going to be at the banquet tonight."

Gage's head snaps in my direction so fast I'm surprised his neck didn't pop. "How?"

"I found someone there finally willing to take a bribe."

"Who?"

"Her case worker. It took a while for her to convince the parole board to let Lake free, but it's done now. She is free and home with us once again."

Gage sits up straighter in his seat. "Take me to her. Now."

"She, Ava, and Riley will meet us at the gallery."

Gage relaxes in his seat a bit before asking, "Riley...That's Ruby's granddaughter, right?"

"Yeah. I'm surprised you remember her."

"I listen to our employees when they talk to us, unlike you."

I shrug. "Speaking of Riley, she will stay with us for the foreseeable future."

That catches Gage's interest as well, probably since I have never let anyone into our inner circle besides Carrie and Jack, and even then, they are kept more on the edge.

"Why?" Gage asks with a hint of apprehension in his tone.

"Recent extenuating circumstances have proven her to be more like us than not. We can trust her, so she can stay as long as she wants."

Gage rolls his eyes. "How cryptic."

I sigh. "I don't want to get into all the details right now. I'm exhausted and agitated, and the last thing I want to be doing is going to this fucking banquet."

"Then let's not," Gage says simply. "I want to go home."

"You know that is not possible at the moment."

"For you. Take me to see Lake, and then I want to leave. I

hate all this posturing bullshit to feed into what you and Ava think is best for us. It won't help anything in the long run anyway. It's all just a matter of time before it's all fucked again."

I feel a pang in my chest as I remember the letter I found tucked into Gage's limp hand when I found him.

You can't save us. It is only a matter of time, and I don't want to live in a world like this anymore. I'm sorry.

"G age..." Guessing the path my thoughts took, Gage looks out the window again. "I don't want to talk about it, Malachai. I just want to see Lake."

I swallow the lump in my throat and focus on the road. I want to see Lake too. She will make this right. She will be able to help Gage in the way I never could.

Chapter Seventeen

LAKE

The ride to the gallery is shorter from Malachai's home than it is from my apartment. The journey goes by even faster because Ava is driving crazier than Riley. I find myself clutching the seatbelt several times as we take turns quickly enough to flip us. Riley looks over her shoulder at me and laughs at my expression, guessing my thoughts correctly.

Soon enough, though, Ava pulls up to the front of the building and passes the keys off to a valet hired for this event. Ava opens my door and helps me out of the back while Riley hops out of the passenger side and falls into step next to us as I look around.

People have already gathered inside in relatively large numbers. I notice a few local news reporters gathered while photographers take photos of people walking into the event. I do my best to ignore them and follow Ava's lead by looking straight ahead as an employee opens the gallery door for us to walk in.

We are greeted by melancholy classical piano music echoing throughout the gallery's interior, which perfectly complements Malachai's works, which have been rearranged for this event. Waiters and waitresses in modern black uniforms walk around, offering champagne to guests as people group in small bunches to socialize.

Riley looks around and then steps a few inches closer to me as she takes in the crowd, who are now, one by one, starting to glance at us curiously. I also ignore them as I feel the suffocating claws of anxiety dig into my chest, making me feel short of breath.

Instead, I look around for Malachai, who I am sure is currently lost in the crowd. Ava also looks around until she sees some familiar faces in the distance. She waves at them, and I notice it is Carrie and Jack Savaadra. They both look sharp in all black and give Ava a big grin. Ava squeezes my arm reassuringly and then leaves us to greet them.

As Ava walks over to them, their eyes drift to where I stand. I see the recognition in their eyes as smiles fall from their faces. I feel a knot in my stomach as I hold their gazes of disapproval. Ava notices this, and once she is within distance of them, she lightly guides them out of sight to talk with other guests.

This time, I am the one to take a step closer to Riley, our arms pressing lightly against one another. Her presence is comforting and grounding, which I need more than anything.

Riley looks up at me. "Do you wanna look for Malachai?"

I swallow and nod while Riley places her hand in mine and guides me through the crowd. It takes a bit of time to find him towards the back of the gallery, talking with people who look essential. Riley stops us about ten feet away from them, and we hang back while still holding on to each other. Riley takes in our surroundings while my focus is locked purely on Malachai.

If you didn't know him, you would think there isn't another place on this earth that he would rather be. Looking closely, though, you can see by the set of his jaw and how he cracks his knuckles behind his back that he is uncomfortable.

I wonder what part of all of this bothers him. On some level, he must have wanted this. If not, why has he worked so hard up until this point? Why would he and Ava create a world in which he is forced to be someone he doesn't want to be?

My internal thoughts are interrupted when I notice movement off to Malachai's left. My gaze follows over to where Gage stands against a wall in the shadows, his hands in his pockets and ankles crossed as he watches Malachai. His brows are furrowed as if he was making the same observation I had just a moment before. Gage's crystal blue eyes glisten with curiosity and apprehension as his gaze begins to drift around the room. I hold my breath until his gaze falls on mine.

There is a brief moment of shock and hesitation before Gage launches himself from the wall and towards my direction. He makes it to me in a few short strides before engulfing me in a hug and burying his face into my neck. I cling to his soft black cotton shirt with all the strength I can muster now.

It feels like the final missing part of me is in place as I tell him, "I missed you so much."

"I love you, Lake," he murmurs into my hair.

I pull away from him enough to cup his face and smile as I try to hold in tears threatening to overflow from my eyes. "I love you too."

He offers me a shaky laugh as his eyes also start to fill. "You look different."

I look up at him. "Of course, I would. You grew like what? A foot?"

He smirks. "Only a few inches. You look good. Healthier."

"You do, too."

I mean the words as I look him over in our proximity. Like Malachai, he has grown into his long form, and while holding him now, I can feel the healthy weight and muscles on his bones. His skin is still the same light shade of porcelain it has always been, but now there is a glow to it. His eyes look tired, but he still has that bright and wondrous look. I reach up and run my fingers through the soft locks of hair hanging in his face before allowing my hand to drift down his face. He grins at me while I perform this familiar motion.

"I missed that," he says while leaning into my hand.

I deepened the caress before I realized the area around us had grown suspiciously quiet. I peeled my eyes off Gage and saw that the people in our surrounding vicinity had entirely stopped their conversations and were watching Gage and me interact intently, especially Malachai.

Malachai has dropped the friendly expression he had plastered onto his face earlier and is now staring at us with an unreadable expression.

I pull away from Gage fully and take a step back. Gage notices my gaze and looks over his shoulder at Malachai. They lock eyes for a moment before Gage rolls his eyes at him and lightly grasps my arm to begin to lead me away from him.

"Come on. I need a drink," Gage mutters.

I feel pressure on my elbow and see Riley grasping at it with a slightly panicked look in her eyes. She probably assumed I was going to leave her.

I pause my walking for a moment and gesture over to Riley. "Gage, this is Riley. Riley, this is Gage. I told you a lot about him."

Riley nods as we begin to follow Gage over to the bar.

"Everything?" Gage asks us over his shoulder.

I smile. "Most."

Gage smiles as he motions to the bartender for three drinks. "How do you know each other?"

The three of us settle into a small huddle while Gage resumes his previous position against the wall. "We were at the same facility but didn't meet until I got released, and they placed us in housing together. Best roommate anyone could ask for."

Riley blushes and nods in agreement while the bartender passes our drinks to me. I hand one to Riley and grasp the other two, bringing one to my lips and then purposefully holding the other down to my side, away from Gage.

Gage looks down at the drink and then locks eyes with mine. A slight smirk plays at the corner of his full lips, signaling he understood my intentions with withholding the beverage. The only problem now is that I look like I am double-fisting two whiskey gingers.

I quickly work on the first one and then set it down on the bar before nursing the second one. I try not to wince at the burn in my throat and stomach so that I don't give away the fact that this is my first taste of alcohol in my entire life. It is fucking terrible.

"Good?" Gage asks me with a devious gleam in his eyes.

I try my best to swallow a cough as I reply. "Yep."

Riley looks up at me with amusement while casually sipping her drink and looking around the room. Her gaze pauses on Ava talking with the Savaadras on the opposite side of the gallery. Her eyes linger a bit too long before her gaze slips back to mine, and she clears her throat before taking a long swig of her drink.

I glance back at Gage, who arches an eyebrow at me, and I just shrug before sipping my drink. He chuckles and steps forward to lean on the bar next to me as he asks the bartender for a club soda. The bartender nods and hands one to him within a few seconds before moving on to the following patrons.

"So, do you know what tonight is all about?" I ask him.

Gage leans back against the wall and thinks that over. "The last time I spoke with Ava, she told me she and Malachai were trying to raise money for a project they wanted to work on involving troubled youth or something philanthropic like that."

"That's a nice thing to do," I state, and Riley nods beside me.

Gage laughs dryly. "In theory, I suppose."

"Do you not like the idea?" I ask while Riley leans against me, resuming her people-watching.

"I'm sure you know why I think this by now, but doing charitable work like that would be ingenuine, bordering on hypocritical," Gage mutters. At the same time, his gaze drifts over to Malachai, who is still staring at us from another corner of the room while blatantly ignoring the person in front of him.

"That better not be booze."

I turn around and see Carrie and Jack behind me. Carrie looks the same as I last saw her, and her husband looks like any other white male in his late fifties or early sixties—clean-cut and balding.

I glance at them briefly and then turn to face Gage again, who does not attempt to hide his agitation at Carrie's comment while taking a long drink of his soda.

I can feel Jack and Carrie's eyes burning holes in the back of my head, so I finish off my glass and set it down on the bar before facing them.

Carrie looks me up and down before nodding and greeting me. "I don't believe we have met officially," she says.

I nod. "I'm Lake."

"We know," Jack states, disapproval clear in his voice.

I sigh and gesture to the bartender for another drink. "And what do you guys know about me?"

Carrie steps forward in front of Jack and holds my gaze

evenly as I start to sip from a new drink. "We never met officially but were at your sentencing hearing. I wanted to know
the truth of what happened, but after hearing it all...We know
what you are capable of."

"Anyone is capable of anything when pushed hard enough.
So stop pushing," I state in as calm of a voice as possible.

Carrie's face reddens at my idle threat, and Jack gently
touches her elbow. I wish I wouldn't let them get to me, but I
am still pissed about the letters.

"What is this?" Malachai asks from behind them while
Ava is hot on his heels, concern written all over her face.

I lift my glass to him and give him a sweet smile. "Just
toasting to my newfound freedom."

I swallow the rest of the glass and set it on the bar again.
My head is starting to feel more clouded than before. I glance
back at Gage, who glances at the empty glass on the bar and
then back at me before slightly shaking his head.

I'm cut off, got it.

I turn from the group and ask the waiter for a glass of
water. He looked relieved that I had decided to change up my
drink of choice, most likely worried I would be the first lightweight to make a drunken scene tonight.

After retrieving my water, I lean against Riley, who looks
like she is about to explode from all the tension in the air.

Malachai glances between Gage and me before leaning
towards Carrie and whispering something in her ear. Carrie
looks pissed but nods and grabs Jack's hand to steer him
towards some people across the way from us to socialize,
leaving the rest of us here.

Gage and Malachai glare at one another as Malachai takes
a step towards him. "What's wrong with you? She has a
fucking concussion, and you are getting her drunk."

Gage shakes his head and looks over at me with worried
eyes. "You didn't tell me she had a concussion."

I put a reassuring hand on Malachai's arm. "Hey, I'm fine. It is my fault. I wasn't thinking about that and didn't tell him what happened."

"What exactly happened?" Gage asks me with concern.

"I'll tell you later." Ava murmurs to Gage.

Malachai looks at me and seems to deflate as he turns from us all and continues up the steps to the higher floors.

I walk over to Gage. "I'm sorry. I wasn't thinking..."

Gage cuts me off as he pulls me into an embrace. "Who hurt you?"

I shake my head. "I'm fine, really, Gage."

"I'll kill them."

"Malachai already beat you to that," Ava chimes in while looking at Malachai's path. "You should go check on him. He is off tonight. We will keep Riley company."

I nod and watch silently as Ava pulls Gage and Riley back into the adjacent crowd. I inhale and exhale multiple times to steady my shaking hands as I slowly ascend the steps to find Malachai.

He is where I knew he would be, in his studio. I hesitate at the door before turning the knob and forcing myself to walk through before I change my mind.

"Can we talk?" I ask, scared of the answer, as I walk slowly to where Malachai is standing. The sunset illuminates him from the glass window.

Malachai breaths heavily as he paces towards me, reaching me in a few quick steps. "I don't want to talk to you."

He gently grabs me by the chin and pulls me within centimeters of his lips. "Then what do you want?"

He inhales the scent of my skin while running his fingers possessively through my hair. "I want to kill that fucker all over again for touching you."

I swallow. "What else?"

Malachai leans back, "I want to hurt you."

155

"How?"

"I want to fuck you raw."

I pull away to look him in the eyes as my breathing quickens with anticipation. "It won't mean the same to you as it will to me."

Malachai's eyes drop from my eyes to my lips. "I think it would."

"Then hurt me," I whisper breathlessly.

Before I can say anything else, Malachai's lips crash against mine as he threatens to consume me whole with a simple kiss. I groan against the taste of his mouth against my own and meet his passion equally.

Without breaking our kiss, Malachai rips at my dress until it is nothing but random heaps of fabric decorating the hardwood floor. My skin burns from where the material tugged before giving into the force of his powerful grasp. When I am down to nothing but my underwear, Malachai grabs me by the throat, forcing me down onto my knees.

Once I am at eye level with his pelvis, I make quick work of his belt, pants, and underwear as he yanks his shirt over his head. I marvel at the beauty of his body as he lightly tilts my head up by my chin. He strokes the long, hard length of himself as he begins to press the head of his length against my lips. Holding his gaze, I allow him to push himself between my lips until I feel him choking off the air at the back of my throat.

"Just bite me if you want me to stop," he tells me as he thrusts in and out of my mouth rapidly as if he cannot wait for another second to be buried to the hilt deep inside me.

I relax my throat as much as possible while digging my nails into his thighs, willing myself to take him for as long as possible as I watch him throw his head back in ecstasy with a deep moan escaping his lips. I meet him with a groan of my own as I begin to taste the salty drip of his pleasure. I take him deeper, obsessed with how his breathing catches when I do so.

I feel like a parishioner on my knees now, worshiping their god of death in the most primal way possible. This is what Malachai has always been to me. A god, my savior, my only reason for existing. I would gladly let him choke me to death now with his cock if that meant I would die while making him feel blind pleasure.

"Oh fuck Lake...." he groans before speeding up his pace and then abruptly pulling out of my mouth.

I gasp for air after being freed from his length. He momentarily holds my gaze in wonder before grabbing my shoulder and pushing me down onto my hands and knees, facing away from him. I focus my vision on the wall before us, where I can see our sharp shadows as Malachai kneels behind me. I feel his index finger hook into my underwear as he slowly pulls them to the side while running his knuckle sensually down the length of my slit. I gasp at the sensation as he presses his head against my opening.

Slowly, he pushes in inch by inch, letting me adjust to his circumference. Once I feel like I possibly can't take another inch of him, I feel his pelvis sitting firmly against me, setting him fully inside. I groan and push back on him lightly, loving the feeling of him inside me where he belongs.

He chuckles softly and reaches around me to massage my sensitive bundle of nerves through my underwear as he starts to move at a slow, deep pace that sets my teeth on edge in the best way possible.

When Malachai has me dripping wet and groaning his name, he fists his free hand in my hair, pulling tightly, setting his rhythm to a new frantic pace as his groans and gasps begin to match my own.

I feel the build-up suddenly peak so hard that I see white, and I am damn near choking on Malachai's name as I try not

157

to scream, but he doesn't let up until a second peak hits me. Only then does Malachai follow me over the edge.

He releases my hair and clit from his perfect touch and digs his nails so hard into my hips that I am sure they are drawing blood, but the pain only makes the pleasure that much sweeter.

I feel his hot semen fill me and drip onto the floor as his pace slows down and finally stops. I think he is about to pull out of me, but instead, he guides us both onto the floor gently so that we are spooning with him behind me while he is still seated deep inside me.

"For the rest of your life, the only marks on your skin will be the ones I leave behind," he murmurs, stroking my hair and leaving a trail of light kisses against my shoulder.

He continues kissing down my arm until he reaches the bruises now uncovered from all the friction and sweat. He also kisses those and even goes as far as to lightly run his tongue along a few of them, causing shivers to crawl up my spine from the mixture of pleasure and pain he is causing with his touch.

"Are you going to go back to the banquet?" I ask him while looking up at the ceiling.

"Fuck no," Malachai murmurs against my skin.

"Why did you do all this if you don't care for it?" I ask him curiously.

"What makes you think I don't care for it?"

I shrug. "Just small things like the set of your jaw when talking to others...the way you hold yourself. It is different from how you hold yourself with me or Ava. It seems...strained..."

Malachai pauses before answering. "I need to make sure we are never victims again."

"You already took care of that eleven years ago, Malachai."

"So Ava told me, but this is different. Money, fame, and

popularity will ensure we are never overlooked or forgotten. There will be no one who could ever touch us again."

"And no one will. Especially now," I murmur more to myself than to him, thinking back to Riley's dad.

"And you accept what I am now and how far I will go to protect us?" Malachai asks with a distinct hollowness in his voice.

"If I am being honest, I don't know Malachai, but I can't forget who you were," I state.

"That person is dead, Lake. They killed him."

My throat tightens. "I know."

"You can't save me," he states.

I blink back tears. "I know, and I don't want to."

"You should move on."

"I can't," I state through gritted teeth.

"You should try."

"I can't."

"I want you to," Malachai states.

"You don't mean that."

Malachai rests his chin on my shoulder. "No, I don't."

He sighs with that admission. I pull myself away from him and gently maneuver him onto his back so that I can place my head on his chest. I listen to the slow, steady rhythm of his heart. It is one of the most beautiful noises in the world, other than his voice.

"I wish I could stay here with you like this forever..." I whisper while tracing the shape of his jaw.

Before he can answer, the door to the studio opens, and I can see the reflection of Gage in the glass window. I stay in my position on Malachai and curl up further against him to hide my naked body.

Malachai lifts his head slightly and groans. "What?"

"Carrie and Jack were wondering where you were. They were about to come up here, but I intercepted them."

Malachai does not move to cover himself and rests his head on the floor. "Glad you did."

Gage sighs while walking further into the room and shutting the door behind him. I stay in my position and watch in the reflection as Gage walks over to us and notices the scraps of my dress on the floor. He sighs again, pulls his jacket from his shoulders, and drapes it gently over me.

I sit up from Malachai and pull the jacket on before facing Gage. "Thank you."

Gage nods and looks down at Malachai. Malachai hesitates a moment before he reaches a hand out to Gage, who grasps it and pulls him to his feet.

Malachai holds Gage's hand as he tells him, "I'm sorry."

Gage gives him a sad smile and nods as he releases Malachai's hand. "Are you guys coming back down?"

Malachai turns from Gage and starts collecting his clothing from the floor as I answer, "I don't think I can go back there like this."

Gage takes in my current appearance as I zip up the front of the jacket to fully conceal myself. It is long enough to cover my mid-thighs.

Gage's eyes trail lightly down my body before he glances away. "Probably not."

I roll my eyes and look back to Malachai, who has already fully clothed himself. His head tilts slightly to the side as he gazes at my legs.

"What?" I ask while fully turning to face him.

"You are bleeding."

I pause, looking down at myself, and see blood running down my thighs from the bloody crescent that Malachai left on my hips from his nails.

"Shit," I mutter and rush to Malachai's office.

The door is unlocked, and I look around until I find a box

of tissues on his desk. I grab a handful to clean myself up as I hear Gage and Malachai murmuring to each other.

"And you were bitching at me about getting her drunk," Gage mutters. "Don't be so fucking rough. Goddamn."

I hear Malachai grumble in agreement as he walks in behind me. "Are you okay?"

I nod as I trash the tissues. "Yeah, I'm fine, love."

Malachai continues to gaze upon me as Gage stares over his shoulder with concern. I feel more naked now than before. I look away from both of them to the floor as I fidget with the edge of the jacket.

"Can we leave?" I ask hopefully.

Gage nods and says, "I'll take you home."

I nod to Gage as I slip past them out of the room. Malachai stops my movement and presses me against the doorway of his office with the length of his body. He gently brushes a stray strand of hair from my face, giving me a charming smile.

"You need to get back to the banquet, Malachai."

"I want to stay with you." He states.

I glance at Gage in embarrassment and sigh before looking back into the black depths of Malachai's eyes. "You can't right now, and I don't have the clothing to follow you back down-stairs. I'll wait for you at home, okay?"

Malachai's lips part a bit before he whispers. "You'll wait for me?"

I give him a brief nod and smile as I hear Gage clear his throat behind Malachai.

"Come on. I want to go," Gage grumbles.

I pull out of Malachai's grasp and step towards Gage, hooking my arm in his as he guides me out of the studio. Malachai follows closely enough behind me to the point I can still feel the heat of his body. I lean in further to Gage to get more support for my sore muscles.

As Gage leads us into the hallway, I look up from the floor and see Carrie and Jack at the end of the hall, slowing their steps as they approach us. Carrie takes in my current state and glares at Malachai.

"Unbelievable," Jack mutters and turns on his heels to return to the banquet.

Carrie forces a stiff smile onto her face. "Malachai? A moment, please?"

"No," Malachai states in a stoic tone.

I look up to him. "Stop that. Go with her back to the banquet. Gage and I are out of place here, and we know it. Do your thing. It will be over before you know it, and you can come home to us."

"She's living with you now?" Carrie asks incredulously.

As I address her, I force myself to keep the venom out of my tone. "It's temporary."

Malachai gives me a devilish smirk. "For now."

I roll my eyes and nudge Gage forward, leaving Malachai in our wake. Gage ignores Carrie and walks right past her as if she is not even there, for which I feel a slight pang of satisfaction.

I release Gage and follow him as he strolls down the stairs to the main floor. He walks opposite the banquet to the back of the gallery, where employees rush back and forth to ensure everything is perfect. A few women give Gage curious glances and flirty smiles as we walk through. Gage openly ignores them and makes a beeline straight for the back exit.

I pause a few strides away from Gage as he tries to push open the back exit to no avail. Gage sighs and looks back at me over his shoulder.

"Well, that's a fire hazard," I mumble.

Gage nods and gives me a sympathetic look.

I sigh. "So the only way out is through the front entrance?"

"Yup."

"Fuck. Well, let's get this over with."

Gage laughs and falls into step next to me as I lead the way to the main entrance and through the banquette. Unfortunately, more guests have gathered, and we receive more than the friendly glances from before. Now, people outright stare, and I feel a blush creeping up my face.

"Distract me, please," I beg Gage as we weave through people.

"What happened to you that Malachai failed to inform me about on the drive over here?"

I glare up at Gage. "Not with that."

"What did he do?"

"Leave it alone, Gage."

"Why?"

I spot Malachai, Carrie, and another man about to take the stage towards the back of the gallery. Carrie glares daggers in my direction, and I look away from them and back to Gage.

"Because I don't want to discuss that here."

"Why?"

I open my mouth to answer him when I bump into someone. I gasp as their champagne spills down the front of my jacket.

"Oh shit, I am so sorry!" The man says.

"It's my fault...I wasn't watching where I was...."

"Lake?"

My heart drops into my stomach at the familiar voice, and I look up into the face of the man I bumped into.

"Will?"

Dark eyes gaze down at me through smooth locks of ebony hair. "Holy shit! It is you. What's it been, like, six years?"

I clear my throat and force a smile on my face. "Yeah."

Gage takes a step closer to my side. "Who is this?"

"Oh, um, this is Will. I met him at Willow Creek. He was the son of one of the board members there."

Will gives me a bright, genuine smile and reaches a hand out to Gage, who reluctantly grasps it. "Nice to meet you. I am assuming you are Gage?"

Gage returns his friendly smile and glances at me. "He knows about us?"

Will's smile wavers slightly as he answers Gage. "Yeah, we used to hang out. Lake told me about you and your family. Is that why you are here? I know this was Malachai's Gallery, but I didn't expect to see Lake here."

"I got released a bit ago," I say while glancing around for Malachai. Luckily, he is still standing by the stage, waiting for his turn to address the crowd, and he is oblivious to this conversation.

"You enjoying your freedom?" Will asks.

I nod. "As much as I can. What are you doing here?"

Will glances around us and waves at a few men by the bar wearing tuxes that almost match his own. "A few of the higher-ups on the force asked us to come to show face for community engagement. I remembered you talking about Malachai, so I volunteered out of curiosity. It turns out he lives up to the hype."

I ignore the last comment and try to rush through pleasantries with Will. "Oh, so you ended up joining the police?"

Will smiles with pride. "Yeah, I just got promoted to detective of the violent crimes unit."

I try to swallow the lump in my throat. "Congratulations."

"Thanks." Will looks me up and down and notices my clothing for the first time. "Should I ask?"

"I would prefer you didn't," I tell him. "We are actually just heading out. It was nice to see you!"

I pull Gage forward, but Will lightly touches my shoulder to stop me. "Wait."

Will pulls his wallet out of his tuxedo and opens it. He removes a business card from it and hands it to me.

"Here. I would love to grab lunch with you sometime. To catch up, you know?"

I offer him a polite smile as I put the business card into my pocket after crumpling it into my fist. I glance back to Malachai, who is thanking the guests for coming from the stage. His gaze falls on us, but his expression of gratitude to the masses does not falter. His eyes linger on Will and me before his eyes drift to other guests.

That...is not good.

"Thanks, Will. Enjoy the rest of the event," I tell him over my shoulder as I damn near drag Gage out of the gallery.

Once we reach the valet, I slow my pace, and Gage hands them a ticket so they can bring us Malachai's car. Gage smirks and looks at me from the corner of his eye.

I wrap my arms around myself tightly. "What?"

"Ah."

I turn more fully to him. "What?!"

"He looks like Malachai," Gage states.

I cringe and look away from him.

"Hey, nothing to be ashamed of. We all get lonely."

"I don't know what you are talking about."

Gage laughs. "That bad, huh?"

"Gage, Malachai will kill Will if he thinks anything happened between us."

Gage sobers at that and mumbles, "Yeah, you're right. I'll drop it."

The valet brings us the car, and Gage opens my door for me. I mumble my thanks as I slide into the passenger's seat while Gage takes the wheel.

Gage pulls away from the gallery and into traffic before breaking our silence. "A lot has changed since that night, hasn't it?"

I roll down my window and toss Will's business card into a trashcan by a traffic light. "It has."

Chapter Eighteen

MALACHAI

I look down at my reflection in my wine glass as I drown out the noise around me. I see a vacant stare looking back at me, and I try to school my features into a more presentable expression for the general public, which is damn near impossible to do so when all I can think of is Lake. What did she see earlier when she gave herself willingly to me in my studio? Did she see the vacant look of a hollow being or the mask I must constantly don to move amongst the bourgeois?

What is she doing now? Did she miss me the second she left my presence as I did her? Does she know that she has awakened a new part of me that I thought was dead and buried along with all the other parts of the boy she left behind years ago when we were ripped apart from each other?

Does she know what she has done to me?

She is perfect—an angel—and mine. She will always be mine.

And that is why I throw back the rest of my wine glass and turn to the man next to me with a casual smile.

"Thank you and your men again for coming. It is always an honor to be joined by our brave men in blue," I say with false enthusiasm.

Dark eyes and pale skin glare back at me from an even darker ebony head of hair. His height is similar to mine. He holds my gaze evenly while taking a long drag from the beer in his hand. He regards me skeptically before swallowing and offering me an outstretched hand.

"Pleasure is all ours," he says as I grasp his hand. "Especially with an open bar."

I chuckle as I let go of his hand and signal the bartender for another glass of Cabernet Sauvignon. "What was your name again? Will..?"

"Will Masters."

"I haven't seen you at any of our previous events in the area. Are you new to the force?"

"No, I've been on it for a while now. I just never opted to come before. As much as I enjoy myself now, this isn't my usual way of having a good time."

I take a sip of the glass in front of me. "What changed?"

Will shrugs while looking around at the guests, wondering about around us as we lean against the bar.

"I guess I would say the guest list."

"Oh? How so?"

He looks back over to me slyly and smirks. "Well, I was interested in seeing your foster sister."

I feign ignorance. "Ava? She is at all of our events."

Will chuckles. "No, not Ava."

I keep my face and tone neutral. "Lake?"

Will grins. "Yeah, I've missed seeing her around for a while now. How is she adjusting to freedom?"

I take a long drink of the wine before answering. "She seems to be doing fine. It's like she never left."

"Is that so? She was locked up for a long time."

I shrug this time. "That doesn't matter. She belongs with us and always has."

"You sure? Maybe she might want something different now that her life is hers again."

"Maybe." I glance around casually, pretending that I am still interested in tonight's events, as I ask, "How do you two know each other?"

Will orders another beer and looks over to me once more. "My dad was on the board of directors at Willow Creek when he was alive, and my mom is a case worker there. They were dedicated to their work, so I spent much of my free time there."

"And that is how you met Lake?"

"Yeah. I met her a few years into her stay. She was an odd one. She wouldn't talk or look at anyone for a long time. She was gorgeous, though. After repeatedly discussing books she liked reading, I finally got her to open up. After that, we were as thick as thieves for a long time."

"She hasn't mentioned you before," I state.

Will laughs without humor. "That's on me. I was young and had an ego on me. Lesson learned."

I nod and let silence envelop us as Will sees one of his buddies by the front entrance wave him over.

"That's my cue." Will slams the last of his beer before tipping the bartender. "Tell Lake to call me when she wants something other than convenience."

He winks at me before getting lost in the crowd. At this moment, I decide to skin him alive the first chance I have.

Chapter Nineteen

LAKE

"Lake..."

I groan and roll away from the voice inches from my face. I don't know what time it is, but I know it's too early to wake up.

"Lake, where is it?"

"Where's what?" I ask as I cuddle closer into Malachai's pillow.

It smells just like him and lulls me back into sleep.

"Lake, wake the fuck up," Malachai says louder as he grabs me by the ankles and pulls me to the edge of the bed in a quick motion.

I let out a squeal of surprise and yank my legs out of his grasp.

"What the fuck is happening?" Gage grumbles from the other side of the bed.

When did he get here? Oh, wait. I faintly remember

talking in Malachai's bed while we waited for him and Ava to get home. We must have crashed out.

I sit up, fully awake now, and glare at Malachai. "Where is what?"

Malachai runs a frustrated hand through his hair and adjusts the glasses on his face while looking around the room. I glance around and see drawers pulled onto the ground and clothes strewn about. I look back at Malachai, who is now glaring down at me.

"Will's business card."

"She threw it out," Gage mumbles as he rolls away from us and curls deeper into the pillows.

"Did you really?" Malachai asks me with apprehension.

I sigh and lay back on the bed. "Yeah."

"Why?" He demands.

"Because I don't need it," I say, crawling back to my spot on the bed and pulling the covers up to my neck.

Malachai hesitates at the foot of the bed, still looking agitated. "Who is he to you?"

"Am I not going to get to sleep tonight?" Gage grumbles at us.

Malachai ignores him and continues to glare, looking more unhinged by the second. Malachai stares at me with rage as he pulls his clothing off in jerky, controlled motions before sitting on the edge of the bed and making no further motion to come close to me.

I sit up again in bed and tug my legs under me.

"I met Will about a year or two into my stay at Willow Creek. He would hang out and read in the same garden I did. We became...close." I tell Malachai.

Gage rolls over to face us as I continue to speak.

"That progressed, and I told him why I was there and about you guys. I was pissed at the time that I hadn't heard from any of you. I was trying to force myself to move on."

"And?" Malachai asks.

"And I couldn't. Will wanted to pursue things between us, and I didn't," I state.

"Why?" Malachai asks again.

"Because I was still hoping that you were alive and I would see you again one day."

Malachai stands abruptly, putting drawers back into place and throwing clothing into the laundry hamper. Gage and I watch him as he silently fumes. After a few minutes, the room looks back to its standard order.

Malachai looks around the room as if he is lost with nothing else to clean. Slowly, his gaze drifts back to me. My heart skips as he walks over to me and leans in like he will kiss me. Instead, he grabs me by the upper arms and bites hard on the flesh between my shoulder and neck.

I let out a hiss between my teeth as Malachai pulls away.

"That was for trying to move on," he says as he crawls over me to place himself between Gage and me in the bed.

I release a huff of disbelief as I rub at the bite and frown at him as he gets under the covers and rests his face against my side. All of his rage is gone, replaced by utter fatigue. Choosing to forgive his momentary outburst, I maneuver us until I lie back on the bed, resting his head on my chest.

Gage throws an arm over Malachai, and within minutes, I hear both of their soft snores fill the room.

We lay together for hours as I gently trace shapes along Malachai's back in what I hope are soothing motions. Looking down at him and Gage now reminds me so much of how we used to sleep when we were younger. The only difference now is that I feel nothing but complete comfort instead of that underlying anxiety that was always there.

Gage tucks his face further into Malachai's shoulder blades and stretches out the arm he had draped over Malachai. His fingers graze my stomach and knot themselves in the fabric there. I let my head drift to the side as I rest my face against Malachai's hair to see if Gage is waking up. He groans in his sleep before settling again, and his breathing evens back to normal.

I hear the door creak open, and I see Ava peek her head in. She slips inside and closes the door behind her with a soft click as she comes to sit at the edge of the bed by my feet. She is wearing a long, black nightgown that dusts her feet, and her hair sticks up at wild angles as if she were tossing and turning in bed.

"Can't sleep?" I ask her.

Ava pulls her legs up to her chest and rests her head on them. "No."

"How did the rest of the banquet go?" I ask softly.

Ava shrugs. "It went how they all do."

"Carrie and Jack didn't give you guys any shit about my exit?" I ask.

Ava smirks. "Not as much as you would expect."

I cringe a bit at that. "What did they say?"

"Same old shit. 'Be careful, blah, blah, blah...'" Ava sighs while rubbing at her eyes.

Without makeup, she looks like the young teenager I had to leave behind all those years ago.

My throat gets tight at the thought. "I missed you, Ava."

Ava gives me a small smile. "I missed you too."

I look back to the door. "Where is Riley?"

"In the guest room next to mine," Ava states.

"Is she doing okay? I haven't gotten to speak with her much."

Ava nods as she crawls over to my right side and lays her head on the same pillow as mine. She curls up by my side and looks up at me.

"She's settling in okay. I have been taking her places to get her out of the house. I don't get the vibe she got out much before now," Ava murmurs.

I nod. "Yeah, she would only leave if I needed anything."

Ava looks up at me sheepishly. "Is she seeing anyone?"

I chuckle. "Not that I know of."

"Hmm...is she...?" Ava asks and trails off, letting the unspoken question hang in the air.

I shake my head. "I honestly don't know, but she seems to like you well enough."

"You think so?" she asks hopefully.

I nod. "What's not to like?"

Ava sighs. "She's been through a lot over the past few days. I don't want to pressure her with anything, so I'm just going to let this lie for now, okay? Can we keep it between us?"

I nod. "Of course."

Ava blushes. "She just looked so pretty tonight."

"She did. You both did," I tell her honestly.

"You did, too. I know you didn't get to stay long because things got out of hand, but did you like the parts that you got to enjoy?"

I think back to Malachai and me in his gallery earlier and blush as I answer her. "Yes. I had a lovely time."

I feel Malachai's grip on me tighten slightly before relaxing. I look up from Ava and notice the time on the clock is about a quarter till five. I sigh and start to untangle myself from Malachai by placing his grip on Ava.

"I don't think I will be able to sleep again," I tell her as I sit up.

Ava takes my place on the bed and relaxes into the pillow as Malachai and Gage readjust themselves in their deep sleep. I walk from the bed to Malachai's closet and rummage through rows of black suits and dress shirts until I find a familiar black hoodie. I hesitate briefly while running my hand along the sleeve before slipping into it. The familiar weight brings me solace as I look for some pants casual enough to go for a walk in. Happy enough with my selection, I exit the closet and meet Ava's curious gaze.

"Where are you going?"

I slip my wallet from Malachai's bedstand into my pocket and then pull on my chucks. "I think for some coffee. Is there any around here?"

Ava shakes her head. "The nearest is by the gallery. Do you want to take my car?"

"Yeah, where are your keys?"

"On the kitchen island."

I wave my goodbye to her and pause at the door. "Do you want me to bring back anything?"

"No, thank you. If these two are up in time for it, we will go for brunch."

I nod and continue my way down the stairs on light feet so that I don't wake Riley up on my way out. I locate Ava's keys on the island and slip into the garage, where my descent is less surefooted once I near the car and see the iron doors that lead to the room below. Part of me wonders what they did with the rest of Riley's stepdad, but I know I shouldn't know the details.

I swallow the dread at that train of thought, slip into Ava's car, and leave the house behind, still coated in evening starlight.

I make no rush to go to the coffee shop, but instead, I take some time driving around town to see what has changed in my absence. There are new stores where old ones used to be and all the regular changes of a growing city. I tell myself I didn't miss much, even though the weight of all the changes hangs heavy on my mind.

I pass our old high school, which is bustling with students in the same outdated school uniforms until I find myself at the end of the street leading up to Malachai's old estate. I can't bring myself to call it my old home or even think of the names of the people who made our lives hell. I don't even know why I came this far from the gallery.

I think back to Ava's letter and feel my heart in my throat as I realize I will always end up here until I return to the willow tree on the estate. Until I do that, I can never be free of this anguish. But as I allow my foot to press forward on the gas, I choke on my breath and hit the brakes.

I can't do this. I can't do this now...Not now.

Shaking my head at myself while wiping away stray tears, I pull an illegal U-turn and head back to the gallery. Once there, I quickly located the coffee shop and parked along the street.

I triple-check Ava's car to ensure it is locked before pulling Malachai's hood over my head and walking through the shop's front doors. I order a chai and then slump into a booth at the back of the shop. I mindlessly scroll through my phone until I see movement in my peripheral vision.

"Lake?"

I groan internally as I see Will picking up a cup of coffee from the front counter. He looks back at me and gives me a bright smile and wave. I wave and glance at my phone before locking it and slipping it into my pocket.

I look back up at Will and see that he is wearing a blue suit with a pristine white button-down and a brown belt with his detective badge hanging from it. He drinks his coffee before adjusting the frames on his face and sliding into the seat across from me.

"Hey, Will." I smile while propping my head up on my hand. "On the job today?"

Will grins at me. "Yeah, I was just trying to grab coffee before the day started."

"Nice. Me too," I say while raising my tea to my lips. It is still too hot, and I feel it singe my tongue.

Will takes in my appearance slowly, lingering momentarily

on the bruising on my face. I silently curse myself for not covering them before leaving the house today.

Before I can make up an excuse for Will, he runs a hand through his hair and leans back in his seat, ignoring the obvious. "So, about last night...."

I sit up straighter and lean back as well. "Yeah, I'm sorry I was so awkward. It was a weird night, and I was honestly caught off guard by seeing you."

Will chuckles, "Well, if we are being honest, I lied to you."

"About what?"

Will offers me an embarrassed smile. "I knew you had gotten released. I only went because I was hoping to see you again."

"Oh," I say, stunned at his admission.

Will leans into me from across the table. "I knew things would be awkward between us after..."

I clear my throat. "I know. I'm sorry..."

Will raises a hand to stop me. "No, I'm sorry. You were in a delicate state after everything, and I made it about me and my bullshit when I should have considered your emotions."

"I'm still sorry, Will..." I tell him softly.

Will offers me a kind smile. "I am, too."

Awkward silence envelopes us, and I glance around the coffee shop, looking for anything to say. My eyes land on his briefcase, and I clear my throat again.

"So, how has work been for you? Got any interesting cases recently?"

Will looks away from me as he answers. "Yeah, I was working a case last night."

My stomach drops at that. "Oh really? Before the banquet or after?"

Will holds my gaze evenly. "During."

I try to keep the anxiety out of my voice. "Was one of our guests a suspect?"

"No," he answers honestly.

I give him a forced, awkward chuckle. "I feel like I'm missing something here, Will. What aren't you telling me?"

"I stopped by Willow Creek to visit you last week, but they told me you had been released already. I wanted to talk to you about it last night. That's why I was hoping to run into you. I figured if I went to Malachai's benefit last night, I would probably see you."

"What does it have to do with me?" I ask him, doing my best to keep a neutral expression.

"Well..." Will pulls a thick manila file from his briefcase and sets it on the table between us. "There has been a series of unsolved murders in the area that I am investigating."

"I'm unsure how I can help you with that, Will..."

Will ignores me as he pulls out a series of crime scene photos and places them before me. I lean back further in my seat away from them as I am met with image after image of people looking like nothing more than scraps of bone and flesh. There are hardly any distinguishing features to even tell who these people were.

Fighting the urge to vomit, I push the photos away from me. "Will, what the fuck?"

"Shit, I'm sorry. I know that was abrupt," he says, pulling the photos back from me.

I stand up to leave. "I don't know anything about that, Will. I'm sorry, I can't help you."

Will grabs my arm to halt my movements. "Wait...hear me out."

I pull my arm from his grasp and stare at him, refusing to sit. "What?"

Will looks down at the photos once more before pulling out a list of names. "Just tell me if you recognize any of these names."

I grasp the list from Will and trail my eyes through the

names. I don't recognize the first two, but the third, fourth, and fifth...Fuck.

I hand the list back to Will. "What is this?"

Will collects the photos and list before slipping them back into his briefcase. "These were people that have been killed over the last year. These are the people in the photos you just saw."

I swallow more nausea. "Who did that?"

Will shrugs. "That's what I am trying to figure out."

"What does that have to do with me?" I ask, hugging my arms to myself while already knowing the answer.

Will gives me a sympathetic look. "The first two names on this list were the prosecutors from your grand jury trial. These other names...You recognize Jim Edwards, Alice Kay, and David Broadbent. They were involved in your case."

Jim was the school counselor who was supposed to report our case to child protective services, but instead, he took a payoff from Michael during a school fundraiser. Alice and David were Penny's employees, critical witnesses to all the atrocities we faced. They refused to testify on my behalf during my indictment.

I shake my head in disbelief and look up at Will. "You don't think I had anything to do with this, do you?"

Will stands. "No! Of course not. But I think you might know who is involved."

I shake my head at Will. "No...they wouldn't do something like that."

Will reaches out to me and lightly rests his hands on my shoulders. I shiver under their weight. "Lake, I think they would. After what you told me about that night...."

I take a step back from Will. "No. You don't get to bring up what I told you in confidence and then use it against me to pin this on my family. We have moved on. Find someone else to blame."

Will gives me a sad smile as I start to leave. "I wish I could, Lake."

Tears of betrayal fill my eyes as I stare at Will. He opens his mouth to say something else, but I turn from him and push through the crowd that has begun to accumulate inside the coffee shop. I look up through the window and stumble as I see Malachai standing outside the shop, looking in at Will with no emotion.

I turn back to Will, who smiles and waves at Malachai like he didn't just show me a pile of photos of mutilated victims. I turn back to Malachai and push through the front doors.

"We need to leave," I tell him as I open Ava's car and slide into the driver's side.

Malachai strolls over to the car's passenger side as rain drips from the sky in a light shower. He opens the door smoothly and then slides into the passenger's side. I look him over as he stares straight ahead, watching the water hit the windshield. I look away from him to the road as I turn the key in the ignition and pull out onto the road.

"What are you doing up?" I ask him softly.

"I couldn't sleep without you," he states while leaning further towards the windshield to look at the raindrops that are a mirror to the ones hanging from the tips of his hair.

My heart leaps at his admission. "Did Ava tell you where I was going?"

"Yes, but you weren't here for a while. Where did you go?"

I shrug, avoiding telling him the truth about the estate. "I was just driving around to see what was different," I say.

"And?" he asks.

I try to hide the sorrow in my tone as I say. "Everything is the same and yet...different. It's weird to see."

Malachai leans back in the seat and turns his head to me. "Where are we going?"

"I don't know...Anywhere away from Will."

"What did he say to you?" he asks curiously, trying to keep his expression neutral.

I sigh and pull over next to a freshly deserted park due to the rain becoming more heavy. Once the car is stopped, I hop out of the driver's seat and drop the keys in my pocket.

After I hear the passenger door close, I feel Malachai walking a few paces behind me as I lead us deeper into the park, away from people and prying eyes, next to a cobblestone bridge. I stop a few feet from it and leave my back towards Malachai.

"Did you kill those people?" I ask him bluntly.

"Which ones?"

"Alice, David, and the other three."

I feel Malachai lightly press his chest against my back as he runs his hand up my hips and under the hoodie to rest them lightly against my stomach.

"Who?" he asks while tracing small circles on my skin and leaning more firmly against me.

"If you don't remember them, then why did Will show me pictures of their mutilated bodies?"

Malachai sighs and leans back slightly. "What did they look like?"

I shudder remembering the images. "They look like they were torn apart."

"How so?"

"I don't know Malachai...Like an animal...They were in pieces."

"So there were rips in the flesh?" Malachai asks.

"Yeah, I guess. Why? What does that matter?"

Malachai rests his chin on my shoulder as he removes his hands from my stomach and reaches forward to graze his fingers along my arms until he grasps my hands. "Because I like using knives. Ones that cut deep enough to kill but not mutilate. Mutilation shows emotion, and I feel none during the act."

"None?" I ask confused.

Malachai gently kisses my ear as he murmurs against my skin. "I feel...Rage. Blinding rage that nothing can distract me from. It is an itch in the back of your mind until it becomes a rash that spreads to every thought you have until the decision is made."

I swallow nervously. "What decision?"

Malachai molds my hands in his to mimic a tight grip as if I were clutching an invisible knife. He mimes controlled slashing motions as if I were his marionette reenacting one of his kills.

"Until you decide to kill them."

I pull out of his reach abruptly and turn to face him.

He holds my gaze for a moment before allowing his gaze to trail over my body. "And then, and only then, a calm begins to consume you until you feel nothing anymore."

"What do you feel now?"

For the first time this morning, Malachai's expression shows emotion as he looks up at me through hooded eyes: "Envy, rage, confusion."

"Envy?"

"I envy Will for getting years with you that I didn't have after the fire. I wish I had been the one you could have confided in. I wish I had talked with you about your favorite books."

I feel my eyes fill with tears, and I blink them back before they fall. "And the rage?"

"I don't like seeing you with another man, even if he approached you first. I want to be the only one in your heart."

"Are you mad at me?" I ask him in a soft voice.

Malachai gives me a sad smile. "Never at you, Lake."

"What is confusing you?" I ask while wrapping my arms

around myself and looking away from his intense gaze that leaves me wondering if he is about to consume me.

"Did Will not ask you about what happened to your face?"

I glance back to Malachai. "What do you mean?"

Malachai reaches up and traces the bruising on my face. "You look hurt. Devastatingly beautiful but hurt nonetheless. If he had cared so much for you before, how could he not be outraged to see you like this? If he wanted you to be his, how could he stand to see these marks and not want to tear apart the person who did this to you?"

My heart clenches painfully at his words as I caress his face and pull his lips against mine. He greets my kiss with equal vigor as I feel his tongue slip into my mouth. I moan against his lips as he lifts me so that my legs are wrapped around his waist, and he presses my back against the foundation of the bridge.

I break our kiss momentarily to look around to see if there are any eyes on us in the vicinity but am interrupted by Malachai as he grabs me by the jaw with his free hand and forces my lips against his once more.

"I need to be inside you," he murmurs as I feel him reach down to start unfastening his belt.

Malachai frees the length of himself from his clothing and then maneuvers me so that I am balanced between him and the bridge as he drapes my legs over his shoulders. He pulls my clothing down my hips so that I am bare enough against him so that he has access to what he wants most at this moment. Malachai smirks at me as he spits into his hand to wet his length before slamming into me hard.

I gasp at the sudden pressure and then groan as he starts moving inside me.

"Tell me to stop if I hurt you," he whispers breathlessly against my neck.

I clutch onto his shoulders and hiss through my teeth before answering him. "But I like it when you hurt me."

Malachai's heavy gaze drifts back to mine with a devious gleam as he brings his free hand up to my throat while his other grasps me firmly on my ass to keep me pinned between him and the bridge. I feel his grip along the arteries of my neck tighten just enough to make me feel lightheaded without obstructing my airway. It feels nice–like nothing else in this world other than him surrounding every inch of me in nothing but warmth and pleasure.

"Your neck fits so perfectly in my hand, Lake. And this..." Malachai groans as he grinds harder into me. "This was made for me. You are mine, and no one else can ever have you. Do you understand? Do you understand that you are mine?"

I gasp and try my best to answer him with what I hope are coherent words. "Yes...Yes, I'm yours."

"Good girl. Because if anyone tries to take you from me, I will tear them apart in front of you and fuck you on their dead body until you forget their name."

I feel a little insane as a laugh escapes me, but I can't help it, even though I know he is deadly serious and would indeed follow through on his words. I think the part of me that is irreversibly damaged loves that I can make him feel this passionate, and I would gladly let him do whatever he wanted to anyone for coming between us.

"I love you, I'm yours," I tell him breathlessly.

As if my words are enough to send him over the edge, I feel his grip tighten on my throat as his hips grind harder into me before he stills.

"Fuck...Lake..."

I allow my head to fall back against the bridge as I watch Malachai come undone. He is so beautiful, especially in the rain.

Malachai holds me in place for a few moments while he

gathers himself before helping me down to my feet. I flex my legs a bit to get the blood back into them as Malachai refastens his clothing. I try to follow suit as I reach down to pull up my underwear and sweats, but Malachi grabs my hand to stop me.

"What are you doing?" he asks with a serious expression.

"Getting dressed?" I ask in confusion.

Malachai smirks. "I am not done with you yet."

Malachai pushes my pants further down as he kneels before me. I feel his cum start to drip from me as he spreads my legs further apart. Malachai watches the fluid run down my thigh with fascination before using his two fingers to collect it and then push it back inside me.

A sigh escapes me as I grasp his shoulders, pulling him closer as his fingers start to move. Malachai holds my gaze as he buries his face between my thighs.

The second I feel his tongue on me, I know I am lost, and there is no coming back from him.

"Oh fuck..." I groan breathlessly as I tangle my fingers in his black curls.

I can feel Malachai grin in triumph against me before he continues his act of adoration. With every carefully planned stroke and caress, I feel the build-up consume me both physically and mentally. He is so beautiful and perfect. Seeing him now on his knees before me gives me hope that, on some level, he feels the same devotion and reverence for me as I do for him.

If he didn't...At this moment, I can't even begin to fathom otherwise with how well he worships me. It is as if he knows exactly what I need to feel nothing but complete ecstasy. Even with all the years of separation, he is still mine as much as I am his.

With this revelation, the build-up crescendos. I bite the back of my hand to stifle my cries as Malachai allows me to come down with soft caresses and kisses along my stomach before he reaches down to help me right my clothing.

I feel like liquid as I lean back against the bridge and watch him in wonder as he ties the bow on the sweatpants that I am wearing. He then trails his fingers along my stomach and chest before lightly grasping my throat once more and pulling me in for an all-consuming kiss. I close my eyes and lean into him as I can taste the mixture of us on his lips.

Malachai pulls us apart as he looks into my eyes. "You are so..."

He seems at a loss for words as I lean forward again to gently kiss his lips.

I smile as I pull back from him. "Come on, let's go home."

Chapter Twenty

MALACHAI

I feel Lake's heavy gaze upon me from across the cafeteria table. It has been days since the attic, and I want to peel my skin off my bones whenever I think of what I did.

After the act, I helped her clean up the best she could, and I went back down to the cellar to await further punishment from Michael as if he would take one look at Lake and know what I had done and what I had taken from him.

But part of me is glad it was me. I love Lake. He will never love or see her for who she is, like I do. He will never worship the ground she walks on. He will never pray every night to dream of her like I do.

No punishment arrived, and the weekend came and went. We were both patched up by Penny's employees and sent back to school like the last few days of horrors never happened. Ava and Gage have given me a wide berth, no doubt sensing the shift in me since that day.

I spare a glance at them now. They sit to Lake's right and talk with themselves and the other students around them. I am glad they do because I don't have it in me to pretend anymore. All I can think of is Lake. All I care about is her and what she thinks of me now.

Does she still love me?

I am terrified that she doesn't, and I need her to love me with every fiber of my being. I want to talk to her., to tell her I love her and that I am so sorry. But I am a coward because if she rejects me, the grief will be all-consuming. It will destroy me.

I glance back at her and hold her gaze for the first time in days. She has an unreadable expression until she offers me one of her sweet, soft smiles.

My heart breaks at the sight, and I push back from where I am seated at the table and run from the cafeteria.

I faintly hear Ava call after me, but I keep going until I am at the opposite end of the school in a deserted hall. I push through the door leading to the men's restroom and grip the end edges of the porcelain sink.

All I can do is suck in short gasps as I hear footsteps in the hall outside of the door. I expect to see Gage walk through the doors; instead, it is Lake. She doesn't look at me as she turns the deadbolt on the door before taking slow, hesitant steps over to me.

"Talk to me."

"Go away, Lake," I gasp.

"No," she says as she takes a few steps closer to me.

I push off the sink and step away from her until my back is flush with the tiled wall behind me.

She halts her steps and looks at me with such sorrow. "Please...Talk to me."

I shake my head. "I can't..."

Tears fill her eyes. "Was it that bad for you? I know it wasn't planned, but was I that bad?"

"God no Lake...You were amazing. It felt amazing. It wasn't that."

"Then what is it?" Her voice cracks as tears begin to fall down her rosy cheeks. "I can't bear to have you keep your distance. I miss you, and I need you. This hurts."

I reach out to her and pull her to me as she cries. She buries her head in my chest as she clings to me. I hold her tightly as I run my free hand over her long hair in soothing motions.

My poor Lake...I hate that I made her cry.

"You know I love you. What happened...I have wanted you for a long time. But not like that. You deserve better, my love. You deserve better than me."

She pulls away from me and looks up at me through thick, wet eyelashes. "I don't understand. I was just glad to have you. I wanted you too."

"I hurt you," I state.

She shakes her head. "No, you didn't. I love you, and I wanted you. You didn't hurt me. I know it wasn't like what you see in movies or read in books, but to me, it was perfect. You were perfect. I don't regret it, and I don't regret you."

"Lake..."

"I mean it Malachai. I just want to make you happy and be as close to you as possible. So please, don't shut me out. Please don't leave me alone anymore."

I caress her cheeks as I look into her eyes. "I will give you anything you want. Anything you need."

I can see she is weighing the truth in my words as she closes her eyes and presses her lips to mine. I tense for a moment before I allow myself to relax into her as she deepens the kiss. I pull her tighter to me as she opens her mouth, and our tongues dance together. I groan at the taste of her and let myself go further as I pull her waist flush with my own.

Lake trails her hands down my chest until she reaches my

belt buckle. I feel her start to loosen it as I freeze and pull back from her.

"Lake..."

She smiles gently at me as she leans in to continue her work and kisses my neck.

"I love you Malachai. I love you and want you. Can you give me you?"

I hesitate a moment more before crashing my lips back to hers. We make quick work of each other's clothing while trying not to break contact, as if doing so would be too much of a wedge between our souls.

I would let her take anything she wanted from me, and in this small bubble of the world we have stolen for ourselves, I let her.

My eyes slowly drift open from the place in between dreams and consciousness as I take in my surroundings. I sit in the chair by my bed once more and see the soft breaths of Gage and Lake rise and fall repeatedly. The afternoon light peaks in from the blackout curtains along the wall and drapes them in a halo of light across their faces. Silence reverberates throughout the house, leaving nothing to distract from this moment. They look tranquil.

I try to commit this image to memory because I can't help but feel like there will be a shift soon, and the sudden peace I have felt at Lake and Gage's return will be shattered.

I wish I could delude myself into thinking I'm just anxious due to the lack of sleep, but my past has been proof that any god does not bless me. It is ripped out of my hands whenever I have some semblance of peace. But this time, I refuse to let go. I will hold on until my nails are ripped from my flesh.

I scratch my neck as I continue to watch them. My skin won't stop crawling. I need an outlet for this energy. I can feel it building slowly, and without dissipating it in slow increments, it will surely consume me, and I cannot risk that now, especially with Will making himself known to us.

What is his endgame anyway?

I had been waiting outside the cafe, waiting for Lake to arrive after I realized she had not already been there. After an hour in the cold, she finally arrived. Not long after, I noticed Will was shadowing her.

The man is not subtle, making it obvious he had been trailing her in an unmarked vehicle. He had probably been trailing her since she left the house this morning, which makes my stomach churn with disdain.

I wondered if Lake had been planning on meeting him there, but that assumption was quickly quashed once she told me she was driving around and seeing the changes in the city. I was distracted from my original thoughts as she got a distant look on her face, and I could tell she was leaving something out of her drive.

I wanted to press her on the matter but decided to let the subject lay. She has earned my trust, and if there is something she wishes to keep to herself, then I should honor that since she has chosen to be honest and open throughout all of our other interactions.

Regardless, the way he approached her this morning was far too familiar for my liking. He made it clear he thinks he can take Lake from me during our last conversation, which is laughable at best. Who the fuck does he think he is? And what does he want with Lake?

My thoughts are interrupted by the soft click of the bedroom door. I turn and look over my shoulder as I see Ava peek her head in. I stand from my place by the side of the bed and take light steps until I slip out of the room, leaving Gage and Lake to their peaceful slumber. I follow Ava to where she leads me downstairs into our shared office. I look over the stark monochrome surroundings and see Riley lounging in one of the chairs adjacent to the desk, with her legs draped over the side as she reads a magazine while still in her pajamas from the previous evening. She ignores our entrance, and I follow suit as I sit behind the desk in the oversized black chair. Ava takes a seat next to Riley and locks eyes with me.

"Any news?" I ask calmly while starting to fiddle with the sharp letter opener on the desk out of habit. I notice Riley's eyes glance at the motion before returning to her reading.

"After you left this morning, I took the time to reach out to some of our contacts on the force to get information on Will Masters."

"And?"

Ava rolls her eyes at me. "And all of what he told you was true. His mother is a caseworker at Willow Creek, but we could not tell who his father was since his birth certificate did not include his name."

"Look into it further. See if you can find a name."

"Okay, you said he mentioned that his father was on the board of directors?" Ava asks.

"That is what he said."

Ava leans back in her seat. "That is interesting."

"How so?" I ask as I flip the letter opener.

"Because when I looked into it, the names were redacted, as were all their meeting times and notes."

I sit up and rest my hands on my desk. "That is...interesting. Keep digging and see if you can find anything further on that. It seems like there might be something to that information."

Ava nods and continues speaking. "Other than that, everything about Will was pretty straightforward. He grew up with his mother in a fairly middle-class home, was on the honor roll throughout school, got his bachelor's in Criminal Sciences, and joined the force right after he graduated at the top of his class. His training at the academy was uneventful and average, based on reports from his superiors. Nothing stands out about him."

"Nothing?" I ask incredulously.

"Nothing other than a couple of parking tickets that were paid off already," Ava says, shrugging.

"What about in his personal life? Any past girlfriends, children, anything?"

"Nothing. Which is the only odd thing about him. Our contact at the force is on the same unit as him and said they hadn't heard anything about him having any disgruntled exes or current girlfriends. No records of children were found."

"His record is almost as clean as my own," I state.

Ava sighs. "On paper, at least."

"Anything else to report?"

Ava glances at Riley for a moment before holding my gaze. "The 'deer' remains were dropped off at the rendering plant off of I-10. They accepted the payment for the disposal. They asked no further questions."

"They never do." I sigh to myself. "Did you pull the cash from the safe?"

"Yes. There were no digital records of the payment. For further convenience, Dad had been hunting with old colleagues from the law firm, so if anyone does mention seeing me at the rendering plant, that is my alibi for being present there. Just doing old dad a favor."

"This is all too convenient," I murmur to myself, saddened more than relieved that it is so easy to buy off others and cover up heinous crimes.

That is why Michael and Penny got away with it for so long. On some level, I despise myself for taking after them to that effect, but as far as I am concerned, the outcome of Riley's stepfather and final resting place is the lesser of the two evils.

Riley is free now. I have only known her for a very short period, but the change in her posture is more relaxed, and her features are more soft.

I killed her demon, and she is finally free. I just wish I could kill my own again since they never seem to disappear.

Chapter Twenty-One

LAKE

I bounce my leg up and down nervously as I wait for the nurse to walk back into the exam room. I look over to Malachai, where he stares at me from his seat, a look of anxiety written on his face.

Stupid...we were so fucking stupid.

I wasn't thinking. I didn't know this would happen. I haven't even bled in years from being so skinny. I didn't realize...

Fuck this is all of my fault.

Penny will kill us.

Michael will...

"Lake?"

I jump at the sound of my name and turn to face the nurse standing in the doorway.

"Yes?" I ask with strain.

The nurse closes the door behind her and steps into the room. "We have the results back. The test was positive," she says.

Fuck...Fuck, fuck, FUCK!

Ringing fills my ears as the nurse continues to talk about my options. I can't hear her, though. All I see is Malachai and how the blood drained from his face as she said the test was positive.

They will kill him.

No, I can say it was someone else. I'll make up a name and lie through my teeth if that is what it takes. He doesn't have to have any part in this.

"Lake, hunny, I need you to look at me and tell me you understand. You are very young and very, very underweight. The risks of pregnancy for someone your age are huge, and you need to start getting prenatal care if that is what you want to do."

I look back at the nurse and meet her concerned gaze. "Yeah...I understand."

"We need to tell your parents. Is there a number we can call?"

"No!" I swallow and still my shaking hands enough to fold them in my lap. "I just...My parents are dead. I don't have anyone to tell...I don't have anyone to help..."

The nurse looks between Malachai and me in confusion before continuing to talk about resources and numbers for us to call. I reassured her I would utilize the numbers as she gets us checked out of the clinic and on our way.

As we leave the clinic, I avoid the glances of curious staff, who no doubt recognize Malachai and me from images from Michael's campaign. I do my best to hide my face more from them as we hurry outside.

I look up and see Gage and Ava right where we left them when we went in. They get up from their spot, sitting behind a bush, and run to meet us.

"Well?" Ava asks with worry on her face.

"Uh...the test was positive..." I murmur, still in shock.

"Shit," Gage murmurs while running a stressed hand through his hair.

"What are we going to do?" Ava asks, panic filling her voice.

"Whatever Lake wants," Malachai murmurs before falling into step beside me as we make our way back to the school.

Ava and Gage talk among themselves as they walk a few paces ahead while they try to take on this problem as if it were their own.

My heart clenches at the sight of them.

"Lake?"

"Hmm?" I ask while looking up at Malachai through my hair. I can hardly bear to look at him.

"Lake, stop," he says as he gently grasps my arm.

I pause in my steps and watch Ava and Gage do the same from my peripheral vision.

"What...What do you want to do?" He asks softly.

"I don't know," I tell him honestly.

"Lake, look at me, love," he says, lightly grasping my chin. "We can make this go away if you want..."

"No!" The word escapes my lips before I have the chance to stop them.

Shock and then disbelief cross Malachai's features. "No?"

I shake my head and hold Malachai's gaze. "No, I mean, I don't know Malachai. I don't know what we are going to do. I don't know. Our situation was so impossible to start with. I kept telling myself that if we held on long enough for a few more years, we could leave Penny and Michael. All we had to do was try to survive that long, but now... there's not enough time. I don't know how to get away from them. They will kill us for this and make it look like an accident. You know Malachai and..."

"Then we will run," Malachai says.

"What?" I whisper.

Gage and Ava step over to us and nod along in agreement.

"Look at us, Lake," Gage says sadly. "They are killing us slowly anyway. We need to leave. We won't make it a few more years as is."

"I don't care what else is out there. Anywhere is better than with them." Ava states.

Tears fill my eyes as I look at us collectively, and once again, I am met with the reality of the situation. "How?"

"We have some time before you start to show. I can find some valuables around the house, and when it is time for us to leave, I will take them to the pawn shop and get us bus tickets that are far enough away that they cannot find us. We will leave and never look back, okay?"

I shake my head. "With a kid too?"

Ava offers me a lopsided grin. "Hey, you knew I would make a kick-ass aunt someday anyway. Gage will be a sick uncle, too. It may be sooner than expected, but we have all made it this far together. We will make it work."

Tears flow freely down my cheeks as I look at my family's determined faces.

My gaze falls on Malachai's the longest. "We will run?"

Malachai pulls me into a tight embrace. "Just say when love, and we will run."

I stretch as I feel myself emerge from a deep sleep. The feel of warm fingers tightening their hold on my hips makes my breath catch in surprise. I roll towards the source of the feeling and rest my head on their chest. Their scent isn't Malachai, and I slowly open my eyes and gaze up into Gage's sleep-heavy countenance.

"Hey," he whispers lightly in greeting as he releases his hold and rubs at his eyes.

"Hey," I echo as I let my head drift back to his chest.

"Still tired?"

"Always."

"Same," he replies as I curl up on his chest while he soothingly pats my head.

The last few weeks since the banquet night have flown by pleasantly, consisting of mornings like this with no other disturbances from Will or anyone else.

I wake next to Gage late in the afternoon and relax with him until we are greeted by Malachai, who ushers us into our day.

Gage has chosen to join me on the night-time cleaning crew, which gives us plenty of time to catch up on all the events that have transpired over the last eleven years of each other's lives that we missed out on.

Riley has been hired as Ava's assistant, and they both handle the day-to-day affairs, leaving the rest of us to focus on our duties in peace without drawing too much attention.

And Malachai...

We spend any free time we find exploring every part of each other, body and soul. So much about us is different and yet the same. I thought the differences would bring me dread, but I have become excited to learn new things about him, such as new likes and dislikes on matters that we used to not have a say in. Now, Malachai is free to choose what he eats and when. He gets to decide what clothing he can wear and how he likes to spend his time.

And he shows as much interest in me as I do him. He wants to know every small detail about me, no matter how inconsequential. It makes me feel special and unique to see that he is as obsessed with me as I am with him. It is more than I could have ever wanted or dared to dream of. We are free, and I can share that with him and my family.

I feel at home and truly happy for the first time.

I glance up at Gage, wondering if he feels as at peace as I do. "How does it feel to be home?"

"This never really felt like home to me before. Nothing has. Well, besides being with you three."

I smile at his admission. "And now?"

He tightens his hold on me. "It is home now that you are here. Also, Riley is a welcome addition."

I smile up at him as I hear the door to the bedroom open and then the sound of familiar footsteps. "Are you both awake enough to function?"

I groan and answer Malachai. "No."

Gage chuckles. "Come join us. You look like death walking right now."

"I'm not tired," Malachai answers as I hear him open the closet.

I roll over in Gage's arms and look to see what Malachai is up to. Malachai is dressed in his usual black slacks, dress shoes, and a button-down that he had rolled up to his elbows. I am starting to suspect this is considered a casual outfit for him. He has a few shopping bags at his feet and starts unpacking things from them and hanging them up in the closet. Shopping for us has become his and Ava's new shared pastime.

"What are those?" I ask curiously.

"I have more items for you and Gage since he has decided to move into the room with us," Malachai murmurs.

"I like your bed better than mine." Gage retorts.

Malachai pauses his work and looks up at us. "Your bed is the same as mine."

"Mine is too big."

"They are the same size."

"I like it better in here," Gage states before draping an arm over his eyes to block out the light of the walk-in closet.

I smile lightly at their banter and think about how hard it was to sleep alone the first few months at Willow Creek. I was always so used to sleeping in the embrace of one of my siblings that when I was finally alone, the bed felt too empty, too quiet, and too cold. Even now, the last few weeks with Gage and Malachai by my side have been the best sleep I have had in years.

I am sure Ava and Gage share my sentiments. I am unsure about Malachai since he seems to be an insomniac.

I sit up enough to prop myself up with one arm. "Malachai?"

Malachai stands up from where he is in the closet and carries more bags into the large restroom.

"Malachai, wait."

"Hmmm?" he calls from where he disappeared inside the restroom.

I groan and crawl over Gage to get to Malachai. He manically arranges items in the bathroom, making room for the toiletries he bought for Gage and me.

"Love, stop," I murmur, placing a hand on his shoulder as he finishes putting the last few items away.

"Why?" He asks with confusion.

I caress his face and trace my thumb over his pale lips and then over his eyes as they close from my soft caress. "When was the last time you fully slept?"

"I don't need sleep." Malachai protests. "I am not tired."

"Bullshit," Gage interjects from where he is leaning in the doorway of the restroom.

Malachai glares at him before standing to his feet and gently removing my hands from his face.

"I can't be tired," he says stoically.

I look back and share unspoken words with Gage, who sighs and walks into the restroom with us before reaching past me and lifting Malachai over his shoulder. Malachai's eyes widen in surprise before he starts to struggle against Gage as he walks him to the bed. The image is comical as they grapple with each other since their heights and statures are relatively similar, but Gage lifted Malachai like he was nothing more than a sack of potatoes.

I hide my smirk with my hand as Gage drops Malachai

onto the bed. He straddles his chest and traps Malachi's arms above his head.

Malachai bucks against Gage as Gage looks at me for help. I hurry to Malachai's feet and remove his shoes before quickly removing his belt and pants. I take Gage's place in straddling Malachi to hold him down as Gage struggles to undo the buttons on Malachai's shirt before giving up halfway down and ripping the shirt off over Malachai's head.

I lock eyes with Malachai and stiffen as I feel him grow hard beneath me from the physical contact of Gage and me. Gage takes in my frozen appearance and lets his hands slide away from Malachai back to his sides from where he is kneeling beside us.

Malachai's pupils dilate slightly as his gaze drifts lazily over to Gage. "Are you sure you want to stay in here with us?"

My cheeks flush, and Gage clears his throat. Malachi looks back at me as a smirk pulls at the edge of his lips. Before Gage or I can react, Malachai pulls out of my grasp and grabs me by the throat as he crashes his lips against mine. He forces my lips open with the pressure of his tongue, and my breath catches in my throat.

As quickly as Malachai is upon me, he is gone, pressed firmly against the mattress once again by Gage, who held him by his throat, almost a mirror to how he had just had me a moment before.

"Enough. You need to sleep," Gage tells Malachai with a slight strain in his voice.

As their gazes are locked, I slide off of Malachai and cover him with the soft fabric of the comforter. I slide into the sheets next to him as Gage gets situated on the other side of Malachai and rolls away with his back to him.

"You two are ridiculous," Malachai murmurs to himself.

"Shut up and sleep," Gage grumbles as he pulls out a book from the side table and flips to the page he left off on.

I cuddle close to Malachai and rest my head on his chest as I flip through channels on the TV until I arrive on a random weather channel. It is interesting enough for me to watch but dull enough to lull Malachi into sleep within minutes. His breathing is slow and even as I listen to the air pass in and out of his lungs. An hour or so passes before I find myself dozing off as well.

I wake from a dreamless sleep to the sound of fabric hitting the bed lightly at my feet. I peek open my eyes and see Riley and Ava at the edge of the bed, piling clothing on top of it.

Malachai groans and pulls me closer to his chest as Gage sits up in bed and places his book back on the side table, much further in it than he had been at the beginning of the day.

"What's up?" Gage calls over to Ava.

"We are going out," Ava calls over to us as she gathers more clothing items.

"Where to?" I ask as I sit up as well, trying to untangle myself from Malachai's grasp.

"I want to go out dancing. Riley informed me she has never been before, and since we are all here, I think it would be the perfect time to rectify that."

I sigh and look down at Malachai, who is peeking at me with sleepy eyes. "Do you want to go?"

He shrugs and looks up at Gage, who shrugs as well.

I look over to Ava and Riley, who both look eager to go out on the town.

I resist the urge to sigh. "What time do you want us ready?"

"Whenever," Ava says as she pulls Riley to the mirror and starts fussing with her hair.

I reach over to the clothing pile and sort out our outfits before I go into the bathroom to freshen up. I then pull on the leather dress with matching boots that Ava had laid out for me. I brush out my hair and let it hang straight down my back as I rummage through the makeup that Malachai had bought for me.

With shaky hands, I try to mirror Ava's work from weeks before with slightly darker eye makeup.

As I finish up, I look at myself from all angles in the mirror and try my best to stifle any self-conscious thoughts I may be having. I have never tried to dress up "sexy" before, and I feel a bit out of my element.

I hear a soft knock on the door before Gage opens it and peaks in.

"Are you ready? Oh...Goddamn."

I fight the urge to wrap my arms around myself. "What?"

He looks me up and down before giving me a silent thumbs up and turning from the room.

I guess that means I look okay.

I sigh and leave the bathroom, where I find Gage leaning against the wall across from the bed, with Ava and Riley huddled close to him. Malachai leans back leisurely against the headboard while scrolling through his phone before he looks up at me.

His gaze immediately heats, and I force myself to take an even breath.

"Are we all ready?" I ask in a soft voice.

All four stare at me in silence.

"What?" I ask again, a bit more defensive.

Malachai ignores me and locks eyes with Gage. "Keep them away from her, or I will."

Gage nods curtly before exiting the room, followed by Ava and Riley.

Malachai walks over to me and grasps my hand in his before placing a soft kiss on the back of my hand.

"You look stunning."

I take in his appearance and see that he had opted to put

on the clothing from earlier that Gage and I had wrestled him out of, with the addition of a leather jacket.

"So do you," I tell him with a soft smile.

He adjusts his glasses on his face before pulling me along behind him to follow the others downstairs. Malachai takes special care to guide me down each flight to ensure I don't roll my way down in these boots, for which I am very grateful.

We all pile into Ava's Tesla, and I am pressed again into the warmth of Gage's and Malachai's arms. As we drive, I rest my head against Malachai's shoulder, and he traces small circles on my knee with his fingers, leaving goosebumps all along my skin.

Once we get close enough to our destination, I hear the harsh bounding of the base that vibrates the car from where we are. I swallow my unease as Ava parks in front of the nightclub and rolls down the window enough to hand a valet the keys.

Malachai slides out of his door and opens the passenger door for Riley before reaching for my hand to help me out of the vehicle.

I pull down the edge of my dress and smooth out the fabric against my stomach. Gage slides out behind me and rests a reassuring hand along the small of my back as we take in the large crowd gathered in a line that circles along the side of the building.

I begin to step toward where I assume the back of the lines starts, but Malachai and Gage halt my movements and gesture to where Ava and Riley have already begun moving toward the front entrance. I hesitate before allowing them to guide me forward as we approach the security guard.

The guard gives us all a slight bow of his head before leading us past a red rope and directly into the depths of the nightclub.

Ava, Malachai, and Gage all make their way to a blocked-off VIP table at the back of the venue as Riley and I take in the image of the ample space while trailing behind them.

I am astonished at how expensive and pristine every detail looks for a nightclub. Lights flash and reflect off of crystal chandeliers and tables. Red and black cover everything that is not adorned with gold. As I walk along, fresh red roses spill down the side of every fixture. No expense was spared in the design of this place.

Ava and Malachi fall into the velvet seating of the table and guide Riley and me down next to them. Gage waves over a server in a slim, classy cocktail dress.

Gage whispers in her ear and then places a wad of bills into her hand before she walks away. He catches my lingering gaze and smiles at me as he slides next to Riley.

"What do you think?" Malachai whispers into my ear.

"It's...amazing."

Malachai smirks and looks satisfied with himself. "Good."

I look around once more. "I don't remember this place being here before. How long has it been open?"

Ava smiles. "We opened it two years ago."

"We?" I ask, dumbfounded.

Malachai drapes his arm over my shoulders. "We own it."

My eyes widen and Riley and I share a stunned look.

Ava nods proudly. "So far, it has been a very lucrative venture."

The waitress returns with a tray of top-shelf liquor for us and places a mock-tail in front of Gage, who graciously takes it from her with a flirtatious smile.

I look around more as we all settle in and pass out a round of drinks. I watch the crowd, enraptured by how people's bodies grind against one another as they dance not twenty feet away from us.

Gage follows my gaze and leans in over the table. "Do you want to dance?"

I hesitate before nodding and looking back to Malachai. He smiles reassuringly and gestures for me to follow Gage.

Gage reaches out a hand, and I grasp it lightly as I let him guide me onto the dance floor. Our movements are awkward at best at first, but after watching those around us, we start to feel the rhythm of the music.

I lose track of how long we dance, but I feel my face begin to hurt from all the smiling and laughing Gage and I do.

I glance back at Malachai and the others frequently but soon notice they have left their place at the table and joined us not too far away on the dance floor.

I feel Gage lightly grasp my hips, and I notice Ava and Riley lost in the feel of each other as they run their hands along one another. There is a look of want and almost desperation on both their faces as Riley finally leans in and crushes Ava's lips against hers.

I look away from them to give them privacy as a shadow passes over my vision. I look up into Malachai's dark eyes.

He smiles down at me as he places his hands above Gage's on my waist and begins to sway with us.

I remember the last time we danced together, and the situation and style were so different that it is almost comical. There had been an innocence to it that no longer exists.

As the music continues, Malachai and Gage close in on me, our bodies pressed flush against one another. I start to feel light-headed from the heat and lightly tug both over to our table again.

Once there, we refill our drinks and cool off for a bit. I try to slow my breathing as I wipe sweat from my brow.

"Thoughts?" Malachai breathes into my ear.

I turn to him and place a kiss firmly against his mouth. As I pull away, I answer him, grinning.

"I like dancing."

Gage chuckles. "Good."

I smile back at him. "Where are the other two?"

Malachai and Gage shrug and return to people-watching as they finish another round of drinks.

Soon enough, I see Ava and Riley walking over from the area of the back of the nightclub, their hair and clothing in noticeable disarray.

I choke on my drink, and Malachai looks over to my line of sight and laughs when he notices them.

"Huh, good for them," Gage murmurs while following our gazes.

They slide into the seat next to Malachai and me. We all order our last round of drinks as Ava tells the waitress to have the valet pull the car around for us.

I get halfway through my drink as I begin to feel the full effects of all the alcohol of the evening. The world tilts a bit, and I blink the haziness away.

I push the drink away from me and watch as Gage collects the glass before downing the other half that I left behind.

Malachai helps me out of our seats as we wait for the waitress to tell us that the car is ready.

As we stand, I start to sway a bit on my feet as my stomach rolls with nausea.

"Hey, love? Where is the restroom?" I ask Malachai.

"Just to the back. Are you okay? You look a bit pale."

I try to laugh off the feeling. "Yeah, I think I am more of a lightweight than anticipated."

Gage lightly grasps me under the elbow and lets me lean on him.

"If you want to get the other two in the car, I can take her to the restroom, and then we can meet you outside," Gage offers to Malachai.

Malachai gives me one last look of concern before nodding to Gage and helping Ava and Riley to their feet.

My stomach rolls as the world tilts, and I grasp onto Gage

as he leads us toward the back of the club and towards the bathroom. I'm not too sure if it is just my impaired balance, but we both almost lose our footing as Gage sways as well.

"You okay?" I ask him as he pushes the women's restroom open and guides us inside.

It is oddly absent of people for a nightclub, but the thought is lost in my head as I stumble over to the sink and turn on the water.

Gage stumbles behind me and proceeds to grab a towel and wet it with cold water before pressing it to my neck.

I watch him worry over me in the mirror and notice his face is almost as pale as mine.

"Hey...are you okay?" I ask him again.

Gage locks eyes with me before turning his head and puking into the sink next to me.

"What the fuck? Gage?"

I reach for him but miss him altogether. The ground wooshes up to me so rapidly that I barely have time to catch myself before my face slams into the floor.

"Oh shit! Lake!"

"I'm..." I try to say, 'Okay,' but the words get lost on my tongue.

I roll onto my side as Gage's face contorts above me. Everything looks like it is underwater, and my ears are ringing.

Gage slumps down next to me and tries to pull me against him. "I think...we were... drugged."

As the last word escapes Gage's lips, the door opens, and I see the distorted features of a man with dark hair and pale skin. I almost think it is Malachai until he walks closer.

Will...

Will looks between Gage and me blankly as he grabs a tray from the vanity by the sink. Before I can lift my arm to block Gage, the tray makes contact with the side of Gage's head with a sickening crack.

Blood immediately leaks from a gash on Gage's head as he slumps down next to me on the floor.

Will watches this with a hollow expression before a smile tugs at the corners of his lips as he kneels in front of us.

"I think it's time we begin the fun," he whispers while trailing his fingers over my lips in a soft caress.

The void of unconsciousness takes me once more.

Chapter Twenty-Two

MALACHAI

"They should be out by now," Riley says from where she is leaning against the front passenger door next to me.

I nod as I tilt my head slightly to the right to see around the range of bodies coming and going from the front entrance. Anxiety twists my gut as I continue to await their arrival.

Over the past few weeks, I have been crawling out of my skin with apprehension, unable to shake the feeling that we are being watched and trailed.

Part of me believed that was my psychosis until there was an incident a few days after the banquet where Will was found lurking around the gallery by security in the exact unmarked vehicle. I immediately instructed the staff to ban him from entering the facility and to let me know if there were any further sightings of him.

Which there were.

One morning, after bringing Lake and Gage home, he was seen again outside our home, taking photos of the surrounding area with another detective. Lake and Gage were none the wiser, but Ava chased them off with threats of litigation for defamation and stalking.

After that, Ava took more precautions, doubling the security detail in our neighborhood and paying a few other cleaners to stay late and arrive early with Gage and Lake so they were not alone at any point in the gallery.

But even with all that, it still did not feel like enough. I have taken to walking patrols of the house when the others are asleep and hanging around outside of the gallery to keep watch over Gage and Lake myself.

Since getting Gage and Lake back, I have felt like a man possessed. We are finally whole, and I can't stand the thought of someone taking my family away from me again. There are no limits I wouldn't cross to keep them safe and untouched.

But I know keeping them trapped at the gallery or home is unfair. They are finally free and need to experience life for all it offers. So, against my better judgment, I agreed to go out today. Besides, where would be safer other than a club we own with staff on our payroll?

I look inside the car and see Ava furiously texting from the back seat. I guess that she is telling Gage to hurry the hell up. He is our designated driver for the evening since he is trying to minimize the amount of alcohol he consumes to help maintain his sobriety.

This makes his stumbling to the bathroom with Lake a bit more concerning because I was watching him all night almost as much as I was watching Lake. The only alcohol he had was to finish off Lake's last drink. I had written off the movement as him losing his balance due to Lake leaning on him.

But still...

I push off from the car. "I am going to go look for them."

Riley nods and follows me as we walk back inside the club. We both make our way back to the restrooms, where Riley walks in to check if they are in the women's room—a minute passes before Riley swings open the door with frantic eyes.

"They aren't in here."

"What?" I snap as I slide past her into the restroom.

I am met with an empty facility. To ensure we don't miss a thing, I slam open each stall individually and look around every corner.

After confirming what Riley said was true, we both charge into the men's restroom to ensure they weren't there. We are met by a few stunned patrons as we search every stall again.

Nothing.

Fuck, fuck, FUCK!

Riley pulls out her cell phone and dials Ava.

I shake my head in disbelief and return to the women's restroom again. I look around once more for any clues to their location, and I notice a red tinge of color on the marble floor as if someone had tried to wipe up a spill quickly.

I reach for the stain, run my fingers along it, and look at the residue left on my fingers. It feels like dried blood...

I burst out into the hallway and reconvene with Ava and Riley.

"Security said they didn't leave out the front, and the bartenders said they haven't seen them since they walked back here," Ava says over the music.

I nod. "There was a lot of blood that was attempted to be cleaned up in the bathroom."

Riley's eyes widen and Ava curses before bringing her phone back to her ear and barking out orders to the staff.

The lights are on within a minute, and the music is cut off. Ava had ordered everyone to stay until we knew more about where Lake and Gage were.

"Malachai..." I hear Riley call from her spot along the back hallway outside the bathrooms.

I look over at her and see her crouched by the floor. I go to stand over her to see what she is staring at and see there is a trail of blood leading to the back fire exit. All three of us freeze before charging out the exit.

I burst from the door first and see more smears and spatters of blood along the concrete before the trail abruptly stops a few yards away from the exit.

"FUCK!" I shout into the air.

I knew... I fucking knew this would happen.

"Call the sergeant and have him send his best officers. I want the footage pulled and reviewed from every streetlight between here and the university within the hour. I don't give a shit what it costs, make it happen, or heads are going to fucking roll." I bark at Ava.

Her face pales as she nods and stares down at the blood while making calls.

Riley hesitantly steps towards me but refrains from touching me—Smart of her. I am seeing nothing but red now, and I feel like choking the first person I can get my hands on.

My brother is gone...And Lake.

My beautiful Lake...

There will be blood for this.

Everything after that becomes a blur as the streets become overrun with police. I separate from Ava and Riley and retrace the last steps of Lake and Gage over and over again until every drop of blood is seared into my memory.

I had promised them both their blood would never be spilled by another as long as I was alive. What a fucking joke.

"Mr. Rosemond?"

I turn from where I am standing again out back of the nightclub in the alley. I turn to the voice and meet the gaze of the Sergeant and five of his other officers. I signal them to follow me further down the alley so their footprints don't disturb the crime scene.

They follow silently until I turn to face them.

"Any news?" I ask them.

The sergeant's face visibly pales, and he shakes his head. "I'm sorry, Mr. Rosemond, but they have not been seen since their arrival here. The security footage and street cameras in the surrounding area were blacked out for the minutes they were abducted."

I inhale and exhale slowly. "And?"

"And?" The sergeant repeats slowly.

Fucking idiot. "And what else are you going to do to find them?"

The sergeant swallows. "We have every available officer patrolling the area, and we are starting to comb through the footage recorded outside the blackout area."

"What else?" I ask through gritted teeth.

The sergeant clears their throat before continuing. "All other efforts will be reported to Ava as the search continues."

"I want everything reported to me."

A few officers step forward, and the sergeant looks at me apologetically. "I apologize, Mr. Rosemond, but we cannot do that now."

I take a step towards him. "And why the fuck not?"

The sergeant blanches further as he removes a pair of cuffs from his suit pocket. "Malachai Rosemond, you are under arrest for the aggravated murders of Jim Edwards, Alice Kay, and David Broadbent. You have the right to remain silent. Anything you say can be used against you in court..."

Oh fuck no.

Before the sergeant finishes speaking, my hands are around his throat, and he is on the ground.

These incompetent fucks are going to do this now? When Gage and Lake's lives are in jeopardy? They choose fucking now to do this instead of putting every officer the focus of Lake and Gage?

Are they fucking serious?

And for some cunts I didn't even kill.

Will…Those were the names Will had asked Lake about when he followed her into the coffee shop. I don't know how he pulled this off, but this is his fucking doing. And the cameras? Only someone with access to the police department could be responsible for that.

I'm going to skin him alive alongside all of these idiots.

I stop feeling anything and just see red…nothing but red—and nothing but the people in front of me who are getting in between my family and me. Nothing will keep us apart, not even them, especially not them…

"Malachai, stop!" Ava screams from behind me.

I feel her claw into my neck to get me off of whoever I have beneath me; I can't even see their face anymore; it's so bloody. I need more. I need more red…

"Malachai? Malachai!"

Who is that? Oh…Riley…

I see Riley in front of me before she swings back her hand and punches me square in the jaw, knocking me off balance enough for the man beneath me to crawl away. Riley uses my disorientation to help Ava pull me away from the other officers.

Riley turns her back to me, and I feel her press into my chest as she looks over at the remaining standing officers who now have their guns raised.

"Wait, wait! He'll go with you! He stopped! He'll go with you!" Riley yells in terror.

"Riley, get out of the way!" Ava screams at her while trying to pull Riley behind us.

Riley yanks out of Ava's grip and reaches for a hand out for the cuffs. "He'll go with you. Please don't shoot. We will make sure he goes with you."

The fuck I will.

I lean forward, ready to push Riley aside to get to the officers. Fuck all repercussions.

Riley turns towards me and grabs me by my jacket. "You are wasting time and causing a scene."

I stare her down, rage still consuming me as a few officers take hesitant steps towards us and place the cuffs on my wrists behind my back.

"We will come get you when we can. We will find them, okay? They aren't gone forever. We will get them back, and we will get you back, too." Ava murmurs as she walks alongside me, and they lead me over to the police cruiser.

I nod once, still unable to speak.

All too soon, I am being whisked away toward the station, leaving nothing but my sister's teary eyes behind in the darkened street.

Chapter Twenty-Three

LAKE

I step into our home's dark doorway and linger with my hand on the doorknob. It's too quiet.

Where is Malachai? He was supposed to meet me after class today to walk to the library. When I went to his class to wait for him, his teacher said Penny and Michael pulled him out of class early before the day ended.

I ended up walking home alone.

I look around the empty foyer with apprehension. There are usually a few workers here or there, but even the gardener was gone when I walked up the drive.

I pause in the doorway and take in the silence. The air is too still, and that overwhelming sense of dread that I am so familiar with is ever-present.

I know in my heart that they know, but I lie and tell myself there is another reason for pulling Malachai out of school early.

I adjust my backpack on my shoulder and close the door with shaking hands. I lock it behind me and pause again, closing my eyes and straining my hearing while hoping and praying

Malachai is about to walk into the foyer to greet me and assure me that everything is fine.

Silence. Nothing but gut-wrenching silence.

I drop my bag at my feet and take a few hesitant steps forward, deeper into our home.

"Malachai?" I call down the hall with a crack in my voice.

Nothing.

"Mal...Malachai?"

Nothing.

I wander through the empty halls, looking through each door, hoping to find him, but nothing greets me but his absence.

After too many minutes, I find myself at the door that leads to the attic stairs. I hear groans of pain on the other side of the door.

I don't want to open the door...

"Just open the door," I tell myself as tears stream down my face.

As if sensing my presence, I hear Malachai let out a shriek of panic from the other side of the door.

"LAKE RUN!"

The door gives way beneath the grip of someone on the other side, and I take a few steps back as I am met with Michael's deadened gaze.

I look at him and feel nothing but terror before turning on my feet and running for my life down the empty halls.

I need to make it to the street. If I can get out, I can get help and save Malachai. I can have someone warn Ava and Gage not to come home and to run. I need to make it out.

"LAKE!" I hear Michael roar from behind me.

Close, he is too close.

I push myself further as I make it to the first set of stairs and take three at a time before slamming into the opposite wall. I turn in time to see Michael reach out, and I let out a scream as his fingers knot themselves in my hair.

I pull free of his stone grip, leaving strands behind with him as I push myself off the wall and continue my descent.

I need to be faster, get out and get help, save Malachai, and save...

My feet barely hit the second set of stairs before I feel a shove between my shoulder blades that knocks me off balance. I reach out to grab the handrail, but my hands miss it by mere centimeters before gravity takes me down at full speed. I feel my ribs hit first with a sickening crack before the rest of me follows.

I can't tell which way is up until I roll to a stop at the base of the stairs. I cough and try to breathe, but my lungs aren't working. It feels like there is no air.

I roll onto my back and watch Michael slowly descend the stairs until his silhouette blocks the light from above us.

"I didn't want to believe them, Lake." He reaches down and grabs me by the hair, yanking me to my feet.

I try to pull out of his grasp again, but my vision is getting fuzzy around the edges, and I still can't get enough air into my lungs.

"I didn't want to believe them when they told me what you did and how you betrayed me." Michael grasps my face with his free hand and grazes his lips against mine.

I bite his lip hard as he pulls away and looks at me with shock.

"I wasn't enough for you, after all, so you used my fucking son against me! My flesh and blood!" Michael screams before hitting me in the jaw.

I fall limp against him. "Please...Please..."

"PLEASE WHAT? What have I not given you?" Michael yells, his voice broken as if I have been the one to hurt him this whole time.

"Please let me go..." I cry.

"I can't do that, Lake."

"Why? Why not? What more can you take from me? I have

done everything you have ever asked of me! I have been good to you. I did everything you wanted. I was the perfect daughter to you." I cry.

"So you went and fucked my son? When you were mine?!" He yells while forcing me to look at him.

How Malachai and he could look so similar yet be so different will never cease to amaze me.

"I was never yours." I choke out.

Michael laughs without humor. "That's where you are wrong. You are mine and will always be mine. No matter what, Lake, you are never going to leave me. This is just a mistake you made, you will see. You will see that you were wrong, and one day, I might forgive you. But for now, you hurt me, Lake. And now I have to hurt you."

I fight with all I have left as he drags me down to the cellar. I fight with every ounce of my being that he has failed to strip away because I know after this, I will have nothing if I am alive to feel nothing at all.

I have to fight for Ava, Gage, and Malachai.

For...

With a sickening crash, the cellar is locked behind us, and I am trapped alone with him again.

I quickly lose track of how long I am in the cellar with Michael.

Nothing...there is nothing left of me.

I lay on the cold cement, hearing Malachai screaming in the distance. I wish I could have seen his face one last time.

I cry silently to myself as I say goodbye.

M y head aches as I feel cold press against the side of my face. I force air in and out of my lungs as they burn like I have just smoked a pack of cigarettes. I cough and pry my eyes open slowly.

Darkness. Endless darkness save for Gage, who lies against the concrete floor, staring past me with wide eyes. The moonlight peeking in from a window is the only thing that illuminates his form. I take in the image of him, which is bound with multiple ropes and a gag in his mouth where blood leaks from the side of it.

I sit up and immediately crawl to him and start to pry at his binds with stiff, cold fingers. I caress his face reassuringly, trying to free him and whispering panicked, nonsensical platitudes.

"You should be more concerned for yourself, Lake."

I turn around and block Gage from the view of our captor, Will. He rests along the wall of what looks like a basement. No,... not a basement. The cellar—the very one that haunts my every waking dream. I look down at Gage and see him staring past Will at the cellar door. I follow his gaze and swallow the scream that is starting to build in my chest.

No...No, we can't be back here. This place was burned.

I look around and see dust covering the pile of my clothing that was discarded here by Michael. I look a foot over and see more stains from the blood that would signal my life from that point would never be the same.

A sob shakes my shoulders as I stare at it. I press back further into Gage and clutch at his trembling form.

This can't be happening.

We can't be here. It was all burned.

"Lake?" Will calls in a sing-song voice to grab my attention, but I can't take my eyes off the stain on the floor. I can't move or even scream like my soul is aching to. I'm trapped in my own body as terror takes hold.

"Lake? How does it feel to be home?"

Home...This was never our home. This was our hell.

Slowly, I look up to Will through tears. He isn't wearing the detective suit anymore. He is wearing a simple gray hoody and sweatpants. His hair is no longer smoothed back out of his face but now hangs loosely down, slightly obscuring his glasses. He looks like...

"Malachai?"

The name slips from my lips as easily as breathing, which was a mistake, seeing as how Will lunges from his place on the wall and pulls me to my feet by my throat. My scream is cut off as his grip tightens. I hear Gage struggle against his binds as his muffled screams echo throughout the cellar.

"My piece of shit fucking brother doesn't exist here. Do you fucking hear me?" Will bares his teeth at me as his grip tightens further.

I whimper and nod. His grip blissfully loosens enough for me to suck in air to my aching lungs.

Will caresses my face with his free hand. "You don't know about that at all, do you? I fear Malachai might not either, even though Michael wasn't that quiet about his extramarital affairs by any means. Makes sense there would be another one of us, right?"

I force air into my lungs as I hold his gaze and see the features of someone else familiar for the first time.

"My mother met Michael at Willow Creek when she was just starting her career as a social worker. I believe you've met her."

I utter the name through gritted teeth. "Shelly."

Will nods. "Did you know Michael was on the board of directors then?"

I shake my head as much as I can.

"It's Funny how the court deemed it suitable to send you to the place run by the same man who made your life a living hell. Don't worry, though. I will make them pay for all of that soon enough."

Will's expression changes as his gaze catches on the tears streaming down my face steadily. His features soften into a look of false gentleness as he leans in and licks the tears from my cheek. I resist the urge to pull away from him or flinch, knowing it will only anger him further.

Will hums softly to himself. "Your skin tastes nice, Lake."

"Let her go, you fucking freak!" Gage yells from below us.

I tear my gaze from Will and see that Gage has managed to free an arm and has pulled the gag from his mouth.

Gage pulls himself closer to us with one arm, his nails digging into the concrete floors below our feet.

Will takes one look at him and laughs while pulling me further away from Gage.

"Or what? What can a junky like you do other than be a waste of space for the rest of us?"

I try to pull away from Will, but he quickly lifts me off my feet and walks me over to the wall where the chain that Malachai had been forced to wear rests on the ground.

Realizing his intention, I struggle harder and pivot in his arms. I dig my nails into his arms and bite hard on his shoulder through his hoodie.

Will lets out a strangled groan before pulling me from his body and dropping me at his feet. Before I can crawl away, he effortlessly straddles my waist while resting his knees on my arms, pinning me to the ground. The bite of the pressure makes me let out a frustrated screech as I am trapped beneath his weight.

Will quickly tightens the chain around my throat. He smiles, admiring his work, before lightly springing back to his feet.

Will pulls a syringe from his pocket before walking over to Gage. I struggle against the chain and reach for Gage, who is watching Will with hate and disdain from where he lies bound on the floor, just barely a few feet out of reach from me.

Will looks down at Gage before placing a foot to his throat and looking back to the syringe in his hand.

"I made sure to bring your favorite. Fentanyl right? Amazing stuff, I hear. Makes everything wonderful and light until you're lulled off into the abyss. I got this just for you. I even made sure I had the right stuff, so I went through the trouble of looking up the report from EMS from the night you overdosed. Or should I say, tried to kill yourself?"

I stop struggling and meet Gage's eyes before he looks away with shame.

Will laughs as he glances back at me. "Didn't know about that, did you? Your precious brother tried to leave you. All the while you were doing everything in your power to get back to him, he decided to opt-out. Fucking weak."

I look back to Gage. "It's ok, Gage. I understand it. I do, and it's ok."

He looks back up at me with tears in his eyes. "I love you, Lake."

"I love you. It's ok. We will be okay, alright? I love you..."

Will sighs as he watches the interaction between Gage and me. "What a shame."

I scream as I watch Will stab Gage with the needle and plunge the syringe down. Gage gasps while holding eye contact with me before his eyes roll into the back of his head, and his head lulls to the side.

"Gage? Gage! Will, please, I'll do anything, please help him! I'll do anything you want; please don't take him from me." I sob while pulling at the chain around my throat.

Will sighs dramatically as he nudges Gage with a foot. "Don't worry, I didn't give him enough to kill him, although I may have pushed it a little fast. I guess we will see if he keeps breathing or not."

We watch silently as Gage's breaths slow unnaturally but even out. I let out a sob of relief.

"Well, look at that?" Will laughs without humor. "That

will take care of further interruptions, at least briefly. Now, you and I can continue our fun."

Will leaves Gage on the floor before he kneels in front of me and begins to run his fingers through my hair. He smiles genuinely at me.

"I have missed you more than you could imagine, Lake. Just remember. Everything I have done up until now has been for you, for your freedom."

I blink back, unfallen tears as I stare at him silently and wait for his next move.

Chapter Twenty-Four

MALACHAI

Silence...I don't hear Lake anymore. Her screams stopped a long time ago.

Is she dead?

No...No, I won't believe it. I refuse.

It will be over soon because now I know what to do.

I hear the floor creak as someone walks up the attic steps. The door opens, and I see Penny. She walks into the room and regards me with a look of disdain.

She doesn't say anything. She just stares at me as I am chained to the floor like a dog.

"Hi, Momma." I spit through bloodied teeth.

When was the last time I even thought of her as my mother and not just another face in my life that brings me dread?

"I always wanted to ask you. Why did you never protect me from him?" I ask, allowing myself to finally let the dam break on the hurt that has been eating me alive for years.

Penny, my mother, just stares at me with the same cold expression.

That's okay. She doesn't need to talk because I know the answer, but I ask anyway. "Why didn't you ever treat me as if I was your child? Your flesh and blood? Was I always that unlovable to you? Why wasn't I enough for you? Why couldn't you have just been a mother to me? I needed a mom all these years, and you just became the person I feared most."

"Stop..." She finally whispers as she takes a step towards me.

But I can't stop. Not now.

"It didn't matter if he hit me or hurt me. What hurt worse was you let it happen. You didn't protect me. You acted like I deserved it. Can you look at me now and say I deserved any of this? Can you say I was at fault?"

"You don't understand." She whispers in a choked tone.

"How could any child ever fucking understand this?!" I scream at her.

She finally breaks in front of me and grabs me by the face. "Because I never wanted you! You were never supposed to be here; none of you were! You have done nothing but make your father mad. Why did you make your father mad?!"

A sob chokes me as I know what I have to do.

I grab her throat as I shove her to the ground beneath me. I let the pain from years of abuse give me the strength to do this.

I don't want to have to do this...

But I squeeze and look anywhere but her face.

"I fucking hate you now. I never did, but now, I hate you and never want to see you again. I want you out of my life and gone. I hate you, I hate you, I hate you!"

She stops struggling after minutes pass, but I can't let go; I need to know it's over. It has to be over, finally.

"You were my mom, and I loved you. Why did you turn me into this?" I sob.

Finally, a numbness takes over as I rise from the ground

and look at the chain on my wrist. I bring the flesh of my arm to my mouth and bite hard until I taste blood. I let the drops saturate my skin until I can pull at the chain hard enough to slip my hand through with a sickening pop.

I look at my now free hand and see where my dislocated thumb hangs loosely out of place. Funny, I can't feel the pain at all.

Without looking down, I step over the body and descend the stairs.

I am not done yet...

I need to find my father.

I sit up from the wall I am leaning against and open my eyes to the view of the detective's office I am sitting in. I pull at my arm, still chained to the desk, and sigh in annoyance.

I allowed myself to doze off while a cop sat in the room with me to watch my every move. Unfortunately, he sits a few yards ahead of me, out of arm's reach.

I would be out of here if he had been any closer.

I meet his glare with one of my own and ask, "You sure you don't have a cigarette on you?"

He rolls his eyes and looks away from me to gaze out the barred window. That is one way I will not be able to exit.

I glance at the clock on the desk and see that another few hours have passed, making it twenty-two hours in total since Gage and Lake were taken from me.

Twenty-two hours...they could be dead by now.

No, I won't believe that.

Before I can start to spiral, the door opens to the young face of another officer. I look him over and see the slight yellow tinge of his nails, accompanied by the smell of smoke still clinging to his clothes. I offer him a friendly smile, and he quickly glances away at the other officer.

Without exchanging words, they switch places, and the young cop sits facing me. He looks uncomfortable as he adjusts himself while avoiding eye contact.

I turn away from him and take in my surroundings for the hundredth time—nothing but a desk, a chair, and a window. There is nothing to use as a weapon and no accessible escape routes. I look over to the floor vent and almost laugh at how small it is—there is no chance of crawling through that.

I relax further into my seat and look back over to the cop. There is only one way out of here.

"Do you have a cigarette I can bum off you?"

"What?"

"Do you have a cigarette?" I ask again. "My lawyer has asthma and didn't bring me my pack while he and I talked in the interview room."

The cop fidgets a bit before saying. "I don't think you can smoke in here."

I roll my eyes. "Come on. Like anyone here really gives a shit about that."

The cop hesitates momentarily before standing and pulling out a pack of menthals. He lights it up for me, not wanting to hand me a lighter.

"Thanks, man," I say as I grab it from him.

His hand is close enough now that I grab his arm with my right hand and slam my fist into his jaw with my left. Fucker is out immediately, and I catch his body before he hits the ground and gently place him down so he doesn't make any noise.

I pick up the fallen cigarette and put it out on the metal desk before bringing my wrist up to my mouth, biting hard and drawing blood. I use the blood to lube the cuff enough to pull my hand out with a pop.

I bite the inside of my cheek to silence a groan of pain as I reset my hand. Once that is done, I strip out of my clothing and pull the uniform off the cop.

After our clothing is swapped, I pull him into the chair I had been sitting in and force the bloodied cuff over his hand, sliding it into place.

I feel a grin creep over my face at my work before walking out of the office. No one bats an eye at me as I walk out the front doors and down the road.

Easy...that was too easy.

I walk unbothered until I am in a park about five blocks from the police station. I find a bush where I had left a water-proof pack full of clothing, money, and a disposable cell-phone. I strip down once more into the grey shirt and jeans that were inside and pull on the sunglasses and baseball cap.

I pocket the wad of cash and flip open the cell, dialing Ava's number.

"Hello?"

"Come pick me up. I'm at Westwood Park by the pond," I say before hanging up.

I reach into the pack and pull out a bag of crackers before stashing the rest of the cop's uniform back into the bag and shoving it in the bush.

I go to a nearby bench, sit down, and feed the ducks while waiting for my sister.

Chapter Twenty-Five

LAKE

I stare at the dining room table's length as I try to remove the ropes that bind me to the chair without drawing Will's attention.

"Are you not hungry, Lake?" Will calls over to me from where he sits to my left.

I stare at the food before me. Will had cooked us mashed potatoes and chicken, and he even adorned the plate with decorative spices.

I swallow a hysterical laugh at the image of Will meticulously preparing this meal for us as he has Gage and me bound in the cellar.

"Feeding myself is quite the challenge with my hands bound like this," I retort, my voice laced with a hint of bitterness that I struggle to conceal.

"If I untie you, will you behave, or are you going to bite me again?" Will asks sweetly while running the tips of his fingers over the ropes cutting into my wrists.

"I don't have another option, do I?" I ask rhetorically as I look over to the head of the table, where I see Gage tied up similarly, staring down at his food with a sleepy, glossy look in his eyes.

Will has repeatedly been dosing him with the drugs to keep him complacent over the last few days, keeping him on another planet.

If Will unties me, I might be able to escape, but with Gage in this state, I don't think he could protect himself, let alone follow basic commands. I don't think I could fight off Will and drag Gage out of here myself. So, for now, I will wait for an opportunity. Until then, I will have to keep my head straight and not give in to the panic coursing through my veins.

"No, you don't, Lake." Will hums in a happy tone.

I look up to him and try to keep my voice even. "Well then, untie me...Please."

Will smiles at me and nods as he pulls a pocket knife from his hoodie pocket and flips it open. While holding eye contact, he cuts away the binds quickly enough. As he moves the knife away from my now free hands, he slowly drags the tip of it from my wrist up to my elbow, hard enough to feel the bite of pressure but not enough to draw blood.

I pull my hands to the front of me and rub at my wrists before picking up a fork and digging into the food. It is possible that Will poisoned the food, but I will have to take this risk to keep him happy and make him think I am compliant.

Will watches me eat for a few minutes before rising from his seat and walking over to Gage. He also frees him from his binds, being much less cautious about knicking Gage with the knife. I watch with disdain as Will looks over the knife, a few drops of blood staining the silver metal's surface.

Will looks over at me and holds eye contact once more as he brings the knife to his tongue, licking away the red drops.

I swallow and look back at my food as Gage slumps forward over his meal. "So, how did you do all of this?"

Will drops the knife to the table beside Gage, who briefly glances at it before he closes his eyes and rests his head against the cold surface of the table, leaving his food untouched. Will sits again next to me as he leans close and gestures around the dining room.

"All of this? You mean the house?"

"Yes...It all looks the same. How did you do this? How was it possible?"

Will looks pleased, saying, "After the fire, Malachai inherited the house and all of my father's assets. He had the opportunity to tear down what remained of the place, but instead, he let it rot. No one ever came to visit this place after that."

"That doesn't explain how it looks untouched," I state as I take another bite. It tastes good but hits my stomach like a rock.

"No one questioned me showing up and repairing the place over the last decade, seeing as Malachai and I both tend to look similar. I could come and go as I pleased. The neighbors even welcomed me as one of their own, never realizing they were talking to the wrong brother or that I even existed."

"You did all of this yourself?" I ask, looking at how damn near every detail looked the same as it once was, from the roof to the wooden floorboards. Even the Victorian doilies looked suspiciously accurate.

Will shrugs. "I've had a lot of time on my hands."

I place my fork down, resisting the urge to attempt to stab him with it. "Why?"

"Why what?" he asks, tilting his head to the side. I cringe internally at the familiar motion performed by someone other than Malachai.

"Why did you do all of this?" I ask, gesturing to the dining room.

Will laughs and looks at me like I'm the insane one. "So you could come home."

"You did this for me?"

"Who else?" Will asks in return.

"Why, though? Why me?" I ask.

Will's smile slips, and he regards me with suspicion. "Why so many questions, love?"

I brace my hands lightly at the table's edge and inhale slowly as I pivot to face him.

"I just don't understand why you would do all this for me, Will."

Will's unhinged smile returns as he leans closer and caresses my face.

"Do you remember the first time we met?"

I swallow and nod. "Yes."

Will leans back as he is lost in the memory. "I never told you this, but I knew who you were before I met you that day in the garden. I knew of you all for years. My father never lied to me about my situation and how I was a bastard of a senator who couldn't stain his reputation by claiming me as his own. That never stopped him from telling me about his beloved sons and daughters and how I would come out of the shadows one day and meet you all."

"That never happened, though. And as the years went on, I began to resent you. I resented the holidays and birthdays you got to spend with him. I resented seeing your faces on the news every fourth of July, and I resented that he had to limit his time with me and keep me his dirty secret, all to keep his little family together."

"And as time went on, I began to hate you all. I hated the torn clothing and empty cabinets my mother struggled to fill while you all could have whatever you wanted. I hated having my dad only visit every few months with false promises and empty gestures. I hated hearing your names and seeing your faces as a constant reminder of everything I would never be. I hated being a bastard and someone not worth acknowledging."

"What changed?" I ask.

"Nothing, not for a long time, at least." Will pauses in thought before holding my gaze once more. "Did you know I was here? The night of the fire?"

My stomach drops. "How?"

"I had finally had enough. I was tired of being a bastard. I was tired of living without. So that night, I came here to confront my father. I was going to demand my place in his life because I'm a fucking human and didn't deserve to be forgotten about and just thought of when it suited him."

"But when I arrived, I heard screaming and saw flames overtake the house. I watched you pull Malachai onto the front lawn and scream for help. I watched Ava run to the neighbors and how Gage repeatedly pleaded for Malachai to wake up. I remember thinking there was so much blood on you and Malachai. It's hard to believe that a human can spill so much yet still be able to move."

"I remember looking around for my father but didn't see him. So I went inside and looked. Every detail of this house has been burned into my memory from looking for him. And when I found him and saw what his precious children did to him...I hated you all the more."

Will smiles to himself once more, his expression not reflecting the emotion in his voice. I lean back slightly and glance at Gage, who is staring at Will from where he is still slumped on the table.

I look back to Will and ask again, "What changed?"

Will smiles at me. "You. I found out that you had been accused of killing your foster parents and starting the fire. Did you know that with all the accelerant you used, the fire burned so hot, there were never any bodies to be buried?"

I look away from him. "I never knew that."

Will grasps my chin and forces me to look at him. "What you did was so gruesome and cold. There were no bodies, Lake, and for that, I hated you and wanted to hurt you for all of the pain you had caused my father. I wanted you to suffer like he had. I wanted you to suffer for taking away any chance of a normal life I could have had with him."

"Then I heard you were to be admitted to the psychiatric facility my mother worked at. By that time, I was already warped. She thinks seeing my father like that broke me, but that is not the truth. The truth was, I was always like this. Maybe that's why my father never acknowledged me. Maybe I was just too much like him."

"But my mother took responsibility and pulled me out of school so I would stop hurting my classmates, and she kept me with her constantly to supervise me. I didn't mind, though; it just brought me closer and closer to you."

"When I finally saw you in the garden, I watched you read in the sunlight for hours. Sweat was beading your forehead, and you looked flushed from the heat, but none of that bothered you. You were so engrossed in your book. I wanted to see those pages stained with your blood."

"But the more I watched you, the harder it was to do it. I don't know why, but I decided to talk to you instead. Talking to you is what changed everything for me."

Tears fill my eyes. "You were my only friend back then, Will."

His smile slips. "I know."

"You have been my only friend outside of my family. So why did you have to change? Why did you have to leave me there alone? Why did you do all of this now? Why are you doing this to me? I cared for you..."

Will offers me a sad smile. "I never changed, Lake. I was always like this. And I always will be."

"And those people in the photos you showed me? You did that to them, didn't you?"

"Of course."

"Why?" I ask once more on a choked breath.

"Because they hurt you, Lake, they all did. Now I am going to ruin everyone who ever hurt us and rebuild everything that should have been ours to begin with."

"Why?" I sob.

"Because I love you, Lake. And I'll never stop." Will murmurs softly while brushing away stray tears from my cheeks.

Chapter Twenty-Six

MALACHAI

I brace myself against the walls as I follow a blood trail leading from the staircase to the cellar.

Please, please don't be dead...

As I round the last hall, I run into a body head-on. Before I can strike at them, I see Gage's wild eyes gazing into mine as he puts a silencing finger over his lips.

He has Ava tucked away behind him. She stares into the open cellar door with a horrified expression before she breaks off from us and runs inside.

We follow behind her, and what I see makes all the air leave my lungs as I fall to my knees beside Lake's limp form.

I pull her gently into my arms and brush her bloodied hair away from her face.

"Lake?! Lake, oh god, please wake up." I cry in a strangled voice into her neck.

I inhale a broken breath and am met with the sweet scent of Lake. My beautiful Lake.

"Baby, please open your eyes. What the fuck did he do?!" I scream to no one.

"I don't know, Malachai ..." Ava cries.

"Malachai, she's bleeding..." Gage whispers.

She's bleeding...She's bleeding so much. But that's not what Gage means. I look at her stomach and see gash marks along her lower abdomen. A foot to our left is the knife that was used to inflict the wounds.

"No, no, no, No! Help me get her up!"

Ava and Gage help me drag Lake across the cellar. She whimpers as we move her, and her eyes flutter open.

"It hurts..."

"I know, I know. You're going to be okay, Lake. You are going to be ok." I try to reassure her.

"Make it stop..." She cries.

Gage sobs as he pulls Lake from my grip. "Here, we are hurting her. Let me carry her."

Gage kneels next to Lake and pulls her into his arm, cradling her against his chest.

We barely make it out of the cellar before I hear the voice that has haunted me since the day I came into this world.

"I can't let you leave," Michael says from behind us.

I look up into the eyes of my father as he lifts a revolver from his side. He aims the barrel directly at Lake and Gage. I step in front of them before I hear a resounding boom and Ava's screams.

After that, there is nothing.

"What the fuck do you mean there's nothing?" Ava yells into the phone, that's been plastered to her ear for several hours.

I open my eyes from where I had dosed against the coffee table and look up at Ava. She paces back and forth in Riley's apartment's living room. Riley and I have been staying here since my liberation from the police department while we search for Lake and Gage. The apartment has become our headquarters, with video surveillance, laptops, and documents.

I blink away the fog of sleep and tune her out the best I can as I focus on what Riley has laid before me. We look over a map of the city in silence and review where Lake and Gage went missing days ago and all the possible roads and allies they could have been taken down.

We also have Will's apartment marked and all of the other places he seems to visit. We have our contacts at the bank pull his credit card records, and the only places he seems to visit are the same sushi restaurant, the coffee shop by the gallery, and a hardware store on the edge of town.

I focus on the hardware store, trying not to let my imagination run wild with all the possibilities of what that could mean. His credit records show he has spent upwards of a million dollars there over the past decade, which leads me to believe he didn't take Lake and Gage to his apartment. There have been no signs of alteration to the foundation there that would account for such a high expense.

That and that no one has seen him there in days, let alone at work. He took PTO for the next month. He plans to be in the shadows with Lake for at least that long. As for what he has planned after that...

Well, I wouldn't put it past him to show up back up to work as if there isn't a body somewhere in a basement. It's not like I haven't done that.

I shake away the thought of Lake lying cold and decomposing somewhere dark and out of reach. And Gage...he is an accessory in all of this. He has probably already been killed.

No, I need to stop getting emotional. That's how I will make mistakes. I need to look at this as objectively as possible.

If I were Will, what would be my end goal? What would I gain from all of this?

I rub my eyes and then look at Riley. "Thoughts?"

"I think he took them."

I agree, but we have to be sure it's him. "What makes you sure?"

"He is the only one who would have bothered to take Gage with him. Anyone else would have just left him bloodied on the bathroom floor."

"And why do you think he took Gage?"

"To manipulate Lake. She would have either gotten away from him by now or killed by him trying to. Gage would be the only reason she is still alive. She would be compliant for his sake."

"And he would know that because he knows about their relationship from when she was at Willow Creek."

I hear a crash from across the room and look up at Ava, staring down at her newly smashed cell phone on the ground. Riley sighs and reaches into her pocket, extending her phone to Ava.

"Please don't break this one," Riley murmurs as Ava gives her a sheepish nod before grasping it and leaving the room.

"She's losing it," I mutter as I watch her exit.

Riley sighs. "We all are."

True. "We need to think back to when they met. Lake said it was a few years into her stay there that she started seeing Will, but he wasn't a patient. Most facilities like that would not allow someone who didn't work at the facility that close to the patients."

"His dad was on the board of directors. That gives him a free pass to wherever he wants on the grounds. It was a private institute run solely by the board. That would make him royalty walking around there."

"Ava hasn't been able to find any information on who his father or mother is," I say with agitation.

"We will figure it out. I know that has something to do with this." Riley states while shuffling through more information on Lake's stay at Willow Creek.

I gaze at a lone photo of Will standing alone outside the gates of Willow Creek. It all comes back to him. Once we know who he is, we will find them, and I'll spend the rest of Will's life making him pay for what he has done to them.

Chapter Twenty-Seven

LAKE

"I'm bored." Will murmurs from where he is lounging on the couch in the foyer. My eyes drift from his lazy form to the doorway a few yards to my right.

If I could just make a run for it...

Then what? I can't leave Gage.

I look down to where Gage trembles, curled up on the couch opposite Will. His breathing is quick, and sweat coats his brow. I run my hands through his hair in a soothing motion, trying to calm him the best I can, but I know the pain of the withdrawals will become unbearable for him soon enough.

Will watches my hand linger against Gage with a look of disapproval. "Does that ever bother Malachi?"

I tilt my head slightly. "Why would it?"

Will sits up and holds my gaze evenly. "Because you're touching another man."

"And?" I ask again, keeping my voice even.

"I don't like it."

"Well, if you hadn't been drugging him for the last few days and then abruptly withholding the drugs, this wouldn't have happened, and I wouldn't be sitting here with him like this."

Will glares at me. "Would you rather I have killed him?"

I sigh. "I would rather you had not brought him along at all."

"If I hadn't, you wouldn't have stayed with me."

I glare back at him. "You don't know that for sure, and you won't be able to since what's done is done."

Will sits up straighter. "What if I let him go now?"

I look away from him. "You wouldn't."

"Would you stay here with me if I did?"

I think about that and decide against lying. "Probably not."

Will's eyes darken. "Why?"

"Because I didn't come here willingly," I state, looking back down at Gage.

He clutches my knee in a death grip before turning his head to vomit onto the floor at my feet.

"Shit..." I mutter as I help Gage get into a sitting position.

"Goddamnit, you have no idea how much that rug cost."

I pull Gage to his feet. "I'll clean it, and it will be fine, I promise."

"Where are you going?" Will asks as he stands to his feet.

"I'm going to help him clean up and then put him to bed," I state as I start walking Gage off to the guest rooms down the hall.

Will has kept us in them for the last few days rather than in the cellar. He doesn't let Gage sleep in the same room as me, but with some convincing and pleading, he allowed him to at least be in the same hall.

Will trails silently behind us as I take Gage to his room and into the adjoining bathroom. Gage leans on me as I wet a cloth, wipe his mouth, and find mouthwash for him to rinse.

"I'm sorry Lake..."

"Shhh...Don't apologize. You would do the same for me." I murmur to him.

"Are you done yet?" Will asks from where he leans against the wall by the central doorway.

"Almost," I call to him before looking back at Gage. "Listen, we just have to wait him out. There will be a moment when he lets his guard down or hesitates, and we will make our move then. And if there's not, I'll make an opportunity. OK?"

Gage nods as I quickly get him situated to not upset Will. He has been more amicable the last few days than when we first arrived, but that doesn't mean he isn't still quick to anger and threats. As long as I do what he says, he doesn't hurt Gage.

"Come on. You need rest. I'll keep Will distracted while you sleep."

Gage holds my gaze and nods before stumbling over to the bed. I pull back the covers, tuck him in, and place pillows under his back to keep him propped on his right side. If he vomits again, I don't want him to aspirate.

I look around the room, find a trashcan, and place it by the bed. "Here, this is in case you get sick again."

Gage nods as Will walks into the room. Will pulls out a pair of handcuffs and locks Gage to the headboard.

I know better than to argue against this after setting Will off about it the other day. This is something he won't budge on, especially now that Gage is coming off the drugs.

Will leaves the room after gazing down at Gage's form for a creepy amount of time. I could almost hear him weighing whether or not he should kill Gage now or later. I know that is what is coming soon, but I hope I can convince him to let him go before that.

I know that is not possible from Will's standpoint. If Gage got freed, he would first tell Malachai where I am, which is the last thing Will wants.

Will wants to keep me here playing this sick game of house for as long as possible, and for Gage's sake, I will.

That is another dilemma for Will, though, because he knows if he kills Gage, I will fight him with everything I have to either get free or follow Gage into the afterlife.

I look down at Gage's trembling form and inhale slowly. I don't know how much longer I can take this myself. Day after day, it has been the same thing. I wake up next to Will, smile, cook, clean, pretend not to be crawling out of my skin every moment, and rise and repeat the next day.

I lie to myself and tell myself for the hundredth time that I can do this. I did it for years while living with the Rosemonds, so what is another day?

"Hurry up," Will calls over to me.

I spare Gage one last look and feel slightly relieved, knowing that if Will is with me, he isn't hurting Gage.

That is another familiar thought from my past that I had hoped I would never have to have again.

After cleaning up the mess in the foyer, I join Will for dinner and sit next to him again. I compliment his food quietly. Tonight's meal is another meticulously arranged platter that looks delicious. I'm sure it tastes fine like all the other meals, but it turns to ash on my tongue.

"How was your day?" Will asks as he picks at his plate.

"It was fine, and yours?" I ask softly, knowing exactly what game Will wants to play now that Gage is out of the picture.

"It was a boring day at the station," Will states, even though he spent the whole day plastered to Gage's and my side.

"I'm sure that's a good thing, though. If it weren't boring, that would mean people were getting hurt."

Will sighs and leans back in his chair. "That's what makes it fun though. The blood, the pain, the screaming, the silence. That's why I became a cop in the first place."

I force myself to swallow the bite I almost choked on. "Ah, I see."

"So if my day was boring, that means it was bad. So what will you do to make it better, Lake?" Will asks, the food in front of him forgotten.

I place my silverware down and force myself to hold Will's gaze. Fuck I don't want to touch him...I don't want him to touch me.

My eyes drift down to the stake knife by Will's plate. I allow myself to fantasize about stabbing him with it. Instead, I pick it up by the blade and extend the handle to him.

"I'll make the day less boring," I tell him softly.

Will's eyes light up as he wraps his hand firmly around the knife. With a swift motion, he pushes our food out of the way with his free hand before reaching up and grabbing me by the throat. He pulls me to my feet before slamming me down on the table. I resist the urge to fight him and relax as much as possible while he climbs onto the table to straddle me at the waist.

Will smiles at me as he moves his knee to pin my right wrist beneath it. A whimper escapes my throat as I feel the bite of pain from the pressure of his knee. Will looks down at me lovingly and traces his fingers from my throat to my mouth. He covers my mouth as he leans down close to my ear.

"Scream for me, love." He breaths.

I feel the sting of the knife as he starts to carve into my upper arm.

I can't help myself.

I scream and scream and scream...

Chapter Twenty-Eight

MALACHAI

Days go by, and there is still nothing. There is no new information or sign of life from Lake or Gage. I'm trying to hold it together, but I feel like I am losing them again with every moment that slips by.

I need to find my family. I need to know they are okay and safe, back in my arms and in my bed.

We have been through too much for it to end like this. I refuse to have it end like this for us. I don't care if I have to tear this whole fucking city apart. I will find them again.

My thoughts are interrupted when Ava enters the apartment through the front door with an unreadable expression. I watch her in silence, seated in the only spot that I seem to exist anymore, at the coffee table, surrounded by useless information.

Ava walks up to Riley. "Your caseworker is calling again."

"Fuck," I mutter. "Put it on speaker."

Riley pales as she presses the answer button. "Hi."

"Riley, what is going on? You and Lake haven't answered the phone in days, and she has missed appointments with her psychiatrist. Where is she?" Shelly asks with concern in her voice.

Riley looks at me with pleading eyes as I scribble down an excuse on paper for her to recite to Shelly.

"She hasn't been feeling well. She lost her voice. That's why she hasn't answered. I thought she said she texted you about it."

"That's bullshit, Riley. The cops called me a few hours ago and told me she had been reported missing. What the hell is going on?"

"Ah..."

"Never mind that I'm at the door. Open it, or I will have the maintenance man open it for me."

"Fuck!" Ava whispers.

"Just get the door," I say while running a hand through my hair. Fuck this is not what we need right now.

Riley jumps off the couch and runs to answer the door. Riley opens it a few inches to see who I assume is Shelly. Before Riley can say anything, Shelly looks around and pushes in through the door.

"What is all this?" Shelly asks as her gaze drifts over our setup to where I sit at the coffee table. "Malachai?"

The hairs on my neck stand up as I get to my feet. "How do you know my name?"

I never spoke to Lake's caseworker directly, as I bribed her to release Lake from Willow Creek. I didn't even give her my name. I was just an anonymous person with a checkbook to her and a motive.

Ava walks over to stand by my side and stares at Shelly with distrust. Shelly ignores my question as she looks at some papers on the kitchen island. Her eyes widen suddenly, and she reaches out to grasp them as she flips through the pages.

"Why do you all have photos of my son?" she asks with a slight tremble.

"Your son?" Riley asks in confusion.

"Will is your son?" Ava asks, taking a step forward.

Before I can stop myself, I am across the room, grasping Shelly by the arms. "Tell me where he is. Now."

Shelly tries to escape my grasp, but I tighten my grip. Ava steps forward and puts a hand on my arm.

"Malachai..."

"Where is Will Shelly? He has Lake and Gage!"

"What do you mean he has them?" Shelly asks in fear.

Ava digs her nails into my arm, but I hold her tight. "He took them from me, and I need them back. He has my family, Shelly. Where the fuck could he have taken them?"

"Malachai, get off of her!" Riley demands as she pulls me back from Shelly.

I stumble a step back as Shelly moves out of arm's reach. She inhales and exhales rapidly as she looks over all of us.

"My son...Is sick." She says while tears flood her eyes. "I didn't know he was capable of this, I swear it. I thought it was just a crush he had years ago on Lake. I never knew he would do this. If I had, I would have never agreed to help get Lake out of Willow Creek, where she was safe from him."

Ava steps in front of me to block Shelly from me. "Tell us everything."

Chapter Twenty-Nine

LAKE

My eyes flutter open as screams fill the hallway. Ava... that's Ava screaming.

She kneels next to a bloody form on the floor. I can't see them from where Gage has me tucked away in his arms.

Where is Malachai? He was just here with us a moment ago. I could feel his warmth against my body, but now it is gone, replaced by Gage's.

I look up into Gage's eyes from where he clutches me to him, his nails digging into my arms. I can't feel the pain of it, though. Everything suddenly stopped hurting.

Gage looks down to where Ava is curled over the form...No, not just a form. That's...That's...

I struggle out of Gage's arms as he slumps down to the ground with me. I place a hand over my stomach to hold in the blood that is leaking from me in a steady stream as I crawl over to Malachai.

His head lulls to the side, and blood leaks from a hole in his temple. His half-lidded gaze stares off past Ava.

I look up to where Michael stares at us with an emotionless gaze. The gun is still in his hand as he gazes down at Malachai.

"What did you do?" I whisper.

Michael doesn't answer. He just runs a bloodied hand through his hair as he lifts the gun once more in my direction. I slump over Malachai to shield his body from further harm and close my eyes.

If I die here, I will at least die with my family. We can be together in the afterlife, which might be kinder to us. We can finally be together without hate or pain.

I wait for another bang to come, but there are no sounds. Instead, I look up and see Ava charging towards Michael with a look of determination and utter rage. She collides with his body, knocking the gun out of his hand.

Gage doesn't hesitate to make his move, and he jumps over Malachai and me to reach for the gun. Once his hand is around the hilt, he screams at Ava, who is fighting Michael like a feral cat.

"Ava, move!"

Ava shoves away from Michael as Gage empties the clip into Michael's chest. The sound and burst of light from the gun leave me momentarily blinded and deaf.

I blink rapidly as I look back down to Malachai. I place my ear to his chest and hear a slow beat. It's too slow.

"Is he alive?" Ava asks from behind Gage.

I don't know if she is asking about Michael or Malachai, but I know Malachai is still breathing. As long as he is breathing, we have a chance. There's a chance we can save him.

I pull myself against the wall and reach down to drag Malachai to the front door. Ava and Gage quickly stumble over to help me. We reach the front door fast once we all have our hands on him.

Gage pulls open the front door for us, and I drag Malachai the rest of the way onto the front yard's grass. Ava spares us one last look before running down the endless driveway toward the neighbor's house. I can hear her start to scream for help once she reaches the edge of the property.

My ears ring as I look down at Malachai once more. His breathing slows as Gage leans over and begs him to wake up.

I look back at the house as the edges of my vision blur again.

"Did you kill him?" I ask Gage.

"What?" He gasps while clutching Malachai.

"Is he dead? Is it over? It has to be over Gage..."

Gage looks up at me with desperation, shakes his head, and looks back down at the gun that is discarded in the grass.

I pick up the empty gun and use the bloodied remains of my clothing to wipe Gage's fingerprints from it before placing it in my grip and turning back to the house.

I walk through the house in a daze until I find the kitchen and turn on the gass of the stove before continuing out back to the shed by the garden. I find what I'm looking for before I stumble back into the house and make my way on unsteady feet to the attic, where I see Penny's lifeless body.

I hardly spare her a glance as I pour the fire accelerant on her. I leave the cap open pouring more out onto the floor as I walk back down to the steps by the cellar, where I find Michael.

I brace myself against the wall as my vision comes in and out of focus. Michael is slumped against the wall as he grasps at the holes in his chest with wide, disbelieving eyes.

I stare at him as I step forward and pour the accelerant on his legs. He looks up at me with panic as I leave a fluid trail from him to the front foyer. I leave the container by the front door as the smell of gas from the kitchen mixes in with the scent of accelerant.

I knock over a candle that Penny had left lit by the front door onto the carpet. I step back through the door and watch as

265

the flame quickly follows the trail of the accelerant into the depths of the house.

I turn away and walk out to Gage and Malachai. Once I reach them, I grab hold of Malachai once more.

"Help me get him further from the house." I gasp to Gage.

Gage nods, and we drag Malachai to the edge of the property, where we start to hear sirens in the distance. I lay down on the road next to Malachai as pain starts to seep back into my body. I cry silently as I curl in on myself on his chest, right as I hear an explosion.

I blink away the memory as I stand in front of the guest bathroom mirror and take in the haunted expression staring back at me. She looks exhausted—like she used to—thin and pale.

I allow my eyes to drift further down and see the uniform from my high school hanging loosely against my skin. Will wanted me to wear it the other day and has wanted me to wear it every day since.

How did he obtain it? The last uniforms I owned burned in the fire.

I swallow bile in my throat as I look back up to the face in the mirror staring back at me. Every day, I see the circles under my eyes grow darker and darker, and I feel something in me start dissipating.

My eyes trail over my flesh, and I let out a shaky breath.

Will Masters

Will Masters

Will Masters

Will Masters

The name over and over again stains my skin in stinging red marks. The blood has long dried, but the damage inflicted will last longer than the wounds take to heal.

I know this because I have suffered this day after day long before I ever met Will Masters. I hate looking at these marks and knowing that if I get free of them, this is just another mark on my already damaged soul.

I close my eyes to the haunted woman in the mirror and meet Will in the hall.

"Lake..." He murmurs as he walks over to me and caresses my cheek.

I lean into his hand and close my eyes in silence.

"I have been working on a surprise for you. A symbol of my love and affection for you. It's outside," he says, stepping back from me.

"Outside?" I ask in confusion. Will has hardly even let us near the windows during the day, much less outside.

He is getting more trusting, if not more brazen.

"The neighbors are too far away to hear you if you scream anyway, and if you run, I would just catch you before you reach them." Will smiles at me, guessing the direction my thoughts had taken.

Run? Scream? I barely have the energy to stand before him. But the thought of going outside brings something of a slight hope as well as a fresh wave of pain I am surprised I can even feel at this point. Deep down, I don't want to go outside. I don't want to see the sunlight behind the willow trees. I want to stay inside, with Gage...I want to curl up beside him and take what comfort I can in his presence, just to forget what is waiting along the shallow shores of the pond.

Will takes my silence as an agreement and grasps my hand firmly in his as he leads me through the manor's halls.

I want to dig my heels into the carpet between us, but I follow him, locked inside a deep part of myself that allows me only to follow behind him.

As we reach the fresh air of the outdoors, I lift my eyes to block the sting of the sun. How long has it been since I have been in the sun? Days? Weeks? How long have we been here?

"Come on," Will smiles, which pulls at the corners of his too-perfect lips.

How cruel is it that sometimes, in the perfect lighting like now, he looks like a splitting image of Malachai? He looks like the one person who I adore most. Sometimes, I wish I could pretend he was Malachai. That would make what I have to do to free Gage and me so much easier.

A sharp gust of wind takes me away from my wandering thoughts as I look at the path that Will is taking me along. My eyes widen, and I dig my bare heels into the ground.

"Will, please..." I beg.

Will gives me a knowing look over his shoulder. "Is there something you don't wish to see over there?"

I nod as I pull against him. "Let's go back inside. I don't want to go over there..."

Will drops my hand and turns to look at me head-on. "Lake...I know I'm...I know I've..."

His gaze trails back to the marks covering my body. A slightly haunted look overtakes his features before he looks away and continues. "Just trust me, okay?"

I want to scream at him for the first time in days and shake him. Trust him? After all that he has done to Gage and me?

But another haunted look crosses his features as he raises his hand to mine again. I let him guide me along again as I struggled to quail the rage boiling in my chest.

The numbness was easier to function with.

But the rage is soon overtaken by the blinding pain I feel cut through my chest as we finally approach the large willow overlooking the estate's pond. My eyes trail from the long green wisps flowing in the wind to the dark roots disappearing into the earth.

I see a freshly carved tombstone there and fall to my knees.

"I remember you telling me what you would have named her had my father not..."

"Don't," I say through gritted teeth as I stare at the name.

Will, for once, doesn't press me on the matter. He crouches down next to me and gazes at the name.

"I thought it was a bit unimaginative, given why you named her that."

"We were teenagers; we aren't meant to be imaginative with naming children," I say as tears swim in my eyes.

"No, I guess not." Will hums as he rests his head on his knees and looks at me.

"Why did you do this? How did you know she was here?" I ask, unable to look away from the stone.

"I remember seeing Ava come here a few weeks after the fire and bury something. Then, when we spoke in the garden, you told me this was where you would have buried her if the hospital and police would have given you the chance. I put two and two together from there."

I feel the tears leak from my eyes down my cheeks. "They never gave me the chance. They never even gave me her ashes. They told me they gave them to the Savvedra's since Malachai was under their care..."

"They will suffer for what they did to you," Will says firmly.

I turn to look at him and feel a shift as our eyes meet. "Thank you, Will... This doesn't change things between us, but...Thank you."

Will nods and looks back to the stone. "I'm sorry, Lake."

"For what?"

"For everything. For her, for this...For..."

I turn away from him and look back at the stone. "Thank you, Will, for giving her what I couldn't..."

I trail off as sobs start to shake me, and I bend over, kneeling, trying to hold myself together. Will sits beside me in silence as my tears dry and the sun begins to disappear behind the clouds.

"Feel better?" Will finally asks.

I nod and look over to Will. He reaches a hand up to my face and pushes a few stray hairs behind my ears.

"Does Malachai know?" he asks while gesturing to the gravestone.

I shake my head. "No...I could never tell him."

Will thinks about that momentarily before asking, "Why did you tell me?"

"Because...I was starting to love you. I wanted you to know me, all of me," I tell him honestly.

"And do you love me now?" He asks softly.

"I'm not sure of anything anymore," I whisper as I look at him and see the man I met in the garden. Back then, he was so gentle. He was beautiful and kind; he was my best friend. How could I not have cared for him then? But now?

Will turns to face me and leans in close to my face. "I just need you to stay with me long enough to realize that you and I are the same. We are meant to be together."

I stare at Will with sorrow. Why did it come to this with us?

I reach up slowly to Will and guide him to the ground by his shoulder. He lays back in the grass and stares at me in curiosity as I rest my head over his heart and close my eyes. Over time, I feel Will relax under me as he runs his fingers through my hair soothingly.

"I can give you time, Will," I murmur to him.

We stay like that until the stars are well into the sky, and finally, Will has to pry me away from the gravestone gently. We find Gage waiting inside the kitchen, leaning against the island.

Exhaustion covers his features as he trembles slightly. He looks between Will and me, noticing the shift between us before he leads the way upstairs to his guest room, where he gets ready for bed under Will's watchful eyes. I avert my gaze as he strips down before us and pulls on some clean clothing that Will left for him. As he finishes that task, he hops onto the bed and places his hand by the headboard, allowing Will to hand-cuff him to it again.

Will reaches for the handcuff and hesitates slightly before reaching for it again and securing Gage to the bed.

Gage glances at me meaningfully as he rolls to his side and buries himself under the covers. Will stares at him again before guiding us out of the room and clicking the door shut behind us.

"Is it okay if I shower?" I ask Will as he leads us to our bedroom.

Will nods in silence as we walk to the adjoining bathroom, and I inhale a deep breath before reaching for the buttons on my white blouse. Will's pupils dilate as he watches my fingers move with shaky precision.

"I'm...going to shower. Join me?"

Will continues to watch me with his unblinking gaze as he steps forward and unbuttons my shirt for me before slipping his shirt off over his head.

I swallow the saliva in my mouth and unzip my skirt down to nothing but my bra and underwear. I turn my back to Will and gesture to my bra.

"Can you unclip this for me?"

I hear him take a step forward and feel his warm hands brush the skin of my back. I allow myself to go to a place deep in my head and resist the urge to shudder.

"What changed, Lake?" Will whispers against my neck as I lean into his touch.

"Nothing's changed, Will," I whisper as I face him and press my lips softly against his.

Will freezes under my touch before crashing his lips hard

against mine. I feel his mouth open and run my hand along his arms, feeling the muscle of years of hard labor under his skin. He traces his hands along my bare skin, and I feel the sting of the wounds he has inflicted over the last few weeks.

I bite his lip to hold in a whimper. Will takes this as a sign to darken our kiss. He nips hard at my lips in return before leaving a trail of kisses down my neck to my shoulder, where I feel him shutter before he bites down. Hard.

I let out a startled scream as he presses his hand over my mouth, blocking the air from my lungs. I groan in pain against his hand before he pulls back and looks into my eyes with an unfocused gaze. Blood drips from his lips as I close my eyes and continue our kiss. Will picks me up to straddle his waist as he walks us to the adjoining bedroom.

Will guides us to the bed, where he lays me out before him before ripping away the fabric of my underwear. Once entirely bare to him, he pauses to run his sharp nails down my chest and abdomen as he admires me,

"You are so gorgeous, Lake," Will says before he leans down to free himself from his clothing.

I reach up and caress him as I would someone I loved. I pull him down to cover me with his body as he presses inside me. I bite into his shoulder at the pain of his length as I hear floorboards creaking from the other room down the hall.

I pull Will closer to me and consume his lips once more, my heart rate picking up in my chest as I hear more movement from the hall.

Will doesn't seem to notice as he digs his nails into my hip, causing another whimper to escape my lips. Will smiles as he reaches his hand up to my throat.

He cuts off enough air to make breathing difficult but not enough to completely obstruct my airway. I resist the urge to cough against the pressure.

"Lake, I love you so much," he whispers lovingly along my skin.

I bury my face in his shoulder as he continues to move. I hear the door to the bedroom open with a soft click as I feel Will tense with his release.

I bury my face in Will's chest to block out what I know is coming next.

A loud crack rings around us, and Will slumps limply onto the bed beside me. I sit up and move out from under him as I look into the enraged eyes of Gage.

He stands wielding a table lamp from the desk by the bedroom door. Bloodied scraps of skin hang from around the wrist that was bound to the bed. His hand was mangled entirely while getting free.

Gage drops the lamp before kneeling before me on the bed. "Fuck Lake, I couldn't get the cuff off, and then I heard you scream."

I force a smile to my face that falls flat. "I'm okay, Gage..."

"You're bleeding again, you're not okay."

I look over to Will's limp form and reach over to feel a pulse at his throat. "He's still alive."

Gage turns his gaze to Will before standing over him. Gage flips Will onto his back and climbs on top of him before repeatedly bringing down the fist of his free hand. I look away from them both and stare at the paint on the wall until Gage chooses to stop.

Gage reaches into Will's pants and pulls out the knife he has used to carve into my skin, extending the handle of the sharp blade to me.

I grasp it in my hand and look down at Will, who is lying beneath Gage, awake and breathing, no less injured from Gage's onslaught of rage.

I adjust myself so that I can kneel next to Will.

"What do you want to do with him?" Gage asks me as he catches his breath.

I grasp onto Will's limp arm as his head lulls to the side to get a better view of what I am doing. I place his wrist under my knee and put my total weight behind it. Will winces at the pressure as I bring the blade tip to his arm.

"I want to play with him."

Chapter Thirty

MALACHAI

"What the fuck?" I ask as I stare at the dwelling I used to call home.

Shelly told us everything about Will, my brother. It is almost comical now that I think of it. Everyone had said we looked alike.

I glance over the landscape before me, dowsed in dim moonlight. The last time I was here was after I got out of the hospital for the first time. I had had my mother and father drive me here to see the place of nightmares everyone had been telling me about. Nothing but a few parts of the first and second floors were still intact, but the rest was burnt to rubble.

Now, I see a white mansion with beautiful blooming flowers flowing along a cobblestone road, leaving shadows in the night. Willow trees flow silently in the distance, leading to a path along a pond.

I feel pain start to grow behind my eyes, as if my mind is trying to force itself back together so that I can remember something important. My gaze lingers along the path to the far-off willow trees.

"Malachai?" Ava whispers at my side.

I look over to her and Riley. "Stick together and take the left of the property. I'll take the right. Try every window and door. If nothing opens, meet me at the back, and we will break in through the cellar."

Before either can answer, I walk off into the night along the right of the property. I wait for lights to turn on at my approach but none do. It doesn't even look like anyone is home. The house itself could be sleeping with how quiet it is.

I try the front door and then go to the back kitchen entrance. I see fully furnished rooms in the windows, almost as if they have been preserved in time for the last eleven years.

As I wait for Ava and Riley, my gaze wanders back to the willow tree by the pond. As if possessed, my feet pull me forward in that direction. I feel my heartbeat in my throat, and for the first time in years, I think something like grief.

Why?

Lake and Gage are in the opposite direction. I need to save them. I need to protect them like I couldn't protect...

My pace slows as I reach the base of the large willow. The moonlight illuminates the epitaph carved into stone.

Willow De Leon
Until we meet again

I read the words repeatedly, and I remember the letter from Ava that Lake had tried to hide from my gaze all those weeks ago.

Lake,

I buried them under the willow tree by the pond. I am so sorry…

I grasp my chest and stare down at the name. I brace myself against the tree, digging my nails into the wood and feeling the bark slip under my nails.

This is…

This is my…

"I'm sorry." A soft, broken voice says behind me.

I turn and see Lake, my beautiful Lake, standing behind me, staring off past me to the gravestone. She looks so pale in the moonlight. Almost like a ghost. Dark circles surround her soft brown eyes, which are usually alight with humor but are now void of anything familiar.

I look from where her hair hangs loosely at her waist, the tips dripping red. It stands out against the haphazardly buttoned white shirt, exposing her stomach above a plaid skirt. I take a step closer to her as I see red marks along her stomach and arms. It looks like someone carved into her skin.

"I should have told you about her sooner, but I didn't think I could. I still don't think I can, but I should have told you about her," Lake says, staring off past me.

I approach her and caress her face before pulling her to me in a tight embrace: Lake, my poor Lake.

"Lake, what happened? Where's Gage? Where's Will?" I ask as I pull back to look at her face and neck. Blood drips from her cut lips, and there is a bite mark between her shoulder and neck. What the fuck happened to her?

"Gage is inside, and Will…Is gone."

"What do you mean he is gone?"

"We let him go. He is gone," she says barely above a whisper.

I pull her to me once more. "Come on, let's find Gage."

Lake still doesn't make eye contact, so I tilt her chin to face me. Her eyes finally drift to mine, and her face crumples.

"I want to go home, Malachai," she sobs as she collapses in my arms.

I lean down and scoop her into my arms. She wraps her arms around my neck in a tight embrace as I walk us back up the path toward the manor. When I finally gaze away from her broken form, I see Gage standing along the route, surrounded by Ava and Riley, who repeatedly try and fail to get him to look at them. His expression mirrors Lake's as he gazes at our approach with hollow eyes.

I walk over to my family while holding the cold and fragile love of my life in my tight grip. I should feel relief that it's finally over, but as I stare into my brother's hollow gaze, I know it's not over.

This is just the beginning.

Epilogue

LAKE

"Where is Malachai?" Gage asks as he walks through the halls of the gallery alongside me.

I hear our footsteps echo throughout the silent building. Everyone left hours ago, leaving Gage and me to our own devices.

"At home. I told him I wanted to hang out with you for a bit here before heading back." I murmur to Gage as we go to the gallery's basement.

I unlock the iron door leading to a steep set of steel stairs. I flip on a few switches and gaze upon rows and rows of canvas storage and display setups. A thin layer of dust is starting to coat everything, even though Malachai's gallery has only been open for less than a year.

As we descend further into the large basement, I run my hand over a few drop canvases covering random storage items.

"It feels wrong...Not telling them about this. About us."

Gage tells me as one of his casted hands caresses my shoulder, slowing my pace.

I shrug. "This is just between us. Why do we need to involve anyone else?"

Gage sighs and matches his pace to my own. I try to slow my excited pace, but I have been thinking of nothing else all day. This was all I wanted to do.

The basement is the perfect place. Gage and I have the keys since we are the nighttime cleaning crew. Well, Ava has one too. She could always come down here at any moment, but that is a risk I am willing to take. This place was just too perfect for us.

We finally arrive at the back of the basement, where I see the steel beam that I welded into a unique display to hold up a large canvas that holds my masterpiece, which is bound to it with thin fiberglass wires.

I walk up to the display and smile as Gage looks on with mild curiosity.

Lake De Leon
Lake De Leon
Lake De Leon
Lake De Leon

The words stain the canvas backward from where Will leaned his bloodied back against it after I was done drawing on him with the same knife that he used to caress my skin with his name.

I look at my wounds, which are starting to scar, and smile at the beautiful symmetry between us. Soon, we will match.

I reach down to Will and caress his face from where he is pinned to the canvas. He looks almost biblical, with a bloodied sheet hanging from his waist and his arms splayed out away from him by the fiberglass wires.

"Will?" I ask softly.

Will groans and opens his eyes to meet my own.

"I need more red."

Acknowledgments

Thank you to my family for consistently supporting me in my writing, whether it be staying up late at night listening to my wild ideas, buying me countless books to feed my reading addiction, or allowing me to express my interests in all things dark and twisted.

Thank you to my Beta Readers, Reyna, and Elizabeth, that spent hours pouring over the pages of this book to make sure I didn't screw up the plot or the spelling too much. This novel would have been a mess without their constant feedback and support.

Lastly, thank you, David. Thank you for all the times you made me feel normal and like I was worth more than I thought I was during my lowest points. You take care of me endlessly, and I will love you forever.

www.ingramcontent.com/pod-product-compliance
Lightning Source LLC
Chambersburg PA
CBHW070639260626
47161CB00007B/2761